"That's better. You don't look s
polished now. You look all r
and kissable."

"I do?" Mallory tilted her he ng into clear, calm blue eyes.

Andrew cupped her jaw. H outh on hers was soft, tentative at first, then more confident. It was a good kiss, a near perfect kiss, all the better because he didn't push things, but let it happen naturally. She rested her cheek against his shoulder.

"Mauve is the pink trying to be purple," she murmured for lack of anything else to say.

"Never can keep those straight." His hand slid along her hair, tucking it back behind her ear. She felt his gaze upon her, smelled a hint of smoke on his skin.

He was wearing his uniform under the denim jacket, she realized with a start—navy blue with the insignia stitched onto the pocket.

The same uniform he wore when he'd abandoned Katelyn to that demon fire.

Dear Reader,

I still remember the night a kitchen fire devastated the heart of my parents' home. Luckily, no one was injured. Others, including many firefighters on duty and off, haven't been as fortunate.

In *Sweet Justice*, Andrew and Mallory find themselves dealing with the fallout of just such a fire, one that injures both a civilian and a firefighter. It all starts with a single bad decision with the potential to send hopes, dreams and futures up in smoke.

The worst thing about most structure fires? They're imminently preventable. Writing this book has reminded me to be safe—and to check those smoke detector batteries!

Cynthia

Check out me and my fellow Harlequin Heartwarming sisters at heartwarmingauthors.blogspot.com.

HEARTWARMING

Sweet Justice

Cynthia Reese

HARLEQUIN® HEARTWARMING™

Recycling programs
for this product may
not exist in your area.

ISBN-13: 978-0-373-36784-9

Sweet Justice

Copyright © 2016 by Cynthia R. Reese

www.Harlequin.com

Printed in U.S.A.

Cynthia Reese lives with her husband and their daughter in south Georgia, along with their two dogs, three cats and however many strays show up for morning muster. She has been scribbling since she was knee-high to a grasshopper and reading even before that. A former journalist, teacher and college English instructor, she also enjoys cooking, traveling and photography when she gets the chance.

Books by Cynthia Reese

Harlequin Heartwarming

Seeds of Trust
A Place to Call Home
What the Heart Wants
Man of His Word
Out of the Ashes

Harlequin Superromance

The Baby Wait
For the Sake of the Children

To my lovely gal pals—Leslie, Bobbi and Fran.
Thanks for talking me down from the ledges.

Acknowledgments

Kathryn Lye and Victoria Curran are the best
editors on the planet—this book wouldn't have
been possible without them. I also owe a huge
debt to my Harlequin Heartwarming sister Karen
Rock, who patiently brainstormed with me to
work out the lives of the Georgia Monroes.

For technical help, thanks goes to Sergeant
Tommy Windham and all the firefighters at the
City of Dublin, Georgia's Fire Department.
Dr. Jean Sumner first gave me the idea of what
injury Katelyn might suffer in a fire. Eric Carney
and Stacy Watson graciously taught me what burn
victims endure during rehab. All mistakes are mine!

Inspiration also came from the Love family—
they've shown me what a wonderful thing a big
family can be.

My critique partner, Tawna Fenske, as well as my
readers, Jessica Brown, Wright and Dusty Gres,
Kandice Williams, and Lee and Kathy Cheek,
helped me tremendously.

And to my husband and my daughter—I owe you
loan-shark big for putting up with my MIA self.

CHAPTER ONE

BLACKNESS.

A solid wall of blackness.

Andrew Monroe crawled farther into the darkness, the grit of the floor biting into his knees, the heft of the fire hose under his right arm. His left hand secure on Eric Russell's turnout gear, the only way he even knew his fellow crewmember was ahead of him.

And the girl they were trying to find? Who knew where she was? Or was she even here?

Eric had called out to her, but the only noise that penetrated the darkness was the rasp of their own breathing.

Captain had said that her roommates weren't sure the girl, Katelyn, was still in the house—if you could call the tumbledown two-story much of a house. It seemed to go on forever, just room after room. It was like so many of the big old homes in this college town—taken over by students in search of cheap rent, and who cared if the place was nothing more than a firetrap?

The roommates, Cap said, weren't even sure this girl, Katelyn, had even come home the night before. No one had seen her since yesterday afternoon.

She was probably out for an early-morning run or getting coffee or had slept over at a friend's—at least, she was if she was lucky.

Whether she was in here or not, it was Eric and Andrew's job to clear the structure and make sure no one was still in the house. So they started at the bottom, intent on working toward the stairs.

Eric moved forward, and Andrew crawled behind. He heard Eric's muffled call for Katelyn again, then his waiting silence.

Only the sound of their air packs answered. Andrew's heart sank. This was a mess, and he could sense time was running out for her if she was in here. She was just a college kid.

Nobody needs to die that young.

Eric pulled up short, and Andrew almost crashed into him. He stayed still, listening. Yeah—there it was again, ahead and above them…on the stairs?

A girl screaming. Even through his mask

and the rest of his gear, Andrew could hear the panic in her voice.

Why do they always go up?

Was she coming down the stairs? In this smoke? She'd be dead—better for her to stay where she was until they could get a ladder setup outside, pull her from one of the upstairs windows.

He felt more than heard her as she dashed back and forth across the landing above their heads.

Hasn't anyone taught you to get on your knees in a fire? Sheesh. You're like a jack-rabbit up there. Slow down, otherwise you run out of air. Get to a window.

Had Eric heard? Andrew signaled to Eric, who was in charge of their two-man sweep team. They needed to radio the captain. As the guy in charge, that was Eric's call to make.

Once the girl was safe, Captain could assess whether it was worth the risk to save this heap of junk.

Eric and Andrew's history of teamwork paid off. Andrew sensed that his buddy had either heard the girl himself or realized that Andrew had.

Eric moved—for his radio? To tell Andrew to make the call?

Andrew didn't have the time to figure it out, because in the next breath, the floor next to Eric gave way. Hot air belched upward, along with a cloud of blackness tinged with an unearthly glow from the flames beneath them.

His buddy would have dropped into that glow if Andrew hadn't had a hold of him. Even so, Eric slipped, his hands scrabbling for purchase, his feet digging into part of the floor that still held. Andrew tightened his grip on him, praying that the floor wouldn't give way beneath them.

C'mon, c'mon, hold still!

For a heart-stopping moment, Andrew was sure they were going to tumble into the yawning pit of darkness below, the heat billowing up…

At least I'm not married. I won't leave a wife like Dad left Ma.

Something in Andrew fought back at that and doggedly held on. They were too young to die in a death trap like this, Andrew was twenty-five to Eric's twenty-eight. Fire couldn't have them today.

Not today. Maybe someday, but not on my watch.

The big firefighter swung sideways and Eric's head rammed into something thick and heavy. The sickening thud reverberated through Andrew's fingers and arm.

Andrew seized the safety strap on Eric's gear and began to drag him away slowly, every muscle protesting at Eric's weight plus the added burden of air packs and boots and turnout gear. The intense heat from the fire and the strain left Andrew gasping.

One more tug. One more pull. And another. And another. Andrew's arms felt as though they would be yanked out of their sockets if he didn't get Eric to a safer spot.

But at least he's breathing.

The blackness got even blacker and Andrew knew what that meant.

The fire's spread.

As Andrew reached for his radio, he felt a shudder in the floor beneath him. He had to get them out before the whole place went. He scooped Eric under the arms again and began dragging him backward, along the line, to the door.

Above him, a girl was screaming, "Don't leave me! Don't let me die!"

Or was it his imagination? Was the fire playing tricks on him?

The front door and help felt an ocean away…and the girl, Katelyn? She might as well be on the moon.

He stopped for a breath. How much air had he used from his tanks to pull Eric this far? How much air did he have left? Unclipping his radio, he managed to wheeze, "Mayday! Mayday!"

Instantly his captain responded, wanting a size-up. Andrew got it out, all of it, Eric, the girl, everything, then returned to the task of dragging Eric closer to the door, inch by inch. Drag. Stop and breathe. Drag. Stop and breathe. Drag—

Hands closed over him—the RIT team Captain had sent in. They scooped up Eric as though he weighed no more than a feather, hauled him away from Andrew.

Above him, another scream.

Or was it only in his head?

Another hand gripped him, pulling him. Andrew's muscles quivered with exhaustion, but even so a part of him wanted to go back for the girl.

He knew leaving her was the right thing

to do. Other firefighters would put the ladder against the upstairs window, go in, find her.

He was done. For now he was done.

Outside, blinking under the glare through the gray October clouds, Andrew drew in deep gulps of cold air. Across the yard, EMTs swarmed over Eric. Head injury, laceration to his leg, maybe a punctured lung from a broken rib.

He didn't even get to say goodbye before they had Eric on the bus and down the street.

His captain strode up beside him, radio halfway to his mouth. "Monroe! Where was that girl? They can't find her. They've done a sweep, but no dice. I pulled them out—the smoke's so bad, and they used up their air in nothing flat. That whole place is about to go."

"You've got to go after her!" Andrew insisted. "Sounded as if she was on the landing above us—as though maybe she was trying to come down."

The captain swore. "The way that floor caved, you can bet the stairs aren't far behind."

"I heard her," Andrew repeated. "I'll go. Send me. I just need a new air pack. I know where she is—at least where she was when I was pulling Eric out."

The captain's radio squawked, seizing his

attention. He turned back, a look of indecision on his face for a moment, then he gave Andrew a quick nod.

Andrew didn't hesitate. He grabbed a new air pack and shot up the ladder, nozzle in hand, with another firefighter, Jackson, behind him.

This time, he didn't hear Katelyn. He climbed inside the window and pushed along the bedroom wall, pawing through what felt like a drycleaner's worth of clothes on the floor. Around a heavy dresser. Over a squeaky toy.

Out the door. Down another hall, this one bare floor, no carpet. Heat seemed to radiate upward through the cracks in the floorboards, and he pushed back thoughts of Eric almost tumbling down into the blackness.

The floor would hold.

They would find Katelyn.

"Fire!" Jackson hollered out. "Stairs!"

Andrew pointed the nozzle and blanketed the area with water.

The smoke, amazingly, seemed to clear, and that was when he saw her—just the shape of her, just a suggestion of a form on the floor. It was a miracle he'd seen her—a second earlier, and he, like the earlier crew, would have missed her entirely.

Andrew crawled forward. Laid his hand on her.

Small. Scarcely bigger than Taylor or Marissa—and his nieces were only twelve.

Still, her deadweight slowed him down as he tried to drag her one-handed back the way they'd come. He was too tired—too exhausted from pulling Eric. He needed to use both hands.

It was almost as if Jackson could read his mind. He clapped Andrew on the back and grabbed the nozzle. Now Andrew set to work, dragging her along the line, back toward the bedroom, over the squeaky toy, through the clothes that would go like fat-lighter kindling once the fire reached this far.

And it would. The glow was getting bigger, marching up the stairs, toward the bedroom door. Jackson was hurrying him now, but he didn't need to, because Andrew knew the score.

They had to get out, out before that fire ate through the staircase and took away the second floor's main load-bearing wall.

Now for the window—daylight, even if it was only a rectangle of gray the color of galvanized steel. The hand-off to Tommy, who was waiting on the ladder—

And that was when Andrew saw how bad Katelyn really was. The disintegrated yoga pants from mid-shin down, the misshapen and blackened bedroom slippers, with their hot pink fur matted and melted. The soot-covered face slack and unresponsive.

I should have called it in when I heard her on the stairs. She was okay then. She was fine. And now... Is she even alive?

Andrew watched as Tommy made his way down the ladder. He watched for any hint that Katelyn was more than a corpse.

Too late. I was too late.

He clambered out onto the ladder and headed down, his heart somewhere in his boots.

Too late. The words echoed in his head with every step on every rung.

On the ground, more EMTs were waiting to take her from Tommy. Quick as a flash they had her on a backboard, a C-collar on— and Tommy was giving him a thumbs-up. His wide grin told Andrew there were some signs of life.

Elation flooded him, and he nearly collapsed on the ground by the ladder as relief pulsed through him.

She's alive!

A win. This was a win. The house could go—and it probably would in a matter of minutes, whether he gave it permission or not.

He looked back over his shoulder to see Jackson on the ground and flames punching through the upstairs windows.

Yeah. Fire could have the house. But it couldn't have Eric, and it couldn't have Katelyn—at least not today.

CHAPTER TWO

THE CHILL ATE into Mallory Blair's bones. The waiting room was empty except for an old man asleep on a couch. He was wrapped in about three dozen blankets and a plump pillow. She found herself fixated on those blankets, wishing for something warm to wrap around her.

Not a blanket to envelop her.

A pair of arms.

Not a pillow under her head.

A strong, rocklike shoulder.

She'd been here before—not here, not in this hospital. All she could think when she took in the institutional furnishings, the flickering fluorescent lights overhead, the overwhelming scent of citrus cleaner, was another hospital. The hospital where a doctor had come out and hemmed and hawed and finally told her that Mom and Dad were gone.

In one instant, the world she'd known—

comfortable, secure, a future ahead of her—
went poof. She'd gone from being—

*Admit it, Mallory. You were a spoiled brat
who had no clue how much you depended on
your parents.*

She hadn't been all alone then.

Katelyn had been with her.

Mallory swallowed the sob pent up in her
chest. If it came out, if she started crying,
she'd lose it. She'd cry for hours or days or a
lifetime, and she couldn't do that. She had to
be strong. She had to think and concentrate
on what the doctor said.

If the doctor ever came back out.

*What if she comes back out and tells you
Katelyn's gone?*

Mallory was still trying to wrap her head
around the little she knew. One minute she'd
been hanging the new shipment of holiday
dresses on the rack, running her steamer over
them to remove the creases and folds, and
the next, some stranger on a phone was telling her…

Accident, fire, medical evacuation by heli-
copter to a burn unit halfway across the state.

And here…after a two-hour drive through
twisty Georgia roads she didn't know, to find
the right hospital in a city full of hospitals…

Down the hall came loud laughter. The corridor was full to bursting with a huge family, tumbling over one another like a box full of rambunctious puppies, more like a family reunion than a crisis. They'd had good news, she guessed. That or they were trying to put the horror of the moment out of their minds.

I should have never let Katelyn talk me into letting her skip her senior year and go on to college in Waverly. I should have insisted she choose a college closer to home. I should have found the money to pay for the dorm, not that firetrap of a house. It's my fault—I pushed for that resident's exemption for her, just to save money, and I shouldn't have.

Mallory's stomach rumbled. It confounded her how she could still be hungry when her sister might be dying behind those double doors up the hall.

Another sob fought its way past her hammering heart.

You might have all the time in the world to eat yet. If she tells you that Katelyn's gone.

The couch groaned as the old man turned on his side, burrowing deeper into his nest of blankets. For a moment, Mallory found herself wondering about his story. What calamity had brought him to this place?

Down the hall, the crowd grew still louder, as one family member ratcheted up the volume level to best another's. More people had come in to join them, and Mallory could see them greeting one another with hugs and back slaps.

This time, she didn't even have a scared twelve-year-old sitting beside her in the waiting room. When her parents had died, there'd been no one left of their family except a hard-of-hearing great aunt on her mother's side they'd never met, and two states away at that. Mallory remembered begging the social worker from the department of family and children services to please, please not put Katelyn in foster care. She could do it—she could take care of her sister.

And see how you've screwed that up.

She pulled her winter coat around her, wincing as the lining ripped in the shoulder seam. The coat was three years old and much mended, but the whole lining needed replacing. She'd been planning on doing it this weekend, in fact…but she wouldn't now.

She had more important things to worry about than a tear in a coat lining. She needed to be grateful she even had a coat.

Is Katelyn cold?

Katelyn hated the cold—it had always been a battle between them over the thermostat, Mallory turning it down to sixty-five to save money, Katelyn slipping behind her and jacking it up to seventy-two.

I'll turn it up to eighty if you'll just come back to me.

Another wail pressed up, out, like a caged animal testing its bars for weakness. She'd just managed to stifle it when she spotted a tall dark-haired guy, shoulders broad in a denim jacket, push through the crowd.

He smiled at the family as he passed, spoke for a few minutes, gestured with the hand holding a big brown paper shopping bag to the cooler he was pulling with his other hand.

He was about her age, and he had a kind smile, the guy did. It seemed so much warmer than the room's chilly, sterile air. She wondered how he was connected to the family, wondered what he had in the cooler. With that many people, they'd need a lot of snacks and drinks. They looked as though they were camped out for the night.

Like me. They're not going anywhere, like me.

He continued on from the crowd, closing the gap between himself and the door to the waiting room with a few easy strides of long denim-encased legs. Mallory realized with a start that he was coming to join her. He must be planning on leaving the cooler here for the family.

The door creaked open. "Hi...are you with the Blair family?" the man asked.

"Uh—yes." She stared at him as he entered, trying to figure out if she knew him from somewhere. Had the stress of the day made her fail to recognize him?

No. She'd never forget his easy smile, the cleft in his chin, the bright blue eyes that seemed to bring a summer sky's joy into the chilly waiting room. His dark hair was closely cropped, but it had grown out enough since his last haircut to have a cowlick right at the crest of his head. Mallory's fingers itched to smooth it down.

"You're Katelyn Blair's...sister?"

"Yes." She struggled to a standing position and extended a hand. She'd been sitting so long and so stiffly that her knees threatened to collapse on her. "I'm Mallory Blair. You must be one of Katelyn's friends."

He dropped the handle of the cooler and gripped her offered hand with a big strong hand of his own, one with long square-tipped fingers that swallowed hers. "Andrew Monroe…and, no, I don't know your sister, exactly. I was one of the firefighters who was at the fire this morning. I wanted to see how she was doing."

Tears stung her eyes at his thoughtfulness. She gripped his hand with both of hers and pumped it with a fierce energy. "Thank you, thank you—thank you so much for getting her out, for giving her a chance—"

She had to drop his hand to swipe at her eyes. "I'm sorry—I'm just a—a mess."

Andrew guided her back to her chair and eased her down in it. He sat in the chair beside her. "I can imagine. She's going to be okay, then?"

"Oh—I don't know. They haven't told me much. They said…" Mallory drew in a shaky breath and knotted her fingers in her lap. She noticed a chip in her nail polish—polish she'd carefully put on just the night before, when all was right in the world.

"Yes?" Andrew prompted. The way he said it was full of patience and encouragement, as though he knew she didn't want to say the words lest they finally seem real.

"She's on a vent. And her feet and legs—they're badly burned. She has twenty percent of her body…burned. The pants she was wearing…and the shoes… They melted in the heat of the fire. How hot does it have to be to *melt shoes*?" Mallory shook her head and closed her eyes tight in a vain effort to banish the image from her head.

"They were bedroom slippers," Andrew said. "Some sort of pink furry ones."

She looked up in surprise. "Bunny slippers. They were bunny slippers. You saw her, then? When they pulled her out?"

His cheeks flared with color, and he ducked his head. "I—er—me and another firefighter, we were the ones who pulled her out. And you're right. It was a really hot fire. This place—" he waved one long arm to encompass not just the waiting room, but the burn center itself "—it's great. They can do miracles here."

"You know it, then? It's a good place?"

"Yeah, oh, yeah. My dad…"

A spasm of pain crossed his face as his words trailed off. He chewed on his bottom lip.

"Your dad what?" Mallory said. She needed to hear something hopeful.

"Well, he was here. There was this warehouse fire, see, and he got trapped in it—"

"Oh, so that's why you're a firefighter," she guessed, laying a palm against his forearm. She should have realized it would be something like that, him giving back after seeing a family member hurt.

"Well, sort of, I guess. He was the fire chief. He—he went in to help rescue another firefighter."

"He's okay now?"

"Uh…no, I'm afraid not. He didn't make it. But—" He turned to her, his own hand covering hers where it lay on his arm. "He was a lot worse than Katelyn sounds—he had burns on nearly three quarters of his body, and, well, it would have taken a miracle for anybody to survive that."

Mallory sagged back into the stiff, unforgiving chair. It wasn't quite high enough to rest her neck, and too straight to find a good position in. "Oh. I'm sorry. This has to be hard for you to come here."

She couldn't have done it—gone to the hospital waiting room in Macon, back home, where she'd heard the news of her parents' passing. Maybe she should have been strong enough, but ever since then, she'd given a wide berth to hospitals of any sort, especially *that* one.

Andrew's face creased into an aw-shucks-it's-nothing smile. "No. I wanted to come. When you're part of the club—this awful, awful club—you know what somebody else is going through, and you... Well, you want to make it better. I'm just sorry you haven't had more encouraging news."

"I haven't had much news at all, but I expect they're busy, and I... To tell the truth, I haven't been here that long—only since about, oh, a little after noon."

Andrew chuckled. "It's after five o'clock already. You're lost to Hospital Time." He squeezed her hand, seemed to realize what he was doing and then moved his own from hers. Mallory felt the waiting room's chill air bite into her at the absence of his warm hold.

Andrew was ducking down, pulling up the bag. He placed it in his lap. "My mom put a care package together for you—she's good about stuff like that. She thought you might need a few things."

"Oh, she shouldn't have—" Mallory protested.

"No, she wanted to. She remembers, see? How it was with her when Dad was...well, here. And she knew the family probably wouldn't want to leave, not this first night anyway. Say, where *is* the rest of the family?" He craned his neck around, spied the old man. "Am I disturbing your... Is that your dad?"

Mallory's throat closed up on her, and this time, she couldn't hold back a tear as it slid down her cheek. Embarrassed at her loss of control, she swiped it away. "Uh, no, that's somebody else. This is it. Just me. Katelyn and I lost our parents in a car wreck nearly five years ago."

"Oh, man."

Andrew's eyes held so much compassion that she had to look away. "It's okay. We get by."

And they had. Until now, they'd made it. It had been tough. It had meant short-selling the house they'd grown up in, letting go of some dreams, working two jobs at times, getting creative to make her paycheck stretch. Katelyn always complained that Mallory pinched pennies so hard that they'd spit out nickels.

She'd kept Katelyn out of the foster care system, and she'd managed to put food on the table, and keep Katelyn in school...

I'll do anything. Anything. Just please, please, pull through, Katie-bug. Please.

"Well, uh..." Andrew cleared his throat.

"Ma wasn't sure how many folks you'd have with you, so she sent a lot." He reached down and patted the cooler.

"I—I don't know what to say."

"Nothing *to* say. Here—this bag, it's got, hmm, let's see…a blanket, a pillow…oh, and Ma sent a toothbrush and toothpaste and some hand sanitizer."

"Oh, wow. I was just wishing for a blanket. She must have read my mind."

"Ma says to tell you that the nurses will give you another blanket if you ask—the waiting room can get kind of cold. Oh, and don't forget that the Southeast Burn Foundation will put you up. Just ask the nurses, and they'll get you hooked up with the right person. They've got this hospitality house for the families, and they provide one good meal a day."

Mallory felt herself blinking back still more tears. So much kindness, and when she'd been feeling pathetically sorry for herself.

"Ma knew, if you were anything like her, that nobody could pry you away from this place tonight, and you'd probably headed up here without much thought of anything but getting here." Andrew patted the lid of the cooler. "She sent, hmm, fried chicken, butter beans, mashed potatoes and sliced tomatoes, and some apple cobbler for dessert. Oh, and tea. I hope you like iced tea, because she sent a whole thermos of it."

"There's no way I can possibly eat all of that…"

Andrew nodded toward the man on the couch, who was now snoring gently. "Share it, then. That old fellow looks as though he could use a good meal. And the apple cobbler will keep for your breakfast."

"Please, won't you have some with me?" Mallory asked.

"Uh…" Andrew ran a hand over his close-cropped hair. "Ma'd skin me alive if she knew I'd eaten up some of the food she sent you."

"I don't want to eat by myself." The confession surprised her. What was it about Andrew Monroe that made her feel so…not alone?

"In that case, even Ma would tell me to join you," he said with a grin and a definitive nod. "She'd surely want me to encourage you to eat."

She managed a small portion of the delicious supper, swallowing it past the lump of fear in her throat. Every time a person in a white coat or scrubs walked by the door, Mallory found herself tensing. Her mind simultaneously prayed they were coming to tell her something and hoped they would go past if it were bad news.

Then, as Andrew was helping her stack the food back into the cooler, the door opened. There stood the doctor, her phalanx of white-coated interns and medical students behind her.

Mallory froze. She felt Andrew take the plastic container of mashed potatoes from her. She turned and numbly accepted the doctor's outstretched hand in its proffered shake. The woman sat in the chair across from her.

"Okay, well. She is…stable. It's been a real battle, I won't lie. We've got her on three pressors to keep her blood pressure up, and she's continuing to need maximum support from the vent. We've assessed the burns to her legs and feet, and, as I told you before, we're dealing with twenty percent of her body surface. The burns are…well, the majority of the higher ones are at least second degree, and she has third-degree burns on her feet. That is serious. Also…do you know if she came in contact with a live electrical wire? She has burns on her hand and torso that appear to be from electric shock."

Mallory shuddered. "I—I wasn't there—I—"

"No," Andrew spoke up. "I was part of the responding fire department. The house didn't have power. We always check and get the power company to shut it off. There's no way she could have gotten an electrical shock. She was fine when I heard her—she was conscious and alert when I had to evacuate a fellow firefighter of mine. She got burned in the time it took for us to go back in after her."

The doctor gave him a dubious look. "The burns on her hand and arm and torso are consistent with, say, a frayed extension cord. Maybe she came in contact with an exposed wire and it knocked her unconscious? It's the least of her worries, but it makes me concerned that we may have missed deeper wounds."

"I can assure you," Andrew insisted. He was leaning forward now. "There was no power to that house, not that I know of."

The doctor held his gaze, turned to take in the curious faces of her flock of junior doctors, and shrugged. "I've seen a lot of electrical burns in my time. And this? Despite what you say, it looks like one. We'll treat it as we see it and keep an eye out for anything else."

She rose from her chair and looked at Mallory. "Do you have any questions?"

"When can I see her?" Mallory husked. "And—and is she—she…" She couldn't form the words.

"You can see her briefly in a few minutes, but I warn you, we have her in a medically induced coma. The next twenty-four hours are critical. Please rest assured that we are doing all we can. It's a miracle that she's made it this far, but…well, if it makes you feel any better, we've seen worse burns."

Then she was gone, her coterie with her.

"That makes no sense," Andrew muttered. "How could she get an electrical burn? She was fine—well, not fine, but—"

"I don't understand." Mallory managed to pull her focus back to Andrew's words. "What happened?"

"It was—well, a little hairy. See, the guy with me fell through the floor."

Mallory put her hand to her mouth. "Is—is he okay? Is he—is that why you're here?" The idea that she'd not even thought of anyone else being injured shamed her.

"Oh, yeah—it was a scare, I tell you. I pulled him up, got him to the front porch.

And he's fine. A cracked rib, a bump to the head. He'll be raring to go in a day or so."

"Oh, well—that's good." Relief sluiced over Mallory.

"Yeah, so—well, just before my buddy went down, we heard her—your sister. We were in the foyer, right at the stairs. She was calling for help on the landing above us, running around like a jackrabbit. Instead of going out a downstairs window, she must have gone upstairs, maybe to escape the smoke? And then she panicked, maybe couldn't find her way out? I know she was conscious and alert then, and the power was switched off. We always check. Anyway, I had to get Eric to the front porch. I got him out, let the EMTs check him out and then I told the Captain I'd go back in and look for her."

"Wait…wait." Mallory struggled to understand the timeline. "You heard her? Right above you? And…you left her? You left my sister in a burning house?"

"Well…yeah, it's protocol." Andrew shrugged one shoulder. "Order of priority. We go after fellow firefighters first, civilians second and property third—a really, really distant third. And she obviously had air—so that meant we had time."

The warmth Andrew had given her with his reassuring smile and his care package coalesced into an icy block within Mallory.

"Protocol?" she choked out. "Why would your...protocol dictate that a civilian is saved after a firefighter?"

Andrew blinked. "A firefighter wouldn't be down in the first place if it weren't for having to go in after the civilian. And—I mean—he's my buddy. I got his back, he's got mine. He would have done the same for me."

"You're saying...that since my sister is a—a civilian, she gets left in a burning house?" This blindsided Mallory. It didn't square with her idea of firefighters running into houses that were aflame or rescuing cats up trees. It didn't sound in the least heroic.

"I guess you could say that," Andrew said slowly. He had a wary look on his face, as though he realized all of a sudden that he had said the exact wrong thing.

"I *am* saying that!" The ice grew inside her, a cold fury that rivaled the chill outside. "You took the time to help your buddy to the front porch, and you ignored my sister?"

"It was a bad injury, and the stairs were too much of a risk for us to go up that way, so Captain said we'd use a ladder—"

"You just said your buddy was fine—a broken rib, a bump on the head—didn't you? Did I hear that right?"

Andrew stood up, took a step toward the door. "Uh, maybe it was a bad idea, me coming here. I just—felt bad. You know. For Katelyn. Because she—" He broke off, ducked his head.

"Because you left her. All this—" She swept her hand at the cooler, the blanket. "It's because you feel guilty, right? You knew you shouldn't have left her."

Andrew passed a hand over his hair, not meeting her eyes, his mouth grimacing. "I didn't *want* to leave her. I do feel bad. But—I mean, my buddy. I had to take care of him."

"Your *buddy* is fine! And Katelyn—Katelyn may *die*." Split-second decisions—with no thought to the consequences—like the guy in the eighteen-wheeler who'd thought he could make the light and instead T-boned her parents' car.

And now another decision just like that—another one was going to cost her the last bit of family she had left on this earth. "You were *there*," Mallory sobbed. "In the house. And you heard my sister calling for help—"

Andrew's face tensed. "Look, I don't expect you to understand. You weren't there."

"Apparently," she shot back, "you weren't there, either, not for my sister. Your buddy? Well, he had gear, right? Gear to keep him from getting burned, and a mask to help him breathe, and—and training—he *knew* what to do in a fire—it was his *job*—but my sister... she's just a *kid*! And all she had on was—was yoga pants and the pink bunny slippers I gave her for Christmas—"

Mallory felt the dinner she'd just eaten rise in her throat, her stomach churning. She put her hand to her mouth and ran from the room. She had to get away—away from Andrew Monroe.

CHAPTER THREE

Three months later

THE EARLY-JANUARY sky stretched out in a deceptive azure blue over the country road Mallory drove down, the sun bright as it shimmered across the asphalt. A sky like that called to mind balmy temperatures, not the forty degrees it was, made even colder by the brisk breeze that feathered through the tall thickets of pines on both sides of the road and buffeted the canvas top of her convertible.

Beside her, Katelyn riffled through the stack of papers. "Yeah, this is the road. See? Stanton Mill Road."

Mallory dared a glance at the brochure from the therapy facility that Katelyn had shoved into her line of vision. The ugly scar on her sister's small hand—a starburst with a long tail—gave Mallory a fresh jolt.

And that's the least of her scars. Mallory pushed away the thought. No, she had to be positive. Katelyn was here, in this car, able to talk, able to get around in her wheelchair. She'd come so far, first at the burn center, and then in an in-patient rehab facility.

And maybe this last round of therapy would actually get Katelyn up, out of that wheelchair, and on her way back to college.

Focusing her gaze back on the road ahead, Mallory said, "So we just keep our eyes peeled for the sign—Happy Acres Farm? Right?"

As if she didn't know. As if Katelyn hadn't begged and wheedled and pleaded, like she was so good at doing. When she'd first mentioned it, Mallory had thought she'd lost her mind. Hippotherapy? She'd never heard of it.

Somewhere, somehow, Katelyn had gotten hold of the shiny, colorful brochure featuring uplifting photos of kids and grown-ups on horses.

Katelyn had always been crazy about horses—why, Mallory couldn't say. Anything that big and hulking, that could tumble you off and trample you, couldn't really be a pet, could it?

Whether it was Katelyn's horse obsession or someone's assurance that hippotherapy would get her out of that wheelchair, the brochure hadn't left Katelyn's possession. Over time, the corners had become dog-eared, the folds so frail that one of them had to be mended with cellophane tape. The brochure had become Katelyn's talisman. Happy Acres Farm, the thing she'd work toward when nothing else would motivate her, when she'd wanted to simply give up.

Mallory couldn't blame Katelyn for those times. Her sister's screams of agony as nurses cared for her burned legs and feet still echoed in her head. And even now, Katelyn had days of unrelenting pain.

There'd come a point during a particularly bad day of therapy when Katelyn had given her scarred legs and feet a disgusted grimace.

"Nobody'll ever want me," she'd said. "I won't ever be able to walk again. What's the point? Maybe I should just be happy with what I've got. I'm alive, okay? Isn't that enough for you, Mallory?"

It wasn't. Mallory had to give her sister her life back—she owed it to their parents. Their mom and dad would expect that, would want her to do whatever she could.

Even if it means getting lost in the middle of the pinewoods of south Georgia trying to find a horse farm.

"Hey! There it is!" Katelyn pointed. She jumped up and down in the seat beside Mallory. "See? Happy Acres Farm! You found it, sis!" She gave Mallory an ebullient punch on her arm.

Sure enough, a big wooden sign with a silhouette of a horse announced the facility. Mallory followed a long post-and-rail fence down to the sign and bumped along the gravel driveway. Here she saw the green metal roof of low buildings—stables, she assumed, and hopefully an office.

"Oh, wow! It's pretty, isn't it? Ooh, Mallory! Look! Horses!"

It *was* pretty—Mallory had been worried that the place wouldn't live up to the bucolic photos in the brochure. The rehab facility surely hadn't—no happy, smiling staff members and triumphant patients to be found in all their time at that facility.

Happy Acres Farm appeared as advertised. Horses frolicked in the cold, crisp air across pastures of impossibly green grass. Beyond them, a pond reflected the blue sky, with clouds of fog still hovering close over its surface.

The stables—if that was what the long, low building was—were fastidiously neat, light green, with dark green trim and shutters. Everything seemed perfectly groomed—and perfectly deserted.

Where were the other patients? Where was the staff shown in the photos? The discharge planners at the rehab facility had warned Mallory that Happy Acres Farm was a small clinic, run by a single owner-operator. Mallory had tried to talk Katelyn into choosing a similar, bigger facility nearer to Macon, where the two of them had grown up and Mallory had lived up until now.

But no. Katelyn wanted *this* hippotherapy facility. And the discharge planners had told them that the therapist was highly qualified— certified in both traditional physical therapy and hippotherapy, and she had certification in counseling. Plus...it was close to Katelyn's college. Maybe her old school friends would encourage her to get better and get back into her classes.

Mallory surely hadn't been able to accomplish that.

"Can you help me with my chair, Mal?" Katelyn's grin was so big, it practically hung off either side of her elfin face. Mallory's heart melted, and her reservations about the place evaporated. Believing it was half the battle—maybe Katelyn would be able to walk again here.

"Okay. We're early, though—"

"I want to see it! I want to go pet the horses!"

Mallory shuddered. Horses were great from a distance—beautiful and graceful. Close up, though?

She loved animals—how many dogs and cats had she and Katelyn fostered over the years? Horses, on the other hand, had big teeth and sharp hooves and eyes that seemed to stare straight through you. She was embarrassed to admit such a phobia, but there it was.

Still, she knew better than to argue with her little sister. The therapist could establish the rules, and Katelyn would certainly listen to her more than she would Mallory. After all, Katelyn had demonstrated time and again that she thought Mallory was an uptight fussbudget who worried too much.

I didn't worry enough.

She took in Katelyn's excitement. Her sister was pink cheeked for the first time in months, her coppery hair, so like Mallory's own, fluffing out around a thinner, still-gaunt face. It was like looking at their mom's photo as a teenager. Katelyn and she had both inherited their mom's auburn hair, but Katelyn had drawn the delicate elfin features of their mother, while Mallory resembled their dad's side of the family, taller, with stronger features.

She sighed and opened the car door. The cool morning air snaked in and she pushed up to a standing position. The cramped confines of her little convertible had been trouble on her knees. She patted the red painted finish, thinking again of the happier day her parents had given the car to her as a high school graduation present.

Not even a year later, and they were gone. She'd struggled to make the payments, not willing to let this last gift from her mom and dad go the way the house had. Now it was paid off—hers forever, or as long as she could keep it going.

She hauled Katelyn's wheelchair out of the tight fit of the trunk. A bag containing their bare essentials and Katelyn's many, many medications was the only other thing stuffed in there. Mallory had hired her former boss's husband and his truck to bring the rest of Mallory's belongings to the apartment Mallory had found in town.

Today…today was a chance to get Katelyn introduced to her new therapist and then settled into the apartment.

She struggled to get the chair unfolded and wheeled up beside Katelyn's door. The wind had picked up, and now it sliced into her and yanked at her hair, pulling it out of the French twist. She'd hoped to appear neat and tidy and organized when she met the staff— the only way people ever took you seriously, she'd found.

Katelyn would have opened the door, but Mallory waved at her to wait. No need for Katelyn to get chilled while Mallory struggled to set the stubborn brake—

"Here, let me—"

A man's hand appeared over hers, big and muscular, competently setting the brake and yanking the chair into instant submission. Half embarrassed at her ineptitude and half eternally grateful, Mallory pushed the hair out of her eyes and extended a hand.

"Thank you—I'm not sure I'll ever get the hang of—"

And then she looked him in the face, saw who he was.

Tall, even against her five-foot-eight-inch frame. Solidly built, with the arms to prove it, which, courtesy of the short-sleeved T-shirt he wore even on this chilly morning, were bare and tanned. The cleft in the chin, the sky-blue eyes, the close-cropped hair—and yes, even the cowlick at the crest of his head.

There was no doubt about it.

This was Andrew Monroe.

CHAPTER FOUR

"Wh-what are you doing here?" she sputtered.

Before Andrew could answer, Katelyn's attempts to get out of the car on her own diverted Mallory's attention. She swung around from Andrew to see Katelyn dragging herself and her useless legs out of the car and to the too-distant wheelchair.

"Wait, Katelyn! Stop!" Mallory warned. "The chair—"

Andrew was two steps ahead of her. While Mallory stood frozen with panic at a possible fall, Andrew had picked up the chair and moved it closer to the car. And then he stepped back, leaving Katelyn to scramble into the chair as best she could.

Just like he did with the fire.

Over the months since the accident, Mallory had thought about what she would say to this man if she ever saw him again. The idea that he would abandon a helpless kid in a burning house… It boggled the mind. Her rational mind could see his point—but her rational mind left her whenever she heard Katelyn's pitiful moans and screams of pain.

So yeah. Mallory did blame Andrew Monroe for Katelyn's agony, for her lifetime sentence in a wheelchair, for each and every angry scar that rippled across her feet and legs and body.

Katelyn was happily oblivious, jabbering away with Andrew, asking about each of the horses, talking ninety to nothing about the farm. Andrew was already pushing Katelyn away from Mallory toward the stables.

"Wait!" Mallory called. "Where are you going?"

Andrew stopped, and Katelyn craned her head around to stare back at her. "Inside, silly," Katelyn said.

"Katelyn—do you know who this is? Do you know what he did?"

For a moment, Katelyn's expression was one of perplexed bewilderment. "Yeah. This is Andrew. He saved my life, Mal. He was the one. Sure. I've only been emailing and text messaging him for—gosh?" She looked up at Andrew, her perplexed expression now replaced with a wide grin. "Two months?"

Andrew shrugged his broad shoulders. "About that. Maybe not quite that long."

"He was the one who sent me the brochure. His sister owns the place. She's gonna help me walk again."

Wind whistled around Mallory, but it was shock and surprise that nearly knocked her to the ground. Emailing? Text messaging? And Katelyn had done all this...and hadn't said a word.

Because she knew you'd have put it a stop to it if you found out.

"Honey, Katelyn, Katie-bug..." Mallory rushed forward and knelt beside Katelyn's chair. "Maybe this isn't such a good idea. We can go to that other place. I mean, they have even more horses than this—"

"No." Katelyn's bottom lip jutted out, making her look six rather than nearly eighteen. "This is the place. I can feel it, Mallory. This is where I've got the best chance. Andrew says—"

Mallory didn't care one whit what Andrew Monroe said. She closed her eyes, closed her mind, tried to find calm and peace and some line of reasoning that would budge Katelyn.

She opened her eyes again as she heard Katelyn say, "And there's not as many patients here, see? I can get more one-on-one treatment with Maegan. Plus, I've been texting Maegan, too, and she's given me lots of tips and—"

For a while now, Mallory had thought it was herself who'd been inspiring and motivating Katelyn. She recalled the gritted-teeth determination that fueled Katelyn after every one of her black, dark episodes, and Mallory had foolishly thought she'd been the one to bring her sister back from the brink.

But no. All along, it had been the Monroes. A dynamic duo, from the sound of things.

Mallory let her gaze move from Katelyn's earnest face up to Andrew's. If for one moment, she'd caught him gloating, seen even the faintest hint of a self-satisfied smirk on his lips, she would have snatched that wheelchair around and dashed for the car.

Instead, she could only see patient forbearance on his face. He wasn't angry or defensive or smug. His hands rested lightly on the wheelchair's push bars. Suddenly, Mallory remembered how strong and comforting his grip was the night of Katelyn's accident, before she'd gone all ballistic on him.

Wouldn't it be terrific if she could actually believe in that quiet strength he exuded?

"Mallory?" he said now. "What will it be? Do you want me to help you get Katelyn back in the car? Or…"

She closed her eyes again, breathed in, breathed out. Weighed her options.

She was here. And Katelyn was happy and believed this place, these people, could help her. And all of their meager belongings were stacked in boxes in a tiny apartment not too far from here, and Mallory had a job here to pay the bills.

What did it matter if she let Katelyn try it? Even if she did decide to move her, at least this way Katelyn would be getting some therapy in the interim. Mallory didn't have to fix this today.

"If this is what you want."

Katelyn squealed with delight. "It is! Oh, thank you, Mal, for not being a pill about it!"

Already Andrew was once again pushing Katelyn toward the stables, and already Mallory was regretting her decision. Where was her resolve? What had her dad always said? "Don't let your wishbone be where your backbone should be."

She wasn't giving in. She was… This was a tactical retreat, that was all. She could be the bigger person here, she decided as she followed Andrew and Katelyn down the pea-gravel path to a white door set in the end of the building.

The warmth inside wrapped around Mallory like a welcome blanket, easing the cold in every part of her save her feet. She glanced down at what felt like two ice blocks shod in her most comfortable heels and kicked herself for wearing them. Heels? To a stable? Boy, she looked dumb. She had been so anxious this morning to get Katelyn from their motel room to here that she'd thrown on her usual "uniform" of a slim skirt, a white blouse, a blazer and...yes, heels to a stable.

The room they were in was more like a living room than an office waiting room—cheery and comfortable, with rough-hewn walls like the inside of a log cabin, sprawly leather furniture, and a kitchen/dining area off to the side. Large paintings of horses and farm life graced the walls, and framed photos of disabled children with a dark-haired woman and various horses were scattered throughout the room. The windows along the back were large and looked out onto the same green paddocks that Mallory had seen earlier. Outside, the horses still ran like four-year-old kids, mindless of the cold.

She found herself drawn to the warmth from a set of gas logs in a corner fireplace, and not just because Andrew had backed Katelyn up to it, as well. Now, for the first time in months, she took the opportunity to look at the man who had left her sister to die.

He wasn't a monster. In her mind, Mallory had made him harder, more calculating. She realized that now as she noticed how compassion seemed to soften the crisp lines of his face. Kneeling beside Katelyn, Andrew was making sure that her little sister was settled in. He tucked a throw from one of the couches around her as if she were seven, not seventeen going on eighteen.

That was reassuring, especially since Katelyn had let slip that the pair of them had been exchanging emails and text messages. Mallory switched her scrutiny to Katelyn. Was Andrew another of Katelyn's frequent "crushes"? It would certainly explain why her sister had wanted to come here, if she'd developed feelings for Andrew. Katelyn could fall so hard and fast with such little encouragement and be convinced that this fellow, this guy, would be her Prince Charming forever.

Mallory smothered an inward snort. There were no Prince Charmings. As soon as a guy heard you were raising your little sister, he was out of there like a shot.

Andrew straightened up into a standing position, and it reminded Mallory afresh how tall and imposing a figure he made. "Hey, my sister's finishing up a phone call. You guys look as though you could do with some coffee. C'mon, Mallory, and I'll show you where we keep the coffeepot."

She followed him into the kitchen area, neat and tidy, surprised to find the counters topped with real butcher block instead of the usual kind. Sliding her hand along the smooth finish, she thought of her dad and his woodshop in the garage, and how he'd been working on a butcher-block island for her mom when…

"You like? Came from trees right here on the property. My brothers and I made these counters ourselves—had the trees sawed into lumber and kiln dried."

Mallory looked up to see Andrew holding a cup of coffee out to her. She slid her fingers along the silky surface of the counter one final time, realizing the hours of sanding that had gone into creating its satiny finish. As she took the cup from Andrew, she said, "They're beautiful. I don't recognize the wood. Is it some sort of maple or oak?"

"Nope, poplar. Ma would have killed us if we'd cut down any of the big oaks on the place. A stand of poplars had to go to make room for the stables, so Maegan asked us if we could use the wood in the construction. Sugar? Cream? It's here. And how does Katelyn take her coffee?"

From the other room, Katelyn called out, "Katelyn takes a little coffee in her cream, that's what Mal tells her. We can't all be tough and fierce and grown up and drink our coffee black like Mallory."

Mallory felt her cheeks heat up. "Think melted coffee ice cream, and you're on the right track," she agreed. "And despite what Katelyn says, I do take a little cream and sugar in mine on occasion." She didn't add that the reason she often drank her coffee black was to save time and money—coffee was expensive in its own right, and Katelyn could drink enough cream and sugar in her coffee for two.

"Melted coffee ice cream? That's an atrocity to good coffee!" Andrew protested. He winked at Mallory, and Mallory found herself grinning back at him. "Especially mine—

you could drink it black. Here, I can't do it to the poor unsuspecting stuff. You'd better."

Quickly she dumped enough cream to float a small boat and a mountain of sugar into the cup. There—exactly the sweet, sticky mess that Katelyn liked.

"Whoa! You weren't joking… Put that in an ice cream churn, and you would have coffee ice cream." Andrew meanwhile had filled a mug that proclaimed "But first…coffee." True to his earlier words, he drank his coffee without fussing over cream or sugar.

His gaze met hers over the rim of the mug: his eyes bright blue, and despite the compassion she saw there, a trace of frank scrutiny still remained. She felt, impossibly, as though he were weighing her true worth against some high personal standard…and had not decided yet whether she measured up. Flustered, she let her own gaze fall to the butcher-block counter.

Once again, the memory of her dad came back to Mallory, and his cautionary quip about wishbones and backbones. That day, so many years ago, her mom and dad had left together for a weekend out of town. She'd been irritated that they expected her to look after Katelyn when what Mallory had wanted to do was go to the beach with her friends.

The last thing she remembered her dad saying as he affectionately ruffled her hair was, "I know it stinks to have to be stuck here, taking care of your sister, but you'll do a good job, and your mom needs some time away. Besides, keeping up with Katelyn builds backbone, right?"

Maybe it hadn't. Maybe if she could let Katelyn stay here, she didn't have any backbone at all. Maybe letting the man who'd abandoned her sister to this fate to begin with was the same as if she'd called up that landlord who owned that death trap and asked if he had any more properties to rent.

No, letting her stay here was worse. Their lawyer had said as much: the landlord was culpable, sure, but any jury would see that the condition of the rental house had screamed buyer beware.

The fire department, though? It was their job to rescue people, to get them out of harm's way.

And then, as she let her fingers reflexively grip the smooth butcher-block, it clicked for Mallory. This whole thing was an elaborate con on Andrew Monroe's part. It would have been like Katelyn to spill everything she knew about the long conversations their lawyer had had with them.

"You know about the lawsuit, don't you?" she blurted out.

CHAPTER FIVE

"LAWSUIT?" ANDREW GULPED down the scalding coffee in a slurp rather than his intended sip. It burned all the way down to his stomach. "What lawsuit?"

Maegan's cheery, "Good morning! You must be Katelyn!" floated through the living room and into the kitchen area. He heard Katelyn's bubbly reply, and the subsequent chatter of conversation. Yep, he'd been right. Katelyn and Maegan would get on like a house on fire.

Mallory was a different story. Here she was, dressed to the nines in an outfit that looked straight off some fashion runway for working women. Who showed up at a stable with heels and a string of pearls? He'd known women like that—even made the mistake of dating a few before he wised up.

Yep, if Andrew had a type, it was high-maintenance Miss Fashion Plate right here in front of him. Lucky for him, he knew that if he scratched off her shiny, polished surface, he'd probably find her core to be all, "What's in it for me?"

One of these days, he was going to figure out that he needed to settle for a good, sensible woman who was comfortable in a pair of jeans, who knew how to stretch a dollar and wasn't all about appearances. Until then? He should steer clear of Mallory's shiny-as-a-new-penny good looks.

Especially if she was considering a lawsuit.

Hearing Maegan talking to Katelyn, Mallory seemed torn. Well, gosh, that went right along with what Andrew had deduced already—Mallory still seemed to focus on him as the cause of Katelyn's woes, was still more interested in placing blame than moving forward. After all, here she was, letting her sister's cup of coffee chill on the countertop rather than getting it to her while it was still warm.

Mallory must have read his thoughts, because she snatched up the coffee, turned on those spindly heels and marched into the den. He heard her as she joined the conversation, noted with some surprise that she seemed to be knowledgeable about the realistic limitations of what Katelyn could accomplish here.

An image of those melted bunny slippers came rushing back to Andrew. Had he left her to die? If he'd called it in when he first heard Katelyn above him—

No. He'd done his job; he'd followed protocol. At some point, you had to cut your losses, evaluate what you had left and make a plan to move forward. He was done blaming himself for that day.

That didn't mean he couldn't be sure Katelyn got the best therapy possible—and Maegan, pesky Irish twin sister or not, was exactly that. He'd seen miracles happen here—kids walking when their doctors had given up on them, an autistic boy speaking after five years of nothing but grunts and shrieks.

The wheels of Katelyn's wheelchair squeaked against the hardwood floor as Maegan moved the operation to a treatment room for her evaluation. She'd warned Andrew that assessment would tell the tale, whether there was any possibility for Katelyn to improve. The kid deserved a break, and Maegan could help her. He knew it.

Even if Mallory Blair didn't seem to know the treasure she had. She must have taken one look at Happy Acres and found it missing the sleek professionalism of a bigger, ritzier operation. A city slicker like her?

She must think we're all stupid hicks.

What lawsuit? What plan was bubbling away in that avaricious mind of Mallory Blair's? Because he knew her type: money, money, money. Had to have money to pay for that car and those clothes and that haircut. Oh, and those shoes—yep. He hadn't grown up with all the sisters he had not to be able to tell those heels, with their fancy design right on the stilettos, were pricey. From the tip of her coppery hair to those teetering printed heels, Mallory Blair screamed high-dollar woman.

He considered who here in Waverly might know about any lawsuit the Blairs could have filed.

Dutch would certainly know—"Dutch" Van der Gooten, the Levi County in-house counsel. Andrew spied a grocery/errand list on the fridge and made his decision: the horses were fed, the stables mucked out, Maegan didn't have another patient coming in until after lunch.

He snatched the list off the fridge, shot off a text to Maegan to let her know he was going into town and forwarded the rehab phones to his cell phone. Grabbing a jacket off the hook by the door, Andrew headed for his truck.

A few minutes later, the downtown section of Waverly came into view, with its three-layer-cake of a courthouse, complete with a frilly little cupola that held a clock tower. He made the block around the town center and continued along the main road lined with recently rebuilt mom-and-pop style shops, past his future sister-in-law Kari's bakery and Mr. Hiram Sullivan's jewelry store. The pocket park's interactive fountain was off, drained of water to protect it against the unusual deep freeze they'd had the past few nights, and, save for a few brave pansies that had weathered the cold, the space looked flat and empty against the crisp January blue sky.

Andrew turned his truck out of the more picturesque downtown area to some newer government buildings that had been built in the 1970s. They were squat and ugly and, to Andrew, like most folks in Waverly, a crime against architecture. He scanned the parking lot in front of the tallest one, a three-story brown brick that still managed to look short.

Yep, Dutch's motorcycle was parked in his usual slot. How a guy as smart as Dutch could ride a motorcycle to work on a day as cold as this boggled the mind. Andrew slammed the truck door and hurried into the warmth of the building.

Dutch's assistant waved him on in, a testament more to the fact that she knew they were buddies outside the office than to him being available. The two of them had played travel ball together for years in the youth and high school leagues, before Dutch had parlayed his considerable talent at batting into a baseball scholarship.

"Hey, Monroe!" Dutch flashed their old sign for a fastball as Andrew came through his office door. It had been Dutch, a catcher a couple of years older than him, who'd made Andrew a better pitcher than he should have been. "What's hanging? You here about the county-city softball tourney? I'm in, man. I am definitely ready for ball."

"With Daniel on the team, I'll probably be warming the bench. He's still got some life in that arm of his."

"That old dog?" Dutch grinned. "You can take him. I've caught for both of you, and sure, he was good when he was young, but he's nearly forty now."

Thirty-eight or not, Andrew's older brother, Daniel, was probably better at pitching than

Andrew would ever be. After all, Daniel had given up a good shot at the major leagues to come back and follow in their dad's footsteps when their dad, the fire chief, was killed in an arson fire years before. Now Daniel was the chief.

Andrew didn't waste time arguing baseball. He dropped down into the stackable office chair that was de rigueur for most of the county offices. "I had something else I wanted to know. Have you heard about any lawsuits against the department? Or the county?"

Dutch's easy smile faded. He leaned back in his chair and clasped his hands behind his neck. "What kind of lawsuits?"

This was the part of Dutch that Andrew didn't know as well, the lawyer side. Already Andrew could see his friend running the angles. Something about law school had turned Dutch into a more calculating guy than Andrew had known as a kid. Or maybe that cynicism had always been there and law school had brought it out.

"Um, well, you remember that big fire in October? The one where the girl got burned?"

"Yeah. The one where you went all cowboy and went back in without being checked out. Believe you me, I reamed out Daniel and the captain on the scene that day. Could have been a nightmare worker's-comp claim if you'd gotten hurt. But you're not suing, are you? Nah, didn't think so. Lemme see, the house was a total loss and the landlord was livid beyond belief. He's not suing us, either. Not that I know of."

"What about the girl? Katelyn Blair?"

"I don't know of any lawsuit that's come down the pike from that. No records have been requested, and they'd better have let me know if any ambulance chasers have been sniffing around. Why?" Dutch sat up and drilled him with the same intensity he'd had during their state championship game, when Andrew had a runner on second and had allowed a walk to first.

If Dutch hadn't heard of any lawsuit... But Mallory had said, "You know about the lawsuit, don't you?"

Andrew started outlining the situation, realizing when he had to backtrack several times to get to the real beginning that it was more complicated than he had admitted to himself. Dutch held up a hand.

"Whoa. Let me call Daniel." Dutch hit a speed dial on his phone and propped himself up on the desk, his elbow planted firmly on a pile of manila folders.

Andrew couldn't forestall a groan. He hated having his big brother dragged into this, because Daniel would go all boss man on him, not just boss man in the fire-chief sense but boss man as self-appointed head of the family.

Sure enough, Daniel was glowering when he came through the door a few minutes later. He moved a box of files from another chair in the office and plopped the chair down alongside Andrew's.

"Now, what's the five-alarm emergency that I had to zip over here for?" he asked Andrew. "Especially when you could have told me whatever it was at supper last night."

"Hey, it wasn't me— Dutch thought—"

"Dutch *knew* he needed to get the facts," Dutch interrupted. "And I wanted to hear Daniel's input. So. Proceed." Their friend leaned back, his expression as intent and calculating as before.

Andrew began again. The false starts had given him some rehearsal and he managed to get the story told in a more efficient, concise way. He held his breath as he waited for Daniel's reaction.

"You don't know of any lawsuit?" Daniel asked Dutch. "Nothing's been filed?"

Dutch shook his head. "Zip. I take it you didn't know about Andrew's big idea here to have a potential plaintiff do therapy at your sister's place?"

"Hey!" Andrew sat forward. "I had no idea that sister of hers was planning on suing! I was trying to help Katelyn. What? Am I supposed to say, 'Uh, no, you might sue us so you can't even think about having Maegan do your therapy?' That doesn't make a dab of sense."

"He's got a point," Daniel said. "I mean, it's a cock-eyed situation now, but at the time, he was— Well, heck, I wouldn't have thought anything of it if he had mentioned it to me. Maegan's excellent at what she does, and I would have felt it unethical to recommend someone else when they would have been my second choice. Besides. Maybe this Mallory Blair won't sue."

Dutch held up a finger. "Ah, but that's why I'm the county's in-house counsel, because unlike so many, I operate from the standpoint of defensive pessimism. She has mentioned the possibility of a lawsuit as if it were a done deal—ergo, there *is* a lawsuit. And that means complications. Maegan could be called to testify against the county—against your department, Daniel, and against you and Eric in particular, Andrew. My legal recommendation? If I were you, I'd suggest that this might prove to be a conflict of interest and you should help her find another rehab facility."

Andrew swore inwardly at the thought that he'd dragged Maegan in the middle of this mess with Mallory Blair. If the woman were the litigious sort, she'd as likely sue Happy Acres as she would the county.

The idea of cutting Katelyn loose rankled him. And it wasn't only Katelyn's enthusiastic response this morning to seeing Happy Acres for the first time. No, he thought back to the night he'd first met Mallory, to the single tear that had trickled down her cheek when she'd confessed that she had no family.

The two girls were alone. Mallory had lost her dad, just like Andrew had, but she hadn't had a family like he'd been blessed with to help her through it. Mallory Blair couldn't be all bad—a tad obsessed with money and appearance, maybe, but Katelyn had told him that her big sister had raised her, and Katelyn had turned out okay, right?

Katelyn…who wouldn't have been so badly injured if he'd only called it in a half minute sooner.

He pushed the thought away. "No. I'm not going to ask Maegan to do that. Katelyn doesn't deserve that—she deserves the best possible treatment, and Daniel's right— she'll get it here. If she's got any shot at all at walking again, it's going to be with Maegan. And you know, Daniel's right about another thing. I'll bet all Mallory wants is for her sister to be happy and healthy, and once she sees what all Maegan can do, the idea of a lawsuit will fade."

Dutch rolled his eyes. "Such Pollyanna attitudes. Whistle right by that churchyard, why don't you? Daniel? You want to set your little brother straight?"

Daniel scratched his chin and stretched out his long legs. His poker face was much better than Andrew's had ever been, and for a long moment, Andrew waited for his decision. "I can see your point, Dutch. It will be a mess if she does sue. Plus, you've got more experience with these things than either of us. Maybe being a lawyer means you're like a hammer. Everything you see, well, it's gotta be a nail."

Dutch shrugged. "Even a broken watch is right twice a day."

Daniel cocked an eyebrow. "In that analogy, are you the broken watch or are we?" He didn't wait for Dutch. "I think we can thread the needle here with a little watchful waiting. You keep your ear to the ground for any signs of a lawsuit, and maybe check out the well-heeled Ms. Blair for any past litigation. And meanwhile, we can let Maegan do what she does best—make patients better. Besides, if it did come to a lawsuit, we did everything by the book that day. We followed protocol, and my guys—even my little squirt of a brother here—were bona fide heroes, and they have the commendations to prove it." Daniel rose to his feet and clapped a hand on Andrew's shoulder. "Bottom line is, Mallory Blair wouldn't have a sister at all if it hadn't been for Andrew."

Unexpected pleasure rushed through Andrew at Daniel's rare compliment. The city had indeed awarded Eric, Chase Jackson and Andrew commendations for bravery following the fire. At the time, it had kind of embarrassed Andrew, and he figured it was mostly because Eric had been hurt, and he and Jackson had only managed to get Katelyn out.

Daniel's praise? That meant something—something that helped take the sting out of any accusing glare Mallory Blair might shoot his way.

CHAPTER SIX

FRANTICALLY MALLORY DUG through yet another box. Nope, no pots and pans, even though it was labeled clearly with the word Kitchen scrawled in her hand. She must have mixed it up with this box of sheets and towels in her hurry to get everything out the door before the landlord charged her another month's rent.

"I'd help you if I could—" Katelyn grunted with effort as she tried to shove another stack of cartons over to maneuver her wheelchair through the clutter of moving boxes.

At the sound, Mallory stopped and looked up. "Don't! You'll knock those over and hurt yourself!"

"Mal…" Katelyn sighed. "Forget it. Let's order a five-dollar pizza. I saw a take-out place as we drove through town. Just tonight, can we please, please, *please* not scrimp?"

For a moment, Mallory was so tempted. She, too, had seen the pizza place, and the last tenants had thoughtfully left a fridge magnet with the number on it. There was the phone... One call, and someone would be winging his way over with a hot, cheesy pizza that Mallory didn't have to lift a finger to get.

Reality came crashing down. "Katelyn... I don't have five dollars." The confession humiliated her.

"What? C'mon. We're not *that* broke. Are we?" Surprise and disbelief flooded Katelyn's eyes...and when Mallory didn't deny it, alarm quickly followed. "Are we?" she insisted.

"Yeah. We are. I'm between jobs, sweetie. I won't get paid for another two weeks, and I had to use our savings for the first and last months' deposit."

"Well...what about your slush fund?"

Mallory couldn't help but smile. Her "slush fund" was an emergency twenty she had tucked behind her driver's license. "I used it to pay Kyle for the gas to move us down here."

"Oh, man, if you used your slush fund, we *are* broke."

"Well—we're not *totally* broke, but I have to have gas money to get you back and forth to therapy and me to work. If worse comes to worst, I can ride your bike or even walk.

It's only a couple of miles from here to downtown."

"A couple of miles! That's an hour's walk! And not even you could bike in heels. No, Mallory, you're not going to walk. We'll... Man. I so did want a pizza."

"Yeah. I can taste the pepperoni. I have some flour and yeast, and we have that block of mozz. And I scored a couple of cans of tomato paste on sale. I think I've still got it— somewhere..." Mallory surveyed the sea of boxes. "We'll have pizza, Katelyn. Maybe not pepperoni, but we'll have pizza."

Katelyn made a sudden choking sound, and Mallory realized she was trying not to cry. Mallory weaved her way back through the boxes and knelt down beside her sister. "What? Are you hurting? I can get your meds."

Katelyn screwed up her fists and scrubbed at her eyes. "I hate this. I hate it. I can't even help you look for the blasted tomato paste. This is all my fault. If I hadn't been so *stupid*, I wouldn't have gotten hurt—"

"No. No, honey. It's not your fault. The house burning down wasn't your fault. You being left there—that wasn't your fault, either—" Was it Andrew Monroe's? Would it make it easier somehow to blame someone for the circumstances of their life?

Yeah. Yeah, it would.

"Can I— Is there any way I can lie down for a while? I'm sorry, Mallory, but I'm so tired…"

Katelyn did look tired. Her earlier energy seemed gone, and now dark circles ringed her lower lids and her pink cheeks had faded back to chalky white, with her freckles standing out in stark contrast. "Sure. The bed's the one thing we can actually get to."

Mallory helped her sister to her cramped bedroom, felt her back ache even at Katelyn's slight weight as she assisted her out of the wheelchair and onto the bed. Katelyn was already drifting off as Mallory pulled the covers up to her chin—over those poor scarred legs and feet.

Mallory felt her own throat close up and she choked back tears as she watched Katelyn settle into sleep. The facility had warned her that Katelyn still had nightmares and that her sleep "wasn't of good quality," as the discharge planners had put it. Mallory wasn't surprised that her sister was tuckered out by seven o'clock.

Rest. And a settled, stable home life, away

from medicinal smells and beeping monitors and nurses that said, "This may hurt a little," when they really meant it would be agony. Yeah, that was what Katelyn needed.

Mallory sighed. She had an apartment to settle and arrange, and a first day on the job tomorrow. Katelyn needed *that*, too.

By eight, Mallory had discovered that the tomato paste and other canned goods weren't in any of the boxes labeled Kitchen, and that her usual organizational skills must have taken a leave of absence when she'd been packing up.

Still, she'd made some progress. The pots and pans were found and liberated, the glasses unpacked.

The last one in the box, a big brown iced-tea tumbler, she set carefully down on the dinette table and examined for nicks or cracks. With a sigh of relief, she realized it had come through the move unscathed. It had been her dad's favorite glass, much to her mom's despair, as it hadn't matched anything else in their kitchen.

Neither Mallory nor Katelyn drank anything out of it. It stayed in the cupboard with the other glasses, a reminder of all the times

Mallory had toted a tall glass of iced tea out to her dad's garage workshop.

With a gentle finger, she skimmed the smooth brown surface—it had been some left-over of the 1970s that he'd found for a quarter at a garage sale. Touching it felt as if she was touching him, that he was a breath away, ready to wrap her in his arms for a reassuring bear hug and a promise that things would get better.

The loud, unfamiliar brring of the door-bell startled her out of her reverie. The rental manager? A neighbor?

Mallory wended her way through the maze of cartons to the door. This apartment complex hadn't appeared too friendly—it was a low-income subsidized complex where people seemed suspicious of newcomers. She'd chosen it in spite of the atmosphere, because it had a stackable washer and dryer, and it was handicap accessible.

Maybe she'd been wrong. Maybe there were neighbors out there who cared enough to introduce themselves.

She looked through the peephole and took a step back.

There, on the tiny stoop, stood Andrew Monroe.

And he was holding a take-out pizza carton.

ANDREW WAS DEBATING between leaving the pizza on the porch and ringing the doorbell for a third time when finally the door swung open.

The Mallory Blair it revealed looked nothing like the one he'd seen before. Gone was the polished wardrobe, and in its place a faded T-shirt and jeans. Her hair was pulled back in a neat ponytail, save for one strand of auburn silk that had escaped across her cheek. The biggest change was her glasses— the dark rims framed her intense green eyes and made her look like some glamorous scientist in a television commercial.

"Hi," she got out. The awkwardness was apparent. "I— How did you—"

"Katelyn's address on her chart. I honestly thought—" he glanced around at the other low brick duplexes. "I thought maybe you'd written down the address wrong. It didn't seem to fit with…uh, what you'd live in."

Did her chin jut out a bit? Yeah, it did.

"This was handicap accessible. And it's just temporary," she cut him off in a stiff voice.

He shifted the pizza to his other hand. "Well, uh, it occurred to me that maybe, what with moving in and all, you guys could do with a pizza."

Okay, so he was a rat and he was actually using the pizza as a pretext for spying on her, which was exactly what Dutch had advised against. In fact, the lawyer's last words that morning had been "Stay away from Mallory Blair. Far, far away, understand? The less you have to do with her, the better."

Apparently, though, Andrew couldn't have picked a better thing to bait Mallory with. The way she was regarding that pizza… Man, her mouth was practically watering. She seemed to be of two minds as to whether she should accept his Trojan horse, but one mind was definitely winning.

"Well, come on in, but please excuse the mess. And Katelyn is asleep, if you've come to see her."

Andrew followed her in. "No, no, it was you—" He broke off and pretended to stub his toe on a carton to cover up his nearly blurted-out confession. This spy business was for the birds.

"What? Are you okay?" She had already bent down and appeared ready to whip off his steel-toed work boot to inspect for damage.

"Yeah, but I hope the same goes for whatever's in the box."

Mallory glanced at the label, which proclaimed it to be Mallory's Shoes. "Oh, yeah, it should be fine. Well—if I marked it right, that is. Apparently I labeled more than a few things wrong, but my old landlord was insisting that I move out before the next due date or pay a full month's rent. I asked if I could pay for a few extra days—"

She broke off as she entered the tiny kitchen, as if she were suddenly aware of what she was saying and to whom. To fill the silence, Andrew supplied, "No dice, huh? Maybe he had other folks wanting to move in?"

Mallory shrugged. "Maybe. I got us out just in time. What's a few mislabeled boxes, right?"

"The pizza okay on the table?" He went to move a big ugly brown glass, but Mallory leaped to intercept him as if the thing was a priceless antique.

She cradled it against her chest, her cheeks pink with embarrassment. "Uh…it was my dad's. I'm sorry. I didn't mean to insult you. It's only… When we had to sell everything… after… Well, there wasn't much left, which was just as well, because we didn't have much space. So…that's my inheritance. My dad's favorite iced-tea glass."

Something about the way she held it so

protectively moved Andrew. He cleared his throat, looked away. "Crazy, isn't it? The things we hold on to? For me, it's my dad's reading glasses. He'd started needing them right before he died, and, well… I still have them. Sometimes…sometimes I take them out and put them on and try to see the world like he saw it. Silly, huh?"

"No," she said in a rush, full of energy and force. "No, it's not. Not when it's the only thing you've got left to hold on to."

Now her mouth curved into a rueful grin. "I do have something we can actually use to drink out of, so let me put this away. Will ice water be okay?"

Andrew kicked himself for not thinking to bring a liter of cola. "Uh, I wasn't planning on staying— I just was dropping this—"

"No, I insist. Do, please, have a seat. Uh— but, you'll have to move that box—"

"No worries." He smiled and waved her away. "You get that ice water, and I'll clear the chairs for us."

After she set two more reasonably sized drinking glasses—dainty stemmed water goblets—on the table along with a couple of ornately decorated china plates, he noticed that she quickly folded cloth napkins into an elegant restaurant-style. "Wow," he commented. "Fancy, aren't we?"

"Well, of course, in honor of your generosity, only cloth napkins will do."

"Not even Ma brings out the cloth napkins much anymore," Andrew commented. "And she's a stickler for things like that. I'm impressed that you've been able to find the china and the napkins in all your boxes."

"That's about all I've been able to find, that and the pots and pans. I thought I'd gotten things down to the bare basics after our last move, but apparently not. And I even held a yard sale before this move."

"You move a lot, then?" *Duh, that was smooth, Monroe*, he thought to himself. To prevent himself from saying anything else, he took a bite of the pizza—still warm, despite the drive and the wait outside for her to answer the door.

Mallory must have been starving, because her pizza slice was history, and she was reaching for another. "This is good! I should wake Katelyn up…"

"If she's asleep, maybe she needs rest more than food. Maegan said she worked her pretty hard today."

"Your sister…" Mallory's eyes filled.

"She's wonderful. So patient and *thorough*. I wish we could have had a therapist like her at the rehab facility. I'm sure Katelyn would have already been walking if we had."

"Maegan is good, and I'm not saying that because she's my sister. Katelyn's in excellent hands, Mallory."

"I—I can tell." Mallory put the second slice of pizza down on her plate and fiddled with her napkin. "She's so good at motivating Katelyn, and that's not always an easy task."

Andrew was surprised at Mallory's comment. "That's…well, your sister seems pretty driven to me. She seems to want to get better and to be willing to put the work and effort in."

Mallory took a bite of the pizza, chewed it thoughtfully, and only after she'd washed it down with a swallow of city water did she answer, "Yes, and no. She has great intentions. She gets started with a bang, but…she's not… I wish she would stick with things, you know? Finish things." She trailed off and seemed lost in thought for a few minutes. And then, abruptly, she answered the question he'd posed a few minutes earlier.

"I only move when I have to. You know, if the rent goes up at the lease renewal. Try squeezing all the things that came from a house into an apartment. Or even a quarter of the things. After every move, I want to sell everything down to a Zen-like bareness. Then I think, 'Gee, I might need that…or what if I miss that?' I sound like a hoarder, don't I?"

Andrew laughed. "You sound like Ma. She has a use for everything. She even saves old toilet-tissue cores so that she can use them to make seed pots for starting our tomatoes early."

"Really? Toilet-tissue cores? How does she do that?"

"You cut the tube in half and then cut flaps into the end of the tube, and then—"

"It folds like a little box! Neat! That's smart!"

Maybe he'd misread Mallory. In her jeans and T-shirt, she seemed more like the girl he should aim for—not the type of glamour girl he had a weakness for.

But she had said *lawsuit*, and Dutch was convinced that such a word was seldom uttered in vain. And the two of them were sitting here eating pizza off fine china plates and cloth napkins…and she couldn't seem to part with an entire box of shoes despite her quest for, what had she called it? Zen-like bareness?

So…who was the real Mallory Blair?

And why was he so intrigued by the apparent contradiction? Hadn't Dutch warned him to stay far, far away?

CHAPTER SEVEN

ANOTHER HARD LOOK at her finances the next morning had caused Mallory to leave the car and its precious half tank of gas parked at the apartment in favor of Katelyn's old rusty bike. She carefully rolled her work clothes and stowed them along with her heels into a backpack Katelyn had discarded some years before.

Thank goodness Katelyn could manage on her own for a few hours. She debated waking her sister before she left, but decided against it. Better to let miffed little sisters lie—and Katelyn had certainly been miffed with her the night before.

She had awoken about a half hour after Andrew Monroe had made a sudden departure, as abrupt and unexpected as his arrival had been. "Why didn't you wake me?" Katelyn had said churlishly as she'd gobbled up her share of the reheated pizza. "Maybe I wanted to see him, too!"

She had accused Mallory of running off Andrew because she didn't like him—which hadn't been fair. Mallory hadn't chased off Andrew. He'd just…gone, before she even had a real chance to wake Katelyn. It was as if a light switch had been flicked. One minute they had been eating pizza together, and the next, whoosh! Suddenly, the man had headed out the door as though he was responding to a fire.

Maybe it was because of the nap, or maybe because missing Andrew had amped up Katelyn, but whatever the reason, she hadn't been able to go back to sleep before midnight. She'd watched sullenly while Mallory had slowly continued to get the apartment's contents out of boxes and into some semblance of order. Mallory knew that eventually her little sister would come out of her blue funk, but it bugged her that the Monroes—both Maegan and Andrew—could have such an impact on Katelyn's mood.

No, for now, she'd let Katelyn catch up on her sleep. She didn't have therapy until late this afternoon, after Mallory completed her first day on the job. She left a note and Katelyn's lunch to be warmed up in the microwave, stowed her own lunch, a PB&J, in her backpack along with a thermos of water and her work clothes and then struck out.

The morning air was frigid but the biking warmed her up fairly quickly. Mallory wasn't a practiced cyclist, but she'd done this before when funds were tight. She only wished that the helmet she'd scored at a yard sale wasn't so aggressively princessy. Katelyn had laughed at it when Mallory had brought it home, saying it had so many sparkles and bling that it looked like a unicorn had sneezed on it.

As Mallory rode into the downtown area, her spirits rose. She liked this little town with its cheerful awnings and bricked sidewalks. She could imagine kids playing in the fountain in the summer, and the whole place seemed alive and vibrant and inviting with its mom-and-pop-style businesses. It wasn't like the dying downtown back in the city—there, for years, the center of town had slowly spiraled into pawn shops and adult-video stores, and only now were the locals finally fighting back.

She'd spied a deserted farmer's market pavilion as well on her way in, and that gave her hope for cheap vegetables later on. Cheap was good, as broke as they were, and Katelyn needed good food to help her regain her strength—not junky food like Andrew Monroe's pizza, despite how tasty it had been.

And free and impeccably timed. Don't forget that. I should write him a thank-you note.

It still bugged her that he'd left so abruptly. Had it been something she'd said? Something she hadn't? He'd disappeared as suddenly earlier that same morning, nowhere to be found after she'd talked over Katelyn's evaluation with Maegan. It had to be about the lawsuit.

The lawsuit.

She was still of two minds about *that*. When an old coworker had visited the hospital and urged her to talk to an attorney, Mallory hadn't wanted to even think about it. Katelyn had been still fighting for her life, and something about suing anybody at that point seemed almost guaranteed to jinx her progress.

Her coworker had insisted, even to the point of bringing an attorney that she knew to see Mallory in the hospital.

Chad had sat down with her, put her at ease right away. "You're not taking anything from anybody," he'd pointed out. "They took something from *you*. They took Katelyn's health away, now, didn't they? Shouldn't they pay the medical bills?"

And so she'd allowed him to look into things. He'd been enthusiastic about the merits of the case—a fireman admitting that he'd left a poor helpless teenager in a burning building? Surely any jury would award them the medical expenses and give them a little money to help recompense Mallory for the days she'd had to be away from work to stay with Katelyn.

Those medical bills… Every single day in the ICU was another ten grand, and it went on and on, setback after setback. Mallory had only been able to afford the bare-bones catastrophic insurance plan for her and Katelyn, with a deductible that was ten thousand dollars, and her coinsurance after that was 40 percent of the negotiated rates of service, until an out-of-pocket max of twenty-five thousand dollars. Already the monthly payments for that deductible and her 40 percent were eating into their tight cash flow, but what else could she do? File bankruptcy? Her parents would have never countenanced that.

No. This was a new day. The county would help pay that debt—what was twenty-five thousand dollars to a big county government anyway? The lawyer assured her that the county carried insurance for exactly this situation—it wouldn't actually cost them anything.

And that was all she needed, those bills paid off, the slate wiped clean, so that she and Katelyn could start over. Mallory had a job, wheels under her that didn't require gas, a roof over her and Katelyn's heads—they would make it.

They had to make it.

She'd passed the shop where she'd be working and pulled to a stop at the traffic light to check the big old-fashioned clock hanging off a bank's granite exterior: 9:30. She had time to duck in somewhere and change clothes— but where? Was the library open?

It wasn't, but the squat and rather ugly municipal building a block or two from the downtown was, and she availed herself of the public restrooms. By the time she locked her bike to the bike rack near the shop and pushed open the door with its carefully scripted name, BASH, on the glass, it was 9:45.

Eleanor Bash, the owner, looked up. She'd been unpacking and steaming something seriously chiffony and yummy to Mallory.

"Good morning! Did I see you wheel by here on a bike?"

Mallory blushed at the thought that Eleanor had spotted her on that old bike and in that terribly childish helmet. "Uh, yeah. Am I late? Should I have come in the back?"

"Gracious, no, but next time, feel free to use the bathroom in the back. I even have a shower in there, if you feel the need. My brother cycles—to the point he shaves his legs, can you believe it? I know all about how a cyclist needs to clean up."

A huge weight lifted off Mallory's shoulders. She'd hoped that her first impressions of her new boss had been right on, and it looked as if they were. "That looks lovely—how can I help?" she asked.

"Don't you just love this color? Lemon yellow probably won't sell until spring, but, oh, I hate the winter!" Eleanor shuddered. "How about you start checking off that packing list? Sometimes this particular company, bless 'em, shorts me, so I have to be extracareful."

The workday had begun, busy enough, though nothing as hectic as the city boutique she'd worked in previously. Eleanor had warned her at the interview stage that if she were looking for high volume, it wouldn't be here—BASH had to mix casual wear with formal wear in order to make it through the year, but the store had a steady business.

Still, Mallory felt calmed by the familiar surroundings of swishing silk and cotton, high heels and the warm, earthy smell of leather bags. And in Eleanor, she'd found a compatriot who understood the importance of line and style and fit.

It was just after Mallory had downed her PB&J that the door alert rang out and a group of three ladies came in. Two were a few years older than Mallory, comfortably but stylishly dressed, but the third woman wore a shell-shocked expression. She looked as though BASH was probably the last place she wanted to be.

The woman was in her sixties, her gray hair in a no-nonsense bun, her face devoid of even a trace of makeup. She was slim, but the khaki mom-jeans-style trousers and the baggy cardigan and button-down shirt did nothing for her. What made her beautiful despite all that was the way her sky-blue eyes sparkled and her warm, self-effacing smile seemed to light up the shop.

"My heavens, can't I go down to the mall and

get something? Or just wear a church dress?" she was asking the two younger women.

"Now, Ma, no, we talked about this. This is Daniel's wedding. You got dressed up for my wedding, and for Cara's, so—"

"Why can't I wear one of those dresses, then? I'll bet they'll still fit," the woman protested.

"Ma! You still have the dress you wore to my wedding? That was fifteen years ago! It's so out of style, you probably couldn't even give it away."

"Styles come back in, don't they?" the older woman replied in a reasonable tone. "And I don't think…" she gestured to a trendy above-the-thigh strapless dress on a mannequin "No, that's not quite right for *me*."

Mallory decided the woman had a realistic view of style, unlike her prior customer, who had insisted that if she had it, she should flaunt it.

The time was right for Mallory to approach her customers. "Hi, there." She extended her hand. "I'm Mallory. Are you looking for something to wear to a wedding? Can I help you find something?"

"Well, aren't you cute as a button? Mallory, you say? Just call me Ma, everybody does."

Beaming, the woman grabbed the proffered hand. "Now, you, you'd look mighty fine in that number—" she indicated the mannequin "—but if you don't have anything…eh, a little more sedate, then one of my church dresses will have to do."

Mallory laughed. "We do, in fact, have something a little more sedate. Can you tell me more about the wedding? When is it?"

"Not till the spring, so gracious only knows why they're dragging me out this early to look for a dress," Ma grumbled. "It's going to be in late May, outdoors at our farm. I don't need to get all gussied up for that, now do I?"

The two younger women, her daughters, Mallory guessed from the marked similarity she saw in eyes that were now rolled heavenward, groaned. "Yes, Ma, you do have to get all gussied up. This is for Daniel and Kimberly," the younger one said. "Now, you made such a fuss over the china patterns—this is no different. It's just like—"

"No, it's not. China, you got to live with, but a dress? I'll wear it once, and then the next time I try to wear it, you'll both be telling me it's out of style."

"What if…" Mallory surveyed the woman. "What if we get you something classic and simple, something that won't go out of style and you can wear to other things?"

"Maybe another wedding?" Ma said hopefully. "Because my other son is getting married soon, too."

"Ma!" the younger daughter protested. "You can't wear the same dress to Rob's wedding that you do to Daniel's—"

"And why not? She just said I could."

"But it will be the same in the pictures!"

"Let's—" Mallory tried to smother a chuckle and couldn't. This woman and her daughters were too precious—for all the squabbling, it was obvious that they loved each other.

Mallory managed to control her laughter before it overtook her completely, and she held up a hand. "Let's try to get your mom a dress she'll love, and then maybe we can find it in a different color for the next wedding?"

Ma stabbed a finger at her. "I like this girl! Yes, ma'am, lead me on to these magical dresses that never go out of style."

They began looking at sheath and column dresses, with Mallory desperately trying to figure out where the wedding would fall on the fancy/not fancy scale. Ma kept insisting that the wedding was not at all fancy, since it was going to be at their farm, while her daughters, who turned out to be DeeDee and Cara, insisted, that no, there must be bling on the dress.

"Kimberly's like me—not fussy a bit. Why, she hasn't even been able to find a dress herself yet—"

The door jangled, and Mallory, who had the store to herself while Eleanor had gone out for a late lunch, craned to see who it was.

When no head popped up over the dress displays, she frowned. "Excuse me—I could have sworn I heard the door open."

"Oh, yeah. It's a girl in a wheelchair. Some nice gentleman opened the door for her and helped her over the threshold," Ma told her. "I saw it all a minute ago while Cara and DeeDee were fighting to the death over sequins. Sequins! At my age!"

Mallory's heart stopped. *Girl in a wheelchair* meant only one thing to her—Katelyn. How had she gotten here? Who had driven her? Was something wrong?

It was Katelyn, sitting proudly just inside the door near a display of the store's newest arrivals.

"Hey, Mal. What do you think, huh? I managed to drive the car all the way down here, all by myself! Pretty cool, if I do say so myself!"

Mallory opened her mouth to—what? Fuss at Katelyn for driving when she hadn't been cleared by her doctor? When she didn't have good control of her legs? Scold her for using part of the gas Mallory needed to drive her to therapy?

Breathe. Breathe, she commanded herself. *She's safe and sound, and how much gas could it have taken?*

Katelyn's announcement, loud and boisterous, had attracted the attention of Mallory's customers. They followed Mallory toward the front of the store like a flock of little ducklings.

"Well!" The smile in Ma's voice was unmistakable. "Katelyn! How nice to see you again! And you're driving? That's good! Maegan will be so proud of you."

Mallory spun slowly back toward Ma, then swung to take in Katelyn's grin. The pieces clicked into place.

This was *Ma*. Ma Monroe—Collette? Colleen? Andrew's mother. The woman who had sent her fried chicken and blankets and pillows.

A paranoid thought pulsed through her

head: Colleen Monroe had never set foot in this shop before today. And Andrew had "happened" to drop by last night with a pizza.

Were they trying to charm her into dropping the lawsuit?

She scrutinized Ma's face as Katelyn jabbered away. No, the woman looked genuinely surprised to see Katelyn here. It was a small town, and most definitely high fashion wasn't Ma's cup of tea, so maybe it wasn't so unusual that she had never been in here before.

"Wait, is this your sister? Mallory?" Ma turned back to her. "Now, why on earth didn't you tell me that?"

"Well—I—"

"Because," DeeDee interjected gently. "You didn't properly introduce yourself, Ma. You used that old, 'Just call me Ma, 'cause everyone else does.'"

"So I did. Now you really know who I am."

"I—I—" Mallory stumbled over her awkwardness. "That fried chicken you sent, and those blankets—it was a wonderful kindness."

Ma laid a hand on Mallory's arm. "And you sent such a sweet thank-you note care of the fire department. People don't bother to write thank-you notes anymore. It made my day, it did."

A pang of guilt coursed through Mallory. She'd written that thank-you note with gritted teeth, carefully packing it up with the cooler, as well as the blankets and pillows that she'd used her not-so-spare change to dry-clean. The shipping cost had been exorbitant in light of her scant funds, but she hadn't wanted to keep a thing of Andrew Monroe's.

"Gracious! Ma!" DeeDee had glanced at her watch. "I've got to go pick up the kids from school!" She shot an apologetic smile toward Mallory. "Can we finish this later? I think Ma's on the right track with this dress, but I have to go, and we're all in the same car."

"Sure," Mallory said uncertainly. "I'll be glad to—"

"Why not bring some of those brochures tonight and have supper with us?" Ma suggested. "I'll look over those pictures and DeeDee and Cara can argue all they want about sequins, plus Kimberly's coming in tonight, so we can ask her how fancy I need to be. I believe I'll be able to think better when I'm home and not amidst all this frippery. That's just the ticket, right?" She laid her palm against Katelyn's thin cheek. "You could do with some fattening up, child, especially the way Maegan will work you. Say, about 6:00? Now, it's plain fixin's, nothing fancy."

"Oh, no—" A feeling of being swallowed up by all things Monroe swept over Mallory. She even found herself taking a step back.

Katelyn interrupted. "Sure! That sounds cool! We can hang out after my therapy session with Maegan, because it will get over about 5:30."

"You come right on down to the farm when you get finished, and I'll put you to work." Ma patted Katelyn's cheek again, and the tenderness of it reminded Mallory of how Mom used to touch her own cheek.

No. She would not, out of stubborn pride, deprive Katelyn of any mothering she could get. Not even if it meant possibly bumping into the here-again, gone-again Andrew Monroe.

CHAPTER EIGHT

IF MALLORY HAD thought she'd been swallowed by all things Monroe earlier, she hadn't even been close. The house was full to bursting with dark-haired men and honey-haired women and boisterous children stair-stepping from diapers to teens.

It also smelled divinely of fragrant steak and gravy. These people believed in eating: on the counters, they were preparing mountains of mashed potatoes, rivers of onion gravy, platters of golden biscuits, bowlfuls of green beans. Mallory's stomach, pinched and cranky from the inadequate PB&J, quivered in anticipatory delight at such a feast.

Her appetite convinced her to stay put while her feet wanted to run. She'd never been good in big gatherings of people—large families weren't her forte.

Now Katelyn on the other hand...

Katelyn had settled into the fray as though she belonged with the Monroes. She sat at one end of the kitchen table, chopping vegetables for a salad alongside two girls about five years younger than her. She laughed and joked with them and with every other Monroe that seemed to wander through the house every five minutes. There wasn't a shy bone in her body tonight, no sullen withdrawn quietness, no bashfulness about her wheelchair.

No, it was Mallory who was bashful.

She managed to wedge herself into a relatively quiet corner by the window where she could observe the family from a distance. There was the big tall jokester—Rob— and he seemed to be connected to a blond named Kari, who was decorating a cake. And Daniel—a tad shorter than Rob, despite being older—was kind of serious, but she could see the longer he stayed, the more relaxed he became.

Andrew, though… He was nowhere to be seen.

Admit it, Mallory said to herself. *You're disappointed.*

Kimberly, Daniel's fiancée, wriggled into the corner beside her. "You hiding out?" she asked Mallory.

"Just staying out of the way. We're kind of

packed in here, don't you think?" Mallory swept a hand toward the crowded kitchen.

"The Monroes can be a little overwhelming at first. I was sure gob-smacked by them," Kimberly admitted.

"Are they always..." Mallory trailed off, not sure exactly what she meant to ask.

Kimberly laughed. She nodded. "Yep. Always just like this. Any excuse whatsoever to get together, to make a party out of things. You should have been down here in October—they had a cane grinding and all the homemade cane syrup you could eat."

Mallory's stomach went from pleasantly hungry to tight and tense at the mention of October. October had found her not at a frolic of cane grinding, whatever that was, but in a burn unit's waiting room, praying that Katelyn would survive.

And all because Andrew had left Katelyn trapped in that fire.

The noise and laughter filling the room must have covered up Mallory's reaction, or maybe something else distracted Kimberly. Thankfully, the woman detached herself and left Mallory alone to watch the rest of the crowd.

As if her thoughts had conjured him up,

Andrew came strolling in the back door, along with a wake of cold air from the darkening winter outdoors.

Katelyn looked up from her carrot chopping. "Howdy, stranger! Where have you been?"

"Well, someone had to get the horses all in for the night. I noticed you didn't offer to help. No, you hightailed it up from the therapy center for Ma's toasty kitchen," Andrew teased. He squeezed past Katelyn's wheelchair at the end of the table to hang up a set of keys on a hook.

"Hey, buddy, I'm a paying customer at this here dude ranch," Katelyn protested. She reached up and punched him on the arm as he slid by again.

Andrew tweaked Katelyn's hair like he would a kid's. "The old dudette ploy, huh? Hang around here much longer, and you'll turn into an honorary Monroe, and then we'll see if you can get away with that."

They bantered back and forth a few minutes longer. Mallory was relieved to see that there was nothing remotely romantic about their interaction—Andrew could have been bedeviling a pesky kid sister. Katelyn, who went all breathy and silly and brainless when one of her crushes ever entered her sphere, didn't show any telltale signs of infatuation.

And that's why you're watching for that, right? Mallory tried to convince herself.

Just then, a toddler, barely steady on her feet, wrapped her arms around Andrew's legs. "Horsey!" she insisted. "Horsey!"

Andrew swung the curly-haired tot up onto his shoulders and galloped around the room, evoking squeals of delight from his rider. His spirited jouncing took him careening into Mallory's hideout by the window. He bumped into her, realized it was her and, his face flaming, pulled up short. He set the toddler down gently on her feet.

"Horsey's all tuckered out, now, sweetie. Go find Uncle Daniel and see if he'll give you a ride."

Off she went, undeterred by all the people and chairs in her way.

"Well, I guess I've made a pluperfect fool of myself," Andrew muttered as he settled alongside her on the wide window ledge Mallory had pressed into service as a seat. "I'm not—well, I don't usually gallop around like—"

A part of her couldn't bear to let him wiggle on the hook of embarrassment. "I thought it was sweet," Mallory told him. "I remember my dad doing that for me and Katelyn."

Some of the tension went out of him then, and he propped an ankle across the other knee, his denim-covered leg nearly brushing Mallory's thigh. His close proximity fueled a confusing flutter of heartbeats, and she found herself scooting over to give him—and herself—more room. Just as she did, she upended a potted plant that was the rightful possessor of the window ledge.

She grabbed for it, missed. She expected the ceramic pot to crash into smithereens on the floor, but Andrew caught it, his strong forearms brushing across her lap. He had the plant by the tips of his fingers.

"Wow—I thought it was a goner for sure—" Mallory reached to rescue the plant, her fingers intertwining with his.

"Ma's African violet has managed to survive us and a whole new crop of grandkids. Couldn't let it go down for the count."

"Hey," Rob hollered, and to her chagrin, Mallory realized the room had fallen silent and everyone was focused on them. "You two lovebirds! If you'll quit playing Twister over there, it's time to eat."

Daniel seemed especially intent, as if

weighing both Mallory's and Andrew's actions. He dipped his chin down, raised a pointed brow at Andrew. Mallory knew a telegraphed message when she saw one—hadn't she done much the same to a recalcitrant Katelyn on more than one occasion?

She felt her face awash with heat and color and tugged at the African violet. "I've got this," she insisted.

Andrew let go of the plant, stood up. His mouth, formerly smiling and relaxed, now set in a straight, ungiving line, with no trace at all of the dimples she'd seen just two seconds earlier. "Y'all go ahead," he said to his older brother. "I need to wash up."

And with that, he peeled off for the hall as though being spotted with her was something shameful. No backward glance, no apologies, not so much as an "excuse me."

The rest of the crowd still seemed to focus on her with intense interest—unlike Andrew, who'd shot off like a cannon.

To cover her embarrassment, she turned, righted the plant on the ledge and brushed off her hands.

Daniel the fire chief is warning Andrew off, she thought, disappointed in spite of herself. Now, why did she feel the need to have the Monroes like her?

That—especially with the lawsuit that Chad might be filing—was a weakness she couldn't afford.

IN THE HALF bath off the kitchen, Andrew splashed water on his face and rubbed it briskly with a towel. He leaned against the sink, his hands planted on either side of the countertop, and stared into his reflection.

Was he trying to prove he was an idiot? Dutch had told him to keep his distance from Mallory, to not tangle up the Blairs any more than he could help into his affairs.

And here he was…

He'd crashed into her not once, but twice, close enough to kiss her. If he'd wanted.

What red-blooded man wouldn't?

Except for the clear signs that she wanted nothing to do with him—hadn't she looked down her nose at his high jinks with his niece Cassie? Sure, she'd mumbled something about how sweet it had looked, but that was manners.

And manners Mallory Blair had in spades. He still remembered the prim thank-you note she'd sent to Ma along with all the stuff

he'd taken to her that night in the hospital—
complete with dry-cleaning tags still attached
to the blanket and pillow.

Andrew shook his head to clear it. He had
a weakness for cover-girl beauties like Mallory, and even if she wasn't contemplating a
lawsuit like Dutch feared, he needed to steer
clear of her kind.

Although, that was hard, with her joining
them for supper. Still…not impossible to keep
his distance. He was glad it was a full house
tonight, where usually it was only Maegan
and Ma, with him coming up to join them
from his apartment over the stables.

Back in the dining room, he realized with
a sinking heart that the only spot left around
the crowded table was by Mallory. No way
to switch without attracting more attention,
so he squeezed in and began to fill his plate.

"You missed grace," Ma pointed out. "You
did say go ahead."

"I did," Andrew agreed, shoveling a little
too many mashed potatoes on his plate.

"Ma, this is so good! Wow!" Katelyn said.
"We haven't eaten like this in… How long
has it been since we've had meat, Mal?"

"You're a vegetarian?" he asked Mallory.
That might explain why she was pushing

around the food on her plate...but it didn't explain the healthy dent she'd put into her own smothered cube steak and gravy.

The glance she shot Katelyn was pointed and freighted with hidden meaning. "Uh, no. It's just—well, you don't need much meat, now do you? And it's awfully expensive."

Katelyn bristled under Mallory's subtle telegraphed message. She rolled her eyes. "Oh, yeah. Why buy meat when you can buy shoes, huh, Mal?"

Shoes? A sudden memory of a big box labeled Mallory's Shoes filled Andrew's mind's eye. The kid was bone thin and getting over a horrible accident, and Mallory put more value in buying *shoes* than putting a decent meal on the table?

Mallory ducked her head and mumbled something, then lifted her chin. "This is wonderful. I'd love the recipe, Ma."

"Oh, me, it's nothing fancy." She began rattling off the ingredients. Thankfully, this seemed to kick the conversation back to easier territory.

Andrew concentrated on eating his meal as quickly as possible so that he could make his excuses. He allowed the conversation to wash over him, trying hard not to notice the resolute self-containment that radiated from Mallory. Was she simply tolerating their company?

Well, hey, we offered her free food. That's more money to buy shoes and fancy duds with.

Maybe that wasn't fair, but it was the first thought that popped into his mind. And what transpired a few minutes later did nothing but strengthen his conviction that Mallory was after the almighty dollar, however she could get it.

The talk had, big surprise, turned to wedding dresses. With two weddings bearing down on the Monroes, it was all Andrew could do to escape endless discussion about stuff that they'd all wear for fifteen minutes and be hot and miserable while they did.

Kimberly was relating to them yet another failed dress hunt when Katelyn piped up, "Hey, Mal could sew your dress. She can sew anything. She was studying to be a fashion designer."

Mallory's fork clattered against her plate, dropping into a hillock of mashed potatoes. She picked it up and daintily wiped off the potatoes before studiously going back to her supper.

"Could you, Mallory?" Kimberly leaned forward, hope in her eyes. "I've looked all over Atlanta for a dress I like, and I can't seem to find one. They're all strapless or too low cut."

"Oh, Katelyn's letting her imagination run away with herself—" Mallory protested.

"I mean, I'd pay—my dress budget is two thousand dollars, but I can't find what I want."

Andrew couldn't mistake the sudden calculating interest in Mallory's eyes. "Well… what exactly are you looking for? If it's not too elaborate…"

Yeah. Suddenly her sewing skills get a whole lot better when Kimberly waves two grand in front of her.

Disgusted, Andrew shoved back his chair. Enough of this woman who valued fashion over basic needs and didn't show a bit of interest in wedding dresses until someone offered her an obscene amount of money to sew one. Two thousand dollars? For a dress you'd wear once? *Highway robbery.*

"Excuse me," he muttered. "I need to see if I locked the stables."

CHAPTER NINE

MALLORY ESCAPED THE hubbub of the kitchen and soaked in the cool quiet of the dusk in the backyard off the kitchen's porch. She shivered, but it was too freeing to be away from all that ruckus to worry about the fact that she wasn't wearing a winter coat.

No, the one winter coat they had between them had gone to Katelyn, as hers had burned up in that fire. Katelyn had complained that Mallory's classic trench coat was too "businesswomany" to suit her. Mallory had insisted. Until she could find a good one in Katelyn's preferred style at the thrift store, Katelyn would have to wear hers.

Maybe with what's left of the two thousand bucks from the wedding dress I can buy Katelyn a new coat, she told herself optimistically.

Kimberly's dress didn't seem to be that complicated—and Ma had even dug up a vintage pattern from the 1950s that was similar to what Kimberly wanted. It was a plain and simple sleeveless A-line, with princess seams, a full tulle skirt and a lace back.

The lace alone will cost two hundred bucks, the pessimist in Mallory countered. *And getting the fit right will be a nightmare.*

She wouldn't let her pessimism talk her out of her good mood. No, even if the fabric and lace and tulle set her back five hundred dollars, as she'd warned Kimberly it might, the bride-to-be was still willing to give her the remainder of the two thousand dollars for sewing the dress.

An emergency fund! A real emergency fund! At that thought, she couldn't help herself—she whirled around in a pirouette of pleasure.

"Better be careful—our Labrador, Jake, digs holes out here, and those spindly little heels of yours are just right for taking a tumble."

Andrew Monroe's sour tone brought her up short. Mallory peered into the gloom. Yes, there he was, standing on the other side of a white post-and-rail fence. He held a largish horse so dark it was rendered practically invisible in the dim light.

"You startled me!" she admitted. "I didn't know you were there."

"I take it you wouldn't be dancing a jig if you had? What's all the sudden happiness for?"

Sheesh. He sounded downright suspicious. Despite her horse phobia, she came closer. "Do I need a reason?" she countered.

"I figure it has something to do with the money you charmed out of Kimberly."

She couldn't help the sharp intake of breath his words, so accusingly delivered, evoked. "I didn't *charm* anything out of Kimberly."

"You *can* sew the dress, right?"

Mallory closed in, not even thinking about the horse now that he'd made her good and steamed. "What makes you think I can't?"

"I didn't say you couldn't. I asked if you could. Can you?"

"Yes. Yes, I can. I was at Savannah College of Art and Design when my—"

The memory of why she dropped out of SCAD slammed into her. Her parents. She owed no sort of explanation to this man of all people—he'd nearly caused her to lose the one family member she had left.

"When what? You decided that shopping was more your thing than sewing? DeeDee told me she and Ma and Cara ran into you over at BASH, that fancy new store downtown. Place like that, you can find a lot of shoes if you don't buy meat, huh?"

"I. Work. There." This, delivered through gritted teeth, surprised Mallory. Why the need to defend herself? Why the impulse to explain herself to him?

A beat of silence stretched out to two, interrupted by the horse's soft snuffling against Andrew's palm. "Oh. I—well, I just thought—"

"You just thought wrong."

She turned with the intent of stomping off, but then slid on the gravel near the fence. Her legs and arms pinwheeled, the horse reared and snorted in surprise and she was convinced she was going to land on her backside.

Exactly as Andrew's quick reaction had saved Ma's African violet, his fingers clamped down on her thrashing arm. He yanked her upright. "Watch it!" he warned.

With shaking fingers she clasped the rough wood of the post-and-rail fence. The horse seemed uncomfortably close, even going so far as to bend down and give her cheek a hot breath of air from its flaring nostrils.

"Uh—uh—can you—put that thing in Reverse?" she asked. No way could she let go of the fence…not without her shaking knees hitting the ground.

"What? Me? Or Pogo?"

"Pogo? Is that the name of that beast?"

"It's a horse, not a beast. Don't you like horses?" Andrew had not removed his hand from her arm, but he had relaxed its grip. Since he had the beast—Pogo, she corrected herself—by its rope, she and it were way too close.

"S-sure," she quaked. "In theory. Pictures. I like horses in pictures."

"Not an animal person, then, I take it? Unless it's made into furs or shoes?"

His sneer evaporated her fear. "Hey, knock it off! I don't wear furs. And I notice those shoes you're wearing are leather. Are you determined to see me in the worst possible light or what?"

MALLORY'S WORDS, SHARP and indignant, speared right through Andrew. He could almost hear Ma's voice in his head about manners and politeness and respecting people, even if they were different than him.

And, boy, is Mallory different from me.

He was close enough to take in her perfume, a flowery scent that put him in mind of tea olives. That had to be pricey. Plus, those silly, probably just as expensive heels of hers had nearly landed her on the ground, and who pranced around on a farm in January in only a blouse and skirt? Where was her coat? Or did that spoil the look?

Still, he cleared his throat and acted as if he had the manners Ma had tried to teach him. Andrew tugged at Pogo's lead and urged the horse back from the fence a few paces. When the horse protested—he must have found Mallory's perfume as interesting as Andrew had—Andrew gave him a pat on the neck. "Easy, fella. Easy."

Now, is that for me? Or for Pogo?

"Thank you," Mallory said to him.

He glanced her way. Her death grip on the fence had relaxed. She *was* afraid of horses.

"How is it that you let Katelyn sign up for hippotherapy if you don't care for horses?" he asked.

"She loves them," Mallory told him. "I— They're so big. And—skittish. I've never been around them."

"Huh. Figured somebody like you would have taken fancy English riding lessons."

"Somebody like— Andrew Monroe, I think you must be determined to get me all wrong." She inhaled deeply, then let out the breath, and he noticed that the air had grown cool enough that her breath misted as it came out of her petal-pink lips. She was so beautiful and glamorous, she could have stepped off the silver screen.

Now she stuck out her right hand across the fence, as primly as if it was gloved in white and she was the queen of all she surveyed. "Let's try this again, shall we? Hi, I'm Mallory Blair, and I'd like to thank you for saving my sister's life."

Andrew couldn't help the moment of hesitation he felt taking her hand. But he reached across the distance to accept her hand and shook it. Her grip was firm, businesslike, but her hand in his felt small and delicate.

"And I can act like Pogo's backside sometimes," he replied. "Here. Let's have a go at this." Her fingers still in his, he lifted her palm to Pogo's neck and guided it along the horse's warm hide.

Her eyes grew wide with fear and apprehension—and interest, he saw. She didn't jerk back. Instead, she let him show her how to scratch Pogo in his favorite-hard-to-reach spot.

"He's—quivery. And shaggier than I expected," Mallory allowed.

"His winter coat. And if you let him know

you're scared, he'll wonder what *he* needs to be scared of. Relax. And…oh, he's looking for this." As Pogo began to nuzzle into Mallory's hand, Andrew slipped an apple slice to her.

"H-how— Is he going to bite me?"

"Nope. Just open your palm and hold it up, like a platter."

Mallory did as he said, then let out a tremulous laugh as Pogo scarfed up the apple slice. "Oh! His mouth feels like the best quality suede!" she said. Pogo reached down and playfully butted her head with the gentlest of taps. "Wow—maybe I should remember that horses don't like to be reminded of shoe factories, huh?"

"Would you like to learn how to ride?" Andrew offered impulsively.

"Me? Are you kidding? I'm terrified of horses—"

"Yet here you are," he pointed out. "Letting ol' Pogo charm the pants off you."

"He *is* a charming fellow."

"And gentle. And now he's decided that he likes you. Maegan uses Pogo for kids who have severe disabilities. He's older than dirt, and patient. You'd be as safe on him as if you were walking on your own two feet—safer, really, than walking around on those heels."

"You think I could learn?" Now Mallory was getting the hang of petting Pogo. She was up on her tiptoes, reaching over the fence and giving the horse an enthusiastic scratch under his mane. And Pogo? He leaned into her hand, showing just how much he liked Mallory's touch.

Just like you.

Andrew shoved the thought out of his head. "Anybody can, given the time and the effort. Dad had us on horses before we could walk."

"It…it would be nice. If I knew about horses and how to ride, it would give me a sense of connection to Katelyn as she's going through her therapy." Mallory gave the horse one more, almost wistful, scratch and stepped back, her hands clasped behind her back. He knew what her answer was going to be before she spoke, and he was right.

"I can't afford lessons."

It was on the tip of Andrew's tongue to retort, "Might cut into your shoe budget, huh?" He managed to swallow the remark. Still, what came out instead surprised him.

"I'll teach you. For free. You know, a few basic riding lessons."

She switched her gaze from Pogo's eyes to his. "You would?"

"Sure. So that you could...understand what Katelyn will be doing."

And you can keep an eye on her and her lawsuit, right? Even to his internal ear, that sounded thin. No, if he admitted the truth, he wanted to share his love of horses with her. No one should be afraid of these big gentle creatures—no one.

"Oh, I don't know..." She had moved closer to the horse now, and she was actually letting him nuzzle her palm. Andrew offered her another apple slice, but Pogo smelled it and quickly shifted his allegiance, snapping up the apple from Andrew's fingers. "You can't have much time."

Andrew shrugged. "Sure, it will have to be when I'm off duty from the department. Part of my job here is to exercise the horses. You can help me by giving Pogo's legs a stretch."

"I'd like that." The smile on her face lit up the evening as brightly as any full moon. "Maybe when—"

Whatever she was going to say was interrupted by a buzz coming from her skirt pocket. Pogo reached down to investigate, but she'd stepped back and drew out a phone.

"Oh, Hi, Chad!" she said. "How odd... I was thinking about calling you earlier, but I figured you were in court." She turned away, the wind snatching something about "records request" right out of her mouth.

A sour feeling permeated Andrew's stomach. Chad, huh? Sounded as though Mallory had a rich lawyer boyfriend.

Which would come in handy if she were angling to file a lawsuit.

CHAPTER TEN

A COUPLE OF weeks after she'd landed the job of sewing Kimberly's dress, Mallory soaked in the quiet peacefulness of the public library and was glad she'd been able to run by before it had closed for the evening. It was an especially soothing balm after the busy week she'd had—every woman in town seemed to need a fancy new dress from BASH in time for Valentine's Day weekend.

The library was nice for another reason. Since Mallory had been coming here, she'd gotten to know one of the librarians, Carole Bingham, who was about her age. At first they'd chatted about the books Mallory had checked out, but as they swapped reading suggestions, they'd found they had a lot in common. She and Carole had even met for a brown-bag lunch a couple of times.

Now Mallory crossed over to the circulation desk to join her.

"Hey, I thought you said the library had

gotten in the newest Lee Child novel, and I put a hold on it for the next available check-out, like you advised." Mallory grinned and asked with a teasing note, "You're not holding out on me to get an insider's sneak peek, are you?"

Carole put her hands on her hips and tried to look offended. "Would I do that? Oh, all right, maybe, but it's not me. Let's see…" She tapped on her keyboard. "Well, you're next, if that's any consolation, but the guy who's got it still has a week and a half before it's due."

Mallory shrugged her shoulders and pushed the books she'd decided on across the laminate countertop. "Maybe he won't take the whole time—I wouldn't. I always read a Lee Child novel in one great gulp. Don't suppose you'd let me know who has it so that I could beg them to hurry up and finish it?"

"'Fraid not," Carole said. She closed the last book after scanning its barcode and pushed the stack across to Mallory. "He's about like you when it comes to reading—voracious, I tell you. You probably won't have to wait much longer. How's the sewing going? And how's Katelyn? Therapy going okay?"

Mallory related the latest on Katelyn's therapy, which was that her sister was getting

stronger and more confident...and conversely
snappier and more easily irritated with Mallory. She didn't tell Carole everything—like
how she'd been avoiding Andrew Monroe, or how she was still waiting on Chad
McGovern, the lawyer, to get back with her
on a date his investigator could start.

Chad had told her the night of the supper
at Ma's that he was confident of the merits of the case, pending what his investigator
turned up.

"The key to the case," he'd told her, "is if
we can prove that the fire department left the
power on. It's a good shot then that a jury
will find the county at fault. And your sister's records indicate that she suffered mild
electric burns—that may have stunned her
and caused her to pass out, which led to her
getting more serious burns."

Chad had repeated that the idea of a firefighter abandoning a helpless teen would create sympathy with the jury.

It had jolted Mallory to realize afresh that
the firefighter Chad was talking about was
Andrew... Andrew, who had just offered her
free riding lessons.

When she'd reminded Chad that he'd told
her they might not have to go to a jury, he

in turn reminded her about all the expenses she'd run up, the job she'd lost, the idea that Katelyn might not be able to hold a job of her own.

She'd protested. "I don't know… I don't want to take—"

"Now, Mallory. What have I told you? *You're* not taking. Someone—the county of Levi—took something from you and Katelyn. And you're Katelyn's guardian, so it's your responsibility to get it back for her. Don't you agree?" Chad pressed her.

She couldn't argue with his logic or his idea that they had to show how the fire department and the county had failed Katelyn. He'd assured her that he'd meet with his private investigator and see when the man could begin doing some discreet digging. That had been all of two weeks ago, and she hadn't heard from him since.

But the awkwardness of knowing that she was responsible for hiring someone to investigate Andrew and the department… It had simply been so much easier to keep her distance.

And Andrew hasn't made it all that difficult for you, her inner voice pointed out. True enough, Andrew hadn't stopped by with any more pizzas, and he'd been on duty at the fire department a lot of the time when she'd dropped off Katelyn at therapy.

Now, standing with Carole, she didn't share any of that. She didn't know Carole quite well enough, for one thing.

And for another… Mallory couldn't figure out what she felt about Andrew Monroe. He was still the guy who had sacrificed Katelyn for his buddy, still the guy who had caused her sister so much pain. Yet the few times she had seen Andrew work with Katelyn, he was gentle and compassionate and encouraging. He wanted her to get better.

Because he feels guilty. Because he knows what he did.

She shoved away the thought and asked Carole what her plans were for the evening.

"My husband is taking me out to an early Valentine's Day supper—got reservations and everything. How about you? Somebody special bringing you flowers and candy?"

Before Mallory could even attempt to evade the question, the library door swung open, letting in a chill gust of air that swirled around her ankles. Carole and she looked up to see none other than Andrew walk through the door.

"Hey, Carole. Somebody called and said you— Oh." He had spotted Mallory, and the expression on his face didn't convey unmitigated pleasure at the surprise. "Hi, Mallory." To Carole, he mumbled something like, "I'll give you a minute," shoved a book on the counter and then dived into the set of stacks closest to the circulation desk.

Carole raised an eyebrow. "Huh. When did you bite Andrew Monroe?"

Mallory eyeballed her right back. "You mean he's not always like that? He is with me."

Carole swiped up the book that he'd left. "You can thank him for one thing—he brought in your Lee Child book."

"He's the one who—" Mallory craned her neck for any sign of Andrew, but it was as if the stacks had swallowed him whole. "*He's* the voracious reader?" she whispered.

"Yep. And I don't know what's eating him if it's not you, because usually you're his type."

"Type? What do you mean, type?"

Carole chuckled as she went about checking the book in. "Hand me that library card of yours, that is, if you do want to read this book."

Mallory fished out her card. "Now give. What do you mean, I'm his type?"

"Andrew Monroe has a particular weakness for… Okay, don't take this as an insult, all right? He has a weakness for pageant queens."

"I'm no pageant queen. I've never been in a beauty pageant in my life!" Mallory was still puzzled. "Not that there's anything wrong with it, but I'm just not the type."

"You look it, though. You look as though you could be a model. And you dress…well, see what you're wearing now—high heels and a pencil skirt and that cute little twinset."

"I came from work—"

"Yeah, and how you managed to pedal that bike of yours in those stilettos—"

"I didn't. I pushed the bike down here. I'll change in the bathroom before I leave for home—if you'll give me a few minutes."

"Sure. No problem. Anyway, regardless of what you're *really* like, I'm surprised Andrew isn't drooling all over you. I mean, you're even prettier than LeeAnn, and she—"

"Who's LeeAnn?"

"LeeAnn Graham. She was Miss Levi County year before last—or was it the year before that?" Carole scratched her chin. "Gosh,

I think it was three years ago. Well, never mind. They were in high school together— she was prom queen and homecoming queen and whatever else queen you can be in high school. He'd dated a whole bevy of pretty girls while he was there, but then their senior year, they got together, and I mean hot and heavy. From the way I heard things, they were practically engaged when they graduated, and everybody kept oohing and aahing over what a fab couple they made. They were like Waverly's version of Brangelina."

It wasn't idle curiosity that made Mallory's stomach churn at the prospect of Andrew being serious about a woman, especially not someone who was Waverly royalty. She couldn't put her finger on exactly why it bothered her. What was Andrew to her anyway? "What happened if they were so perfect for one another?"

"Oh, but they *weren't*, don't you see? For all of Andrew's good looks—I mean, *he* could be a male model, but then all of the Monroe boys are extremely pleasing to the eye, no?" Carole waggled an eyebrow. "Lee-Ann was not a country girl, even if she did live in Waverly. She was town, through and through, and she was not happy with how he wanted her to spend time with his family out on their farm. Horses? She was allergic. Farming? Her idea of hunting and gathering was the drive-through at a fast-food place, and her idea of a good time was to go out shopping or for a mani-pedi or a trip to the beach or Atlanta or somewhere with bright lights and lots of loud music, which is okay on occasion, but that's *all* she wanted to do."

"They couldn't have lasted long, then," Mallory murmured. She still didn't see a trace of Andrew moving around the stacks.

"Longer than they should have, more's the pity. He was besotted with her, and she was so mean to him. He didn't get hit with a clue stick until she changed her major and transferred from the college here to a school up near Atlanta. She said she was going to be a dental hygienist, but I think she dropped out and married... I can't remember his name, but it was some city guy with pots of money."

"Ouch."

"Oh, no, that wasn't the worst of it." Carole leaned forward conspiratorially, dropping her hushed tone even lower. "She dumped him when he joined the fire department. Said she wasn't going to date anybody with a blue-collar job. Now, I tell you, what was the girl thinking? She was dating a Monroe, wasn't she? Didn't she have a clue that it's practically a Monroe birthright to be a firefighter? And what's wrong with a girl who doesn't like a firefighter? Huh?"

Mallory couldn't fathom the idea of someone turning her nose up at a person because of the job they had—and Andrew, no less. Anger on his behalf burned through Mallory. She'd met plenty of LeeAnns in her line of work, and she didn't care a fig about them. They treated shop clerks and assistants and anyone in the service industry like second-class citizens.

"How long ago?" she asked.

"A couple of years now? Maybe longer? He didn't exactly learn his lesson, because he started dating a series of pretty faces who was essentially a carbon copy. They lasted all of about six months each. And since the last one…" Carole frowned. "Hmm. I haven't heard of him seeing anybody. Maybe the fire department and his work out at Happy Acres keeps him busy."

"Well, if I do remind him of his ex-girlfriend, I wish he'd learn not to judge a book by its cover. I'm not her, and not a thing like her, and it would be nice if he wouldn't take his anger out on me," Mallory said.

"Maybe you should try to get to know him better—because you're right. You're not a bit like LeeAnn. I mean, you and he both read. You're both nice—" Carole was warming to the subject now, a definite matchmaking glint in her eye.

Mallory knew something Carole didn't— she knew about the lawsuit. It would underscore Andrew's poor opinion of her when he found out for certain what the suit was about. Why bother getting to know him?

She gathered up the books and interrupted Carole before she could gather any more steam. "Hey, do I still have time to change clothes?"

Carole glanced at her watch. "Yikes! It's past closing time. My boss will have my head." Then, without asking Mallory, Carole gaily called out. "Hey, Andrew! You're in your truck, right? You'd take Mallory home, wouldn't you?"

Mallory groaned. She turned back to glower at Carole, only to receive a wink. Behind her, she heard Andrew clear his throat and reply:

"Sure, Carole. As a favor to you, sure."

CHAPTER ELEVEN

ANDREW'S TRUCK WAS bare bones in the luxury department. Mallory hadn't realized they still made trucks with vinyl bench seats and no carpet. The radio was strictly the AM variety, the windows operated with a hand crank and the only nod to creature comforts was the welcome heat pouring out of the vents.

Taking it in reminded her of her dad's truck—of her dad, in fact. Unlike her mom, who loved gadgets and accessories, her dad was of the mindset that any accessory on a vehicle was simply one more thing to break. Mallory closed her eyes, slid her palm against the vinyl that was patched with duct tape and sighed.

"It's not a Rolls Royce, I know that," Andrew snapped.

His words brought her back to the present. "What?"

"The truck. I know it's not up to your standards. But it's bought and paid for, and it runs like a top. Plus, it does what it's designed to do—which is farm work."

"It's fine," she insisted. "I'm grateful that you…" What? Offered to give her a lift? No, Carole had practically twisted his arm, appealing to his gallantry. "That you're giving me a ride home."

"It's too dark for you to be riding that fool bike anyway," he grumbled. His hands flexed on the steering wheel, and his jaw tensed, as though he were biting back more words.

"I didn't expect to be at the library so long." The urge to explain and defend herself irritated her. She made an effort to change the conversation to something else before she could pile on more excuses. "Uh…thank you for bringing back the book."

As he braked at a stoplight, Andrew turned to her. "What book?"

"The Lee Child book. I had placed a hold on it, and I was—"

"You like suspense novels?" His brows lifted in surprise. "You read?"

Exasperated, and her urge to be more charitable to him quickly evaporating, Mallory retorted, "And why are you so blown away by that? Yes, I read. I love to read. And suspense thrillers are just one of the many, many kinds of books I enjoy. Why on earth do you think I was in the library in the first place?"

"Oh, I dunno. The fashion magazines?" he quipped.

"No, I don't go to the library for the fashion magazines! What kind of brainless idiot do you think I am?"

They locked eyes, Mallory not backing down from his surprise, which was now morphing into frank interest. A horn beeped behind them. Andrew swore, released the clutch and stepped on the gas. The truck took off with a start, jerking Mallory sideways. She flung out a hand, searching for something to brace herself with.

That something wound up being Andrew's shoulder.

It was a warm and solid shoulder, well defined even through the fabric of his jacket. She managed to pry her hand loose a second before it became socially awkward.

"Sorry," he muttered, glancing in the rearview mirror.

Now Mallory's temper began to boil in earnest. That was all he could say? Sorry? When it was obvious he was painting her with the same brush he painted all his former girlfriends? She pulled herself straight and tall in the seat and asked, "When will you stop pretending you know anything about me and get to know what sort of person I really am?"

The question must have startled him almost as much as the horn beep had, because he slowed down, then sped up, then slowed down again as he approached the courthouse. Abruptly he pulled into one of the parallel parking spots along the curb, stopped the truck and turned to her, arms folded, mouth straight and unbending.

"All right. Tell me what I should know about you."

A flutter of nervousness shot through her. "Well, you don't have to be a jerk," she said.

If anything, his mouth compressed all the more tightly. She had the sudden urge to do something, anything to make him smile, so that she could experience again the easy kindness he'd first treated her with.

"I'm trying to *stop* being a jerk," he told her. "You say I don't know you, that I have the wrong idea about you. So...fix it."

Mallory put her fingers to her eyes, leaned against the cool glass of the passenger side window. "You know, forget it. I don't know why it's important to me for you to see me in a positive light."

"It's important to you? That I like you?"

The trace of wonder in Andrew's response completely undid the earlier edge to his words. She lifted her eyes and stared at him.

"Well, of course, nobody wants to be disliked."

Was that disappointment that flashed across his features? He shrugged and said, "If it makes you feel better, tell me where to sign up for the Mallory Blair fan club and I—"

"See? That!" She jabbed a finger at him—too close, because it brushed the denim of his jacket. Yanking her hand back to her side of the truck, she swallowed. "I don't have a fan club. I don't need one or want one or... sheesh. I just..."

She trailed off. He was waiting for her, silent and steady and giving absolutely zilch encouragement. She took in a deep breath, let it out and then plunged ahead.

"I like to read. A lot. And cook. And I sew—but you know that. I like to bike. I'm afraid of horses—you know that, too—but I love almost every other critter out there. I'm not good at parties, and I'm a disaster on the dance floor because I have two left feet. I prefer the mountains to the beach. My favorite color is coral, but I can't wear it because it makes me look like an overripe strawberry."

Some of the rigid tenseness in his frame seemed to leave him. He relaxed against the vinyl bench seat and propped his jaw against his hand. "A disaster on the dance floor?"

"Completely. I could manage to step on your toes even if you were levitating two feet above the floor. I have absolutely no sense of rhythm."

"That's a shame. I love to dance."

She could just bet he did. He was probably a great dancer—probably he and Her Royal Highness LeeAnn had torn up more than a few dance floors in their time together.

"Your turn," she prompted.

"Hmm...okay. Don't tell Ma, but I still hate cabbage. I love to read, too, but only mystery novels, and, uh, what are they called? Biographies. I hate all those TV shows and movies about fire departments because none of 'em are accurate, and about the only thing I actually do watch on TV is the weather and the news. I'd rather ride a horse all day than bike ten minutes anywhere. If I'm not on a horse or at the station, I like to fiddle around with wood and building things. I have absolutely no clue what color coral is, but I'll bet it looks good on you, despite what you said a minute ago."

Her cheeks suddenly felt red-hot. "It's... orange trying to be pink. Or maybe pink trying to be orange."

"Like the sunset?"

She couldn't answer him at first, because he had his fingers out, gently tracing the curve of her cheek, his thumb idly following the contour of her cheekbone into her hair. And to her horror, she was sliding closer to him, the bench seat suddenly making all the sense in the world.

"Exactly like the sunset—except not the mauves or the lavenders—"

"Wait, the mauve, is that the purple one?" He didn't seem to be too interested in colors because his fingers were moving back, finding the oversize pin she'd used that morning to skewer her hair into a bun, pulling it out. Her hair tumbled down. "That's better. You don't look so polished now. You look all rumpled and kissable..."

"I do?" She tilted her head up, staring into blue eyes that seemed as clear and calm as a Caribbean lagoon.

Now he cupped her jaw in his palm, tugged her closer...and she followed his lead. His mouth on hers was warm and soft, tentative at first, then more confident. It was a good kiss, a near perfect kiss, all the better because he didn't push things, but let it break naturally and allowed her to lay her cheek against his shoulder.

"Mauve is the pink trying to be purple," she murmured for lack of anything else to say.

"Never can keep those straight." His hand slid along her hair, tucking it back behind her ear. She felt his gaze upon her, smelled a hint of smoke on his skin.

He was wearing his uniform under the denim jacket, she realized with a start: navy blue with the insignia stitched onto the pocket.

The same uniform he'd worn when he'd abandoned Katelyn to that demon fire.

Mallory pushed away from him. Fumbling with her hair, she began to wind it up into a bun again.

"Hey. What's the deal?"

She jabbed at her hair with the oversize pin, missed because her fingers *would* tremble so much, jabbed again and got a huge swath of scalp instead of hair. "Uh, Katelyn," she gabbled. "I need to get home."

"Katelyn's out at the farm. She was staying for supper," Andrew said. "Ma suggested I bring you out to eat, too. She seems to think you can't afford to eat a decent meal—" He stopped abruptly, but Mallory didn't prompt him to finish. No doubt he was going to say something about how Mallory preferred to spend money on shoes rather than buy what it would take to cook one of Ma's "decent meals."

She's right. I can't afford it if her definition includes great huge slabs of meat, Mallory said to herself. Her pride wouldn't allow her to confess that. Now that she'd managed to corral her hair, she felt more put together, more able to resist the charms of Andrew Monroe. "Katelyn would prefer to eat junk food three times a day if I'd let her."

"I'll bet you're into that paleo diet, where all you eat is brown rice and nuts and berries." Andrew shook his head and put the truck into gear.

"A paleo diet wouldn't actually use rice," she corrected.

"See? You look the type that would know stuff like that. Vegetarian, I'll bet. No rib eyes for you."

The image of a steak, complete with succulent wafting smells of sizzling, smoky fat, appeared to Mallory as realistically as any mirage of water to a man thirsting in a desert. When was the last time she'd had a rib eye?

No. Dwelling on what you didn't have—on what you *couldn't* have—was a recipe for disaster and dire unhappiness.

And what she couldn't have was a good, juicy prime rib...or Andrew Monroe.

ANDREW CHECKED HIS rearview mirror and saw the headlights of Mallory's little convertible bouncing up and down as the car negotiated the ruts of Ma's drive. She'd insisted that he drop her off at the apartment so she could drive her car out to the farm.

Now, why had he kissed her? He'd completely blown his promise, just that morning, to Dutch and Daniel. The county attorney had shown up at a training fire they were holding and buttonholed Andrew, then drew Daniel into the impromptu conference.

The good news: no official papers filed yet at the courthouse.

The better news: neither Mallory nor Katelyn had a history of any sort of litigation.

The bad news: using the name Chad McGovern for a start, Dutch had most likely discovered that Mallory's mysterious attorney friend was an aggressive personal-injury attorney, one who had racked up a sizable track record and fortune chasing ambulances. He had a reputation for leaving no deep pocket untouched—and he tended to dip his fingers into even shallow pockets if there was a nickel to be lifted.

Dutch had minced no words.

"This guy's a pro—this is how he makes his bread and butter. Lawyers like this work on contingencies, so they're after the deepest pockets they can find. McGovern has sued counties, cities, corporations, small businesses and even Fortune 500 companies. What he's after is to make things so unpleasant that the target will offer to settle out of court for a huge sum—including an obscene amount for attorney fees—and then he takes a cut of the award," Dutch had explained. "And once he takes a case, according to my buddy, he sinks his teeth in and doesn't let go. The only people who use him are truly committed—they don't seem to care what dirty tricks he employs to get them their settlement."

"Unpleasant?" Daniel had asked. "What kind of dirty tricks are we talking about?"

"Everything just south of what could get him disbarred or brought up on ethics charges—he's famous for dragging up skeletons out of people's personal lives."

Andrew shrugged and stared off into the rumbling flames of the condemned house that was being used as a training fire. "We don't have any skeletons. Let him dig," he insisted.

Dutch shook his head. "You don't get it, Andrew. This guy could ruin your career—ruin Maegan's career. He could take her license if he set his mind to it, as collateral damage."

Daniel rubbed his chin. "We can't let that happen. I won't let that happen."

"Look," Andrew suggested. "What if I talk to Mallory? What if I straight up ask her if this is the guy? If I tell her—"

"No!" The word came in unison from both Daniel and Dutch.

Andrew lifted his hands. "Whoa. It was just a thought."

In the end, he'd assured Daniel that he wouldn't divulge any forewarning they might have about a pending lawsuit. He'd treat Mallory the same as he would any relative of any patient of Maegan's.

Now it was Andrew who rubbed his chin in puzzlement as he parked the truck and sat there, considering. Not ever before had he kissed any woman even remotely connected to one of Maegan's patients.

And besides that…hadn't he learned anything about women from his disaster with LeeAnn?

You just have to keep picking the same woman over and over, don't you? When will you ever get it through your head? The last one was supposed to be the last one.

Maybe Mallory was as different as she insisted…but all the signs pointed to someone who was simply out for money and the good life. Look how she'd sighed over having to ride in his pickup. He'd bet she was more accustomed to traveling in luxury sedans and sports cars.

A tiny tap came on the truck window, startling him. He peered out of the condensation already gathering on it to see Mallory standing by the door.

Scooping up his lunch box from the floorboards of the truck, he slid out and slammed the door. It creaked ominously, reminding him that he needed to grease those hinges.

"I didn't thank you properly for taking me home," she started.

"Don't mention it. It was no bother."

His words must not have been exactly what she was after—or maybe it was his tone again, because even to his ears, he sounded brusque. Well, excuse him for being tired and out of sorts—he'd had to pull almost an extra half shift today to get in his training. That and his moral tussles over what he should and shouldn't say to Mallory had exhausted him.

Keeping her at arm's length did not, in any way, shape or form, feel natural to him.

Andrew saw the hurt in her face. It made him feel as guilty as seeing Katelyn in that wheelchair. He brushed past her and headed for the house, the gravel crunching underfoot. "Ma's probably got supper warming on the stove for us," he tossed over his shoulder. "I didn't know you were coming along until late…"

Give him enough rope and he'd hang himself. After he'd nearly slipped up earlier about Ma's invitation, he hadn't planned on telling Mallory that he'd refused Ma's earlier request to invite her out to eat. He'd planned on avoiding Mallory at all costs after Dutch and Daniel had double-teamed him.

"I wouldn't want to…horn in." Mallory's words drifted through the cold night air. The expression didn't sound right in her city-accent. It was as though she were trying too hard to fit in.

Like LeeAnn, at first.

"Eat if you want, don't if you don't," he shot back. "I'm hungry. You can dither all you want."

And with that, he stalked toward the house, figuring that a girl as quick on the uptake as Mallory Blair could find her own way to a meal ticket.

CHAPTER TWELVE

MALLORY GROUND HER teeth in frustration. What was with this hot-and-cold routine? True, she'd been the one to back off first after that kiss...

That kiss didn't bear thinking about. *Stupid, stupid, stupid.*

She followed in his wake up the graveled path, up the steps to the back porch and to the screen door that he'd let slam in her face.

A moment later a sheepish Andrew pushed the door back open. "Sorry," he mumbled. "I wasn't thinking."

"That's right, Andrew Monroe!" Ma scolded him. "You most certainly weren't thinking, or else you wouldn't act like some knuckle-dragging Neanderthal. What would your father say if he were alive? He'd skin you, that's what he'd do!" Ma shook her head and transferred her attention to Mallory. In a gentler voice, she said, "C'mon in, honey. I try to raise these boys with some modicum of manners."

"Ma!" Andrew protested. "I'm not thirteen anymore!"

"Well, then, act like it." Ma bustled around the kitchen, retrieving plates and silverware and uncovering delicious-smelling food from big pots on the stove. "Mallory, get your supper. Daniel and Maegan have already eaten, and Katelyn—"

"She shouldn't have invited herself—we have something waiting for us at the apartment," Mallory insisted.

"Oh, shush! She said you'd fuss at her, but I do like the company. All my girls seem to have something else to do this week, and the house is so quiet," Ma explained. "I'd already told Maegan to bring that child up here after they got finished. Do you know? She even walked a few steps on her own today?"

A breath caught in Mallory's throat. She'd missed that. She missed such a monumental accomplishment because she was mooning over Andrew, letting him kiss her and charm her with his supposed ignorance of mauve and coral. Her parents would have never put something like that—that trivial—ahead of making sure her or Katelyn had the support they needed. Hadn't her parents been at every football game she'd ever cheered at?

Hadn't her mom gone to every honor's day and school play that either of her daughters had been involved in?

"She walked?" Mallory asked. "Really walked?"

Even Andrew seemed to be jolted out of his grumpy mood by the news. He'd stopped what he was doing, his big hands soaped to the elbows at the kitchen sink, his mouth a perfect O of surprise. And then he whooped with delight. He reached over and yanked Mallory up, mindless of his sudsy hands, and whirled her around the kitchen.

"She walked! Did you hear that, Mal? She did it!"

Mallory couldn't tell what made her heart do its double-tap—the good news about Katelyn or the way that Andrew's face lit up when he was truly happy.

"My word, Andrew, the girl's going to get drunk if you keep spinning her around like that. And besides, you'll wake up Katelyn. She's taking a nap on the living room sofa."

"Oh, gosh, Ma, sorry!" This time, no note of churlishness fouled his words. Andrew set Mallory back down so suddenly she wobbled on her heels. His big mitts had left two damp spots on her sweater, but no harm had been done. "Where's Maegan? I want to hear all about it! Did she record it?"

"Maegan's gone down to her office. Said she had to catch up on paperwork. You'll just have to bide your time, but you never were the patient sort, were you?" Ma patted Andrew on the cheek. "Now eat, the both of you, and I'll tell you what Katelyn told me. That girl was plenty excited, let me tell you."

Mallory allowed Ma to tempt her into a big plate of meatloaf and all the trimmings. She couldn't help but elbow Andrew in the ribs as he made a move to skip the cabbage.

"Aren't you forgetting something?" she teased as she stood by the stove. "You need your leafy greens."

He groaned. Under Mallory's pointed gaze, he shook his head in mock resignation. "Oh, all right. It won't kill me to eat it."

Their convivial mood held all through supper as Ma regaled them with tales of Katelyn's triumph. She had walked—even though she'd almost given up before she'd actually taken those three steps without so much as Maegan's hand on her back.

It was all Mallory could do not to wake Katelyn up from her slumber and hug her. She waited as long as she could, trying not to rush through the delicious supper, insisting on washing her dishes, before she tiptoed into the living room.

There was Katelyn, still asleep on the couch. Ma had covered her up with a soft quilt. Katelyn's hair fanned out across a snowy white pillowcase, her mouth slack, her face so much younger in sleep than her seventeen years.

Mallory's heart ached as she watched over her sister. How many nights had she done this very thing? Countless times right after their parents died, after Katelyn had sobbed herself into a fitful sleep. And still more when Katelyn was in the burn unit after the accident.

But...it wasn't an accident. Chad had warned her about thinking of it in that way. An accident, he'd pointed out when they'd first met, was something that happened despite everyone's best efforts, and leaving Katelyn to nearly die—that wasn't anybody's best efforts.

Or it shouldn't have been.

Mallory sighed, her good mood deflating. She had not watched over Katelyn, not then and not today. What if she'd fallen? What if

Katelyn had wanted her to be there, to see her triumph?

Mallory sat back, careful not to wake her sister. She took in the room and its cozy furnishings, so unlike their cramped apartment with its wickedly uncomfortable futon that served as a couch. Lit by a single lamp on an end table beside the sofa, this room was anchored by a fireplace with the remnants of a fire still crackling in it. The mantel held a host of photos of the Monroe clan, including a particularly cute gap-toothed grade-school picture of a much-younger Andrew.

The big easy chair looked as though it were Daniel's, what with the table beside it full of trade magazines about firefighting and a big blue binder with the county insignia on it.

In black magic marker, in a neat print, the words *Policy and Procedures Handbook* were scrawled across the front.

Policies and procedures...

Mallory rose from the sofa and crossed to the chair. On her way, a floorboard creaked beneath the big braided rug. She halted, checking over her shoulder to make sure that Katelyn had not awoken, and neither Andrew nor Ma had heard her sneaking across the floor.

Silly. Daniel wouldn't have left it here if it had been confidential. I could probably get a copy of it down at the municipal building.

Still, stealth ruled her actions. She perched on the edge of the easy chair and began flipping through the pages. Yes, there indeed was the policy that Andrew had quoted back to her almost verbatim, about priorities during a rescue. And...

She flipped forward a few more pages, consulted the typed table of contents at the front of the binder and then leafed through until she got to the relevant section.

Priority shall be made to ascertain that no power or gas is flowing to a structure, so as to safeguard residents entrapped in the structure and rescue personnel responding at the scene.

It was followed with detailed directions for how to obtain that knowledge, from a meter check to a call to the utility providers, and a special proviso for residents with solar panels or generators.

Yes. There it was, in black-and-white, captured in plain, no-nonsense Courier font. The fire department should have made certain no electricity was going to that house.

The memory of that ugly starburst scar on

Katelyn's hand burned into Mallory's brain. It was the only scar that her sister couldn't hide with long sleeves and long pants, and her doctors were certain it had been caused by contact with a live electric wire.

Katelyn had wept over that scar. For some reason, whenever she saw it, it bothered her almost as much or more than the scars she could hide.

But that scar was definite proof that the Levi County Fire Department had not followed proper procedure. They had almost cost Katelyn her life.

CHAPTER THIRTEEN

ANDREW CAME DOWN the darkened hall toward the dim yellow glow of the living room lamp. The fire must still be going, he decided, because it was warmer the closer he got. He and Daniel and Rob needed to talk Ma into adding more insulation into the old drafty place. Their dad would have insisted on it.

His dad. Not for the first time since Ma had invoked Dad's name earlier that evening had Andrew questioned his gruff manner with Mallory. His father was big on respect for women. More than once, Andrew had been grounded for even a hint of rolling his eyes at Ma.

"You respect Ma and your sisters— everybody, regardless of who they are," his dad had told him. "They got their own troubles, just like you. Last thing they need is you piling your baggage on."

That was what he'd been doing, he figured, tossing onto Mallory's load a suitcase or two of his own guilt about the fire. Never mind that he'd done his best. Never mind that he'd followed procedure.

You got her out, he reassured himself. *Katelyn is here today and walking—walking—because you found her.*

The walking part was a big deal for him. Maegan had been so pessimistic about Katelyn's chances to walk. She'd pointed out that Katelyn had already gone through arduous therapy already. Maegan's focus was to give Katelyn the confidence she needed to tackle life, even if it was in a wheelchair.

Andrew paused for a moment in the hall and took in a large framed photo of the last group shot with his dad, just before Daniel had headed off to chase his dream of becoming a major-league baseball pitcher. All the kids surrounded Ma and Dad, like points on a clock. Daniel was at the twelve position, and everybody else fell into place from there.

And there Andrew was, the youngest, trying to appear older and tougher than his twelve years. He still remembered that day, cooped up in the photographer's studio, itching to get out to the ball fields with his buddies. He could still feel the bite of the dress shirt's collar that Ma had starched to a fare-thee-well, hear the crackle of the new pants Ma had bought for the occasion, the pinch of the dress shoes he'd had to shine to a high gleam.

And…yes. He could still feel the weight of his dad's hand on his shoulder. It wasn't a scolding. It was a gentle reminder: patience.

No, Andrew decided. Dad wouldn't have cared one whit for the way Andrew had treated Mallory. He'd probably have advised him to be polite and keep his distance and certainly, certainly not pull Maegan into any professional risk.

Andrew squared his shoulders and vowed to be more like the man his dad would have wanted him to be. He moved toward the living room, intent on apologizing to Mallory for his earlier behavior.

He found her in Dad's—now Daniel's—chair, her head bent over something. A glance at the sofa told him that Katelyn was still asleep.

"Do you think we need another log on the fire?" he asked, just above a whisper.

Mallory jerked up in surprise. Her face paled, and she slammed the covers of whatever she was reading shut, sliding it in the crevice of the seat. "Uh—not for me," she got out.

Something about the way she was looking directly at him while busily ditching the book—a binder, actually—aroused his suspicions. He closed the gap between them, posing in as casual a tone as he could muster, "You're sure? It can be drafty, especially when you're reading. What are you reading anyway?"

A splash of embarrassed color lit Mallory's cheeks, and her hand on the binder instantly stilled. She shrugged. "Uh—actually—" She pulled it out and looked at it as if she needed to read the marker-scrawled title. "Policy and Procedures Handbook"... Katelyn always says I'd read the back of a milk carton."

Her chuckle wasn't as carefree as she'd meant it to be, Andrew thought. Still, he tried to give her the benefit of the doubt. Maybe she had been bored, waiting for Katelyn to wake up. Maybe it had been in the chair and she'd had to move it.

Yeah, right, maybe she really, really wants to be a firefighter when she grows up, especially if she can do it in designer turnout gear.

Cynical sarcasm bubbled up in him before

he could tamp it down. Aloud, he responded with, "Yeah, you will read anything. That stuff will put me out like a light, even when I've got to study it for tests. Works better for insomnia than any sleeping pill they could ever come up with."

"Oh, yeah," Mallory said, forcing a laugh. Her hand smoothed over the cover. "Dry stuff."

"Yeah? Don't tell Daniel. He and Rob were the ones who drafted most of that." Andrew's own laugh sounded as forced as Mallory's had. He ignored it and pushed on. "Here's a pop quiz—what do you remember reading?"

She opened her mouth—that pretty mouth he had kissed not even two hours before—and closed it. "Gracious! It was, you know..." Mallory waved a hand over her head. "How you guys keep everything straight, I don't know. And you, er, you get tested on it?"

"Sure." Andrew glanced down at the binder, realized the corners of some pages had been folded over in an unintentional dog-ear when she'd slammed the book shut. Now he reached across, again with the most casual air he could manage, and took the book from her. He slid a finger between the dog-eared pages, and then opened the book.

Was it his imagination, or did her entire body seem to relax? No, she was definitely less tense. Andrew didn't remark on it. Instead, he read aloud, "Vehicles shall be refueled when the gauge shows three-quarters or less on the dash of the truck. All power tools shall be refueled after each use. Portable fuel cans shall be maintained in a full… Oh, yeah. Riveting stuff here. You'll be out like a light, just like Katelyn is."

Uttering Katelyn's name served as some sort of signal for Mallory. She leaped up and said, "Gosh, is it that late? I guess I'd better wake Katelyn—"

A twinge of remorse pulsed through Andrew. Here he was, letting his suspicions take hold, and he was probably driving Mallory away with his thinly veiled interrogation. And causing trouble and pain for Katelyn.

Katelyn, who'd already gone through enough torment for three lifetimes.

"You don't have to—"

Even as he began his protest, Mallory bumped past him, causing the notebook to spill out of his hands. He reached down to scoop it up, realized Mallory's hands were reaching for it, too.

She laughed again, that shy awkwardness

that he'd cast in such a sinister light a moment ago. "Here," she said. "Before I catch trouble from Daniel for abusing his masterpiece. And no, I have to work tomorrow, and I think it's past time for us to get going."

"I'll help you—"

"No!" The word was sharp and cut through the cozy living room air. It served to rouse Katelyn, who fluttered her eyes open in confusion.

"Wh-what time is it? Is it—morning?" Katelyn mumbled.

Mallory knelt down beside the couch. "No, sweetie. It's just after eight o'clock. C'mon, sleepyhead. We've got to get you in the car and get you home. I hear you had a huge day today."

"Yeah!" Now Katelyn seemed more awake. She pushed up on one elbow and shoved aside the quilt. "I walked, Mal! I walked!"

"I wish I could have been there," Mallory told her, and in those words, Andrew could hear something else: the same aching protective pride that Ma's voice held whenever she'd learned of some new accomplishment one of them had achieved.

Katelyn scrunched up her features in a clear expression of never-you-mind. "Oh, you would have told me I might fall or to take it easy, or stop at the first step—I did it, though! I did it."

"You did. And you'll do it again. Right now I think we'd better head home."

Andrew stepped forward to help transfer Katelyn into the chair. He stopped, though, when Mallory seemed to guess what he was about to do and halted him with a discreet but definite hand signal.

Puzzled, and more than a little miffed, he watched as Mallory allowed Katelyn to struggle into the wheelchair on her own. Andrew noticed the older sister's hands clench nervously, her knuckles white, as Katelyn bumped her way into the chair.

She's letting her do it for herself, Andrew realized. *She's following Maegan's advice about allowing Katelyn to be more independent.*

Finally, after a full five minutes that seemed like an eternity, their patience was rewarded with Katelyn self-confidently wheeling up the hall and toward the kitchen. She was chattering a mile a minute, telling Mallory all about the steps she'd taken that day.

Mallory loves her. She wants what's best

for her. She trusts Maegan. Maybe there won't be a lawsuit after all.

Andrew dropped his gaze from Mallory and Katelyn's departing backs to the binder in his hand. Along the top edge, he could still see one of the folds among the pages.

He flipped the binder open, let his eyes take in the text. At first, he saw nothing but dry-as-dust procedures he knew by heart about chain of command on a scene.

And then his eye hit upon a paragraph in the middle of the page.

Priority shall be made to ascertain that no power or gas is flowing to a structure, so as to safeguard residents entrapped in the structure and rescue personnel responding at the scene.

His heart sank. In an instant he knew that this was what had so captured Mallory's attention that she hadn't even heard him coming down the hall.

She and Chad the ambulance chaser still had their eyes on the coffers of Levi County—and whoever else might be blocking the way to their money tree.

CHAPTER FOURTEEN

A WEEK AFTER Andrew's kiss, Mallory still didn't know which way was up. She'd even started avoiding the library because Carole kept pestering her about how things were going with Andrew.

Now, as she pushed her mop across the apartment's faded vinyl kitchen floor, she considered what her real answer to Carole might be.

I'd love to give myself over to the moment, but I'm too busy trying to prove that he screwed up?

No, that wasn't right. After her clumsy foray into Daniel's policy and procedures manual, with Andrew catching her redhanded, Mallory had sworn off any further investigation. Best to leave that to the professionals, she'd thought.

But Chad had seemed impressed that she'd found the information. Since his investigator had been tied up with another case, he had urged her to keep digging.

He'd called her again this morning, and she'd had to admit she hadn't found anything else beyond trying to balance work and cleaning.

Mallory had today off, and she'd not even thought of using it to "investigate" Katelyn's case. Instead, she'd given the apartment a thorough cleaning. It was easier when Katelyn was gone, not sacked out on the futon, glued to her phone, surrounded by snacks.

Mallory had finally given in and subscribed to one of the online streaming services to take advantage of the complex's free, if poky, Wi-Fi. Maybe that had been a mistake. It was supposed to be a carrot to tempt Katelyn into getting back into her schoolwork.

The "carrot" had turned out to be another distraction, another, "Oh, Mal, I will, sure… This episode ends in, uh, seven minutes."

At least when it came to therapy, Katelyn was raring to go. Mallory had dropped her off earlier, then beat it back to the apartment to give the unoccupied futon a good going-over with the vacuum.

Now she thought about her conversation

with Chad. She wandered back into the living room and sank down on the freshly vacuumed futon. A scrap of paper torn from an old sales circular, with a phone number in Katelyn's handwriting scrawled on it, lay on the floor. It must have fallen out when Mallory had been shaking out the cushions.

Chad had warned her that the longer they waited, the more evidence the county could hide—and they would, despite her convictions to the contrary. When she'd protested that the Monroes were good people who'd honestly been trying to help, he'd laughed wryly.

"Oh, ho, ho. They're pulling *that* stunt on you, huh? Where they're so nice and so helpful and they bend themselves into a pretzel trying to accommodate you?"

He'd warned her not to fall for it, to keep in mind that, more than the money, they needed to make sure the county was held accountable.

"You want them to *hurt*, Mallory. You want it to sting when they write that check out. You want to make sure they hurt so bad that they'll never do something like this to another kid in Katelyn's shoes."

When Chad had mentioned shoes, all Mallory could think about was the melted pink bunny slippers. For her, they symbolized the horror that Katelyn had been put through.

What Chad said made sense, Mallory had conceded. "I can see that. And that's what I want, too. For them to admit they made a mistake, and to be sure it will never, ever happen again."

"That's my job—and looks like it will be yours, too, Miss Nancy Drew, because I'm putting *you* in charge of digging up some more evidence. Here's what we need. We need a timeline of what happened that day. Who did what. They've got a report somewhere— probably in triplicate, knowing the county. You go in there, say that, uh…" Chad had paused, considering. She'd heard the clear snap of his fingers as he'd hit upon an idea. "Say the insurance company needs it for their records, that's it. And if you can find out if any of the firefighters who responded had disciplinary write-ups in their records—"

"What?"

"You gotta have leverage, Mallory. That's what's going to keep this thing from going to a jury trial. If there's anything they don't want to come out in open court, county governments will pay big just to sweep it all under the rug."

And with that, he'd gone, leaving Mallory staring at the scrap of newsprint with the mysterious phone number in hot pink ink. Afraid it might get lost, she picked it up, walked over to her wallet and tucked it in the change compartment. She'd have to remember to give it to Katelyn—

Katelyn!

A glance at her watch told her it was past time to head out to Happy Acres. So intent had she been on mopping every smidge of dirt and dust—and if she were honest, every thought of Andrew—out of existence, she'd let the time sneak up on her. That and Chad's phone call had vaporized the block of time Katelyn had been at therapy.

Mindless of her jeans and sweater, Mallory grabbed her purse and keys, jumped in the car and headed off to pick up Katelyn from therapy.

A few minutes later, as she leaned on the farm's white rail fence and watched Maegan work with Katelyn on a ponderously slow gray horse, Mallory used the sneakered toe of one foot to ease a cramp in her calf from all her mopping and cleaning. She needn't have hurried. She could see that now. Maegan always scheduled Katelyn as her last patient, and many times she took an extra few minutes to work with her.

Was it like Chad said? A way to make nice and get them to forget about the suit?

Mallory lowered her chin to the rough wooden rail and drew in the crisp air perfumed with Ma's fragrant hyacinths. The weather had warmed up to the point where she had driven out to the farm with the top down on her convertible, inhaling tea olives and Carolina jessamine and the wonderful smells of early springtime in Georgia. Even here, the air smelled of grass and woods eager to throw off the damp sogginess of winter.

A vibration through the rail fence caught her attention. She looked across to the other pasture to see Andrew astride a huge gleaming black horse, thundering over the deep green grass toward a group of barrels. Her breath caught as she watched the pair. They moved as one, Andrew almost an extension of the horse, around the set of barrels in a tight figure eight.

She found herself drawn to him as though he was lodestone. Easing alongside the fence, she approached the paddock where he was.

Andrew hadn't seen her. He was intent on putting the animal through its paces. He could have been on the cover of a rodeo poster: a battered Stetson atop his head, his back straight, the reins loosely but confidently held in one hand. His plaid button-down, faded jeans and dusty boots made a sharp contrast to the glistening, heaving horse.

Mallory couldn't fathom how he made the horse do its delicate two-step around those barrels. The turns were so sharp and fast that she found herself holding her breath, praying that he wouldn't take a spill.

And then it was over. The horse, following some unseen signal from Andrew, slowed to a trot, and then to a walk. Andrew leaned forward, giving the animal a pat on the neck, talking to it.

"Easy, boy. That's a good guy, you're getting the hang of it. And they said I'd never break you!"

The horse's sides were heaving, but he tossed his head high in response and let out a neigh, as if to say, "Sure, I can!"

She couldn't help it. She laughed with delight. She stopped herself before she broke out in a clap, remembering what Katelyn had told her about horses and blind spots and how easily spooked they could be. And this huge creature, twitching from his velvety muzzle to the tip of his long tail, looked as though he'd take any excuse to rear up on his hind legs.

Andrew wheeled the horse around in response, his frame relaxing as his gaze fixed on her.

"I'm sorry…but he looks so smug and self-satisfied," Mallory apologized. "As though he's conquered the world."

Andrew lifted a shoulder and nodded. "From his point of view, I reckon he has."

"Did you really break him yourself?" she called.

He walked the horse over closer to the fence. "I did. He was a rescue… He and about four other colts had been pretty much left to fend for themselves. If you'd seen him then, you wouldn't recognize him now. Skinny— and skittish. Didn't trust people."

I can see his point, Mallory thought, taking in the horse's liquid eyes, which studied her with a hefty dose of suspicion. Down the center of the horse's nose was a large white blaze, stark in contrast to his inky blackness. *Why should you trust a world that keeps handing out bad stuff?* "He still looks nervous."

"Oh, man, this is nothing. He was barely halter trained when I got him, and nowhere near able to endure a saddle. Little by little I've got him to this point."

The idea that Andrew, so busy with the fire department and helping Maegan, would patiently coax a skittish, abused colt into becoming this magnificent creature astonished her. The energy and patience and faith it must have taken!

"What's his name?"

"Joker—and no, I didn't name him. That was all he had when he came to us, and I didn't want to take that from him. Besides, it's a good fit. He's been known to have fun at my expense."

"Can I—" She lifted her hand, and then pulled it back.

"Go on. That's right. Lift your knuckles up to him—that's how you say hi to a horse." Andrew slid off and led the horse closer. Once again, she found herself being tutored in the ways of these giants.

Joker reached out, but instead of sniffing her hand, he nosed at her hair. His muzzle grazed her, tickling as it explored. Mallory stood stock-still, paralyzed with fear at such a close encounter with a horse.

Joker didn't seem to notice. Instead, he moved over to sniff the other side of her head. Then, more like a friendly Great Dane than a horse, he gave her a swipe on the cheek with his tongue.

"Joker! Mind your manners!" Andrew scolded. "She does not want your sugars!"

Mallory wiped away Joker's "sugars" with the backside of her arm. She saw that the horse had taken a step back, and, honest to goodness, looked as sheepish as a dog who'd eaten the morning newspaper. "Does that mean he likes me?" she asked.

"Yeah," Andrew said. He regarded the horse and then Mallory with a measure of surprise. "Yeah, and that's amazing! He's standoffish with most everybody but me. Even Maegan, and she can charm almost any horse."

"Wow. Then, I guess I should count that as a high honor," she told him. "I thought horses could tell you were scared of them."

Andrew reached up and gave Joker a welcome scratch in what was apparently a favorite spot. The horse leaned in and nuzzled him…then stretched out his nose and touched Mallory's hair.

Her heart hammered less than it had the first time, but still she stood quietly. When she saw Andrew make a move to pull the horse back, she said, "No. Please. Maybe it's my hair color."

"Oh, your hair. I remember. It smells like strawberries, and Joker loves 'em. That's what I'd use to reward him when I was first training him."

Inexplicably Mallory felt a sense of letdown. Joker hadn't liked her, hadn't felt the strange kinship of abandoned orphans that she'd felt for him. He'd only liked her shampoo—

"Wait. How do you know what my hair smells like?"

Andrew cleared his throat, stared at the horse. "You know. When we…when we kissed. In the truck."

Of course. His own scent of wood smoke and clean soap came back to her as strongly as if they were still in the cab of his truck. Before she could figure out how to fill the resulting awkward silence, Joker leaned back in for another hit of her strawberry shampoo.

"I guess I should go."

"No, no, wait—if you don't mind. He likes you. I mean, not just your shampoo. You're wearing sneakers for a change. And I need to walk him to cool him off. Sometimes when he knows it's time to call it quits, he gets cantankerous, but if you'll walk with us—"

She burst out laughing again. "What? Am I horse bait?"

Andrew's lips pressed together. Some of the cheerfulness dimmed in his eyes. "Only if you want to be. I guess you don't. After all, you haven't taken me up on those riding lessons."

His derisive observation made her mind up for her. "Will it spook him if I climb the fence?" Mallory asked.

"Not if you do it slow. Do you even know how to climb a fence?"

Mallory sniffed. "How hard can it be?" And with that, she put one foot up on the bottom rail and began to swing herself over. Joker didn't seem too unhappy that she was joining them—in fact, he gave her another big fat snuffle and a welcoming nicker.

"Ha," she said to Andrew. "Guess I showed you. How is it that you can have so much faith in a horse and none in me?"

"I— That's not exactly fair, is it?" he asked.

"Exactly where do I need to lead this horse?" Mallory began walking backward, Joker obediently trotting after her. "Because it seems to me that me and my strawberry hair form an irresistible combination."

"I can't believe it. Only a few weeks ago, you were shaking in your stilettos fifty feet from a horse. And now look at you." Andrew shook his head. "You want to lead him?"

Mallory's confidence melted away. "Uh, I'm not that brave."

"Okay. But how about that riding lesson? I can teach you how to take Joker's bridle off, and how to groom him. That's part of my first lesson anyway."

Mallory swallowed. Andrew's eyes seemed to hold a dare. "You mean me? In an itty-bitty stall with that great big old critter?"

"What happened to 'me and my strawberry hair being an irresistible combination,' huh?" He pointed behind her. "And the stables are where you're supposed to be leading him. But take the long way because I'm—I mean *he's*—all out of breath."

Instantly she was the one all out of breath— as she obediently walked backward for a few steps, watching Andrew. His smile lit up his face and erased all traces of the suspicious doubts he seemed to harbor about her. What would it be like to be the sort of girl who could make Andrew Monroe lose his breath?

The sort of girl…

Carole's words came back to her, about Andrew's past girlfriends and how he'd never seemed to find a way to make any of those relationships work.

The bubble of joy inside her grew a touch smaller, not quite gone, but not the great big levitation device it had been. She turned around and walked toward the barn.

"What?" Andrew protested behind her. "Was it something I said?"

No. Something I'm not. I'm not one of your glamour girls who can flirt and make small talk. I don't spend all my days having mani-pedis or going shopping. These days, the idea of a shopping spree is turning me loose with ten bucks in a Goodwill thrift shop.

Another thought dogged that one: the thought that it wasn't fair to either one of them to get tangled up in so much as a flirtation. Even if Chad was wrong about what motivated the Monroes to be so nice, Mallory needed a clear head so that she could look out for Katelyn's interests.

She hadn't been there for her when Katelyn had needed her. Mallory owed it to her to be there now.

CHAPTER FIFTEEN

ANDREW COULDN'T QUITE believe it. He actually had Mallory Blair on a horse, in riding boots, and she'd managed to ride around the paddock in a slow walk.

Sure, the horse was Pogo, who wouldn't have cared if somebody held a dance party atop his back, and the boots were a spare pair of Maegan's. But you couldn't ignore the fact that Mallory was on a horse.

She was trembling, though. "It—it's pretty high up here. How tall is this horse?"

"Pogo? Kind of on the shrimpy side. Joker's three hands taller. You're telling me you're afraid of heights and you walk around on those stilts you call shoes?"

"Those stilts, as you call them," she quipped, "won't actively try to buck you out of their soles."

"Trust me, the last time Pogo even thought about bucking, people considered subprime mortgages a great investment. Are you—"

A squeal of delighted surprise came from the other side of the fence. "Andrew! You got my sister on a horse!"

Pogo stayed still as a stone and didn't make a liar out of him by so much as even offering to startle at Katelyn's shout. Andrew watched as Mallory, beaming with accomplishment, turned the old horse toward Katelyn, who sat in her wheelchair, Maegan behind her.

"We wondered where you guys were," Maegan called. "I saw Mallory's cute little car, so I knew she was here."

"I take it you two are finished with Katelyn's session?" Mallory asked. "I guess I'd better call it quits." For a moment, she looked around, her face tense, obviously considering something. She twisted in the saddle and stared below at the thick rye grass covering the pasture. "Uh, how exactly do I get down from this thing?"

Katelyn let another peal of laughter escape her. "Andrew, why didn't you videotape this? I've never seen Mal so unsure what to do. She *always* can figure out how to boss me around."

Mallory took the ribbing good-naturedly. "Katelyn, I'm glad you got to see me out of my element. And I'm *really* glad Andrew didn't have that video camera you were hoping for."

Andrew admired her willingness to be made fun of, almost as much as the courage that it taken her to climb on Pogo to begin with. He knelt down and offered a knee.

"Woo-hoo, Andrew! Popping the question already?" Katelyn teased. "You move fast!"

"Uh, no— I—" Above him, Mallory had reacted with the same embarrassment at Katelyn's juvenile teasing that he had. He shook it off. To Mallory, he said, "Give me your hand and slide down until your feet touch my knee. And you, squirt," he called over his shoulder at Katelyn. "I'm sure Mallory's got some embarrassing photos of you when you were, say, eight. We'll post them on every social media site we can think of."

Katelyn blew a raspberry. "Maybe you can, but I'm safe if you're depending on Mallory to think up where to post it. She's above all that social media stuff."

That surprised him. He figured Mallory would be like his other girlfriends—posting every nanosecond of her life online.

Andrew's stomach flipped.

His other girlfriends. He'd actually thought that.

He cleared his throat to cover his discomfort. "I can only be a gentleman so long. This grass may look soft, but a pebble's digging into my knee."

"Oh! Sorry!" Without a moment's hesitation, Mallory slid off the horse and into Andrew's hold. For a beat or two, he held her there, the two of them close enough for him to get another intoxicating whiff of the strawberry shampoo that had so enchanted Joker.

Still, what held his attention even more than the feel of her waist in his palms was the way her eyes sparkled and her chin lifted up. Confidence—Mallory Blair had conquered something, even if it was just poking around a paddock on Pogo.

Something he had helped her achieve.

"Well, if you two are all done…" Andrew couldn't miss the teasing note in Maegan's voice. He let go of Mallory as though she were molten iron.

"I'll see to Pogo," Andrew said and tugged at Pogo's lead. Pogo, stubborn old mule of a horse that he could be, didn't cooperate. He jerked his head in protest, pulling so hard that the lead came out of Andrew's hand. Then he stepped back smartly and nudged Mallory.

"No, you old thing," Andrew snapped, embarrassed at the horse's rebellion. "No apples for you, not until we get you groomed."

"Are you sure I don't need to help you groom him?" Mallory asked. As he shook his head no, she reached up and stroked Pogo. "I'll bring you some next time, okay, old boy?"

Next time?

He hadn't dared to hope for anything beyond today. Maybe he was reading too much into Mallory's willingness to try riding a horse. Still, it showed that she trusted him. And if she trusted him...

Maybe she was beginning to trust him about Katelyn, too. Dutch had said that every day that went by without a lawsuit being filed meant the odds went down that she'd actually file.

Mallory climbed over the fence and joined Maegan and Katelyn on the other side. She rested one hand on Katelyn's wheelchair.

"Ma says she's got plenty of supper if you want to join us," Maegan offered.

Andrew found himself looking forward to another meal with Mallory—especially this relaxed and easygoing side of her—but his hopes were dashed.

Mallory shook her head slowly. "I'm sorry, but...I'm going to have to pass you up on that. I have falafels that I've already made at home. Will you give your mom my regrets?"

"Oh, Mal! Don't be so stiff-necked!" Katelyn protested. "Ma's a better cook than you are. I hate falafels!"

Mallory's mention of a food Andrew had heard of but had never tried served as a reminder of her citified ways.

Maegan chuckled and patted Katelyn on the arm. "Boy, do I know what you go through," she said. "Daniel's the same way. Ma says she wishes she could have convinced him to eat more vegetables when he was six and refusing to eat his cabbage."

Mallory arched an eyebrow toward Andrew. "Some of us are way past six but *still* refuse to eat our cabbage," she commented.

Katelyn negotiated her chair toward the house. "Well, I'm going to check in with Ma and see if she's got any pie or cake for a snack. Mallory never buys any junk food."

A flare of irritation arced across Mallory's features. "Katelyn, you know we can't—" She cut her words short, glancing in Andrew's direction. What had she been planning to say?

Whatever it was, Katelyn was in full little-sister mode, not listening to a thing her older sister had in mind. She was powering the wheelchair toward Ma's porch and back door, her thin arms pumping up and down to move the wheels.

"Katelyn!" Mallory trotted after her. "Katelyn Blair, you stop this minute— How do you think you'll even—"

By dent of an incline and Katelyn's wiry muscles, the girl had reached the bottom of the steps. Now she was leveraging herself out of the chair, pulling herself up first the bottom step, then the second, then the third.

Maegan was impressed to the point of letting loose a long, low whistle of approval. "I need to use sibling squabbles and Ma's baking for motivation more often."

Relief more than anything else pulsed through Andrew. Katelyn was getting stronger, better, every day. In the beginning, she didn't have the balance and coordination or muscle strength to make the trek across the yard, much less up those steps. He allowed Pogo to wander over and nibble on grass while he joined in with Maegan's clapping.

Ma pushed open the back door and poked her head out. "What on earth?" she asked. And then she spotted Katelyn, who was clinging to the banister post at the top of the steps with shaky determination.

Andrew called out, "She's doing tricks for cake. You got any?"

"No cake, but will a coconut pie do? I just got a double-size one out of the oven. C'mon in, and, land sakes, help that child before she falls over from grinning so big."

The screen door slammed shut, and Maegan rushed forward to assist Katelyn. Andrew walked over to retrieve Pogo, tugging him away from another hillock of grass and starting for the barn. Behind him, he heard Maegan's effusive praise of Katelyn's effort. He craned around for a second look, and that was when he noticed it.

Mallory was frozen in place. Her face was shut down, her fists clenched by her hips.

Of the four people who'd been watching Katelyn, Mallory was the only one not over-the-moon happy about the girl's achievement.

MALLORY'S HEART SLOWLY ratcheted down from its rat-a-tat, and she drew in a long, slow breath. Maegan had reached Katelyn's side by now and was yanking the wheelchair up to the porch, then easing Katelyn down into it. Mallory took a step forward, relieved that the spell that had frozen her to the ground had broken.

When she'd seen Katelyn pull herself out of that chair and cling to that railing, she was sure her sister would come crashing down. She could visualize broken bones, torn muscles, an instant setback to the gains Katelyn had so painstakingly achieved over weeks and months. And yet Mallory couldn't run to her. Couldn't move. Couldn't save Katelyn from herself.

What kind of sister was she?

And what kind of people were these Monroes that they rewarded such heedless action? Oh, she knew the answer to that. Mallory had seen enough pictures around Ma's house to recognize that the Monroes from childhood on had engaged in all manner of heart-stopping activities—bucking horses, bungee jumping, high diving, even a parachute jump. Apparently what passed for a fun family activity was anything that could give them an adrenaline buzz.

What did she expect anyway? They were a family of firefighters.

How on earth could they ever see the risk Katelyn was taking by shinnying up some steps?

Mallory trudged up those same steps and entered the kitchen, which was now humming with laughter. Katelyn sat at the table, inelegantly wolfing down a piece of golden-brown coconut pie, with Maegan and Ma enjoying the spectacle of a hearty appetite.

Great. Mallory dropped into a chair beside Ma and felt distinctly sorry for herself. Now Katelyn would not have an appetite and most likely would refuse to eat the falafels Mallory had made for supper: cheap, filling and nutritious.

She didn't want them to feel sorry for Katelyn and her...not because of money. The only "sorry" she wanted uttered was from Andrew: a simple "I'm sorry I left her there" would have been a great start.

Katelyn's accident had been another before-after line of demarcation for Mallory, just like her parents' death. Before the accident, things were fine, stable, they were doing okay.

After the accident?

Mallory had lost her job and run up her credit card balance. They'd had to move, and she'd had to figure out how to pay for the thousands of dollars in bills. And those were the fixable things.

Thinking about money reminded her of the wedding dress she'd been working on for Kimberly. She cleared her throat and managed to squeeze a question into the hubbub of conversation. "Wasn't Kimberly supposed to be down this week?"

"Sure is," said Ma. "They have some days off from school. She said you had something ready for her to try on."

Mallory hedged, "It's only the muslin. Before I start to work on the dress proper, I need to check for fit."

Katelyn piped up, "If she worries over the real dress any more than she does that muslin, I won't be able to live with her. She's like 'don't touch that, Katelyn,' and 'watch your glass of milk, Katelyn,' and 'you moved my scissors three-quarters of an inch to the side—'"

Mallory gritted her teeth to keep the defensive retort bottled up. When Katelyn had an audience, she could be twice as ruthless as she was now.

Any laughter she netted from her teasing would only encourage her, Mallory knew. Katelyn was getting revved up for the snarky, cutting remarks that always seemed to cause people to roar at Mallory's expense. Katelyn never failed to portray Mallory as a dull, boring stick-in-the-mud. Any sort of defense on Mallory's part only served to emphasize the point.

Then something unexpected happened to short-circuit the whole cycle: Ma reached over and patted Mallory's hand. "We seamstresses can get mighty tetchy about our scissors, can't we?" The solidarity she felt through Ma's touch warmed her.

"Oh, yeah," Mallory conceded. "Katelyn can't seem to understand that it's impossible for me to cut anything if my scissors aren't where they're supposed to be."

Ma nodded in agreement. "Tell me something I don't know. One of the times I got the maddest with Andrew is when he got hold of my best scissors, the ones I saved *only* for cutting cloth—"

Maegan slapped her palm to her mouth. "Oh. My. Word. Mallory, I came the closest to not having a little brother—" She dissolved into gales of laughter.

Beside Mallory, Ma's shoulders shook, as well. "Oh, that poor dog…"

"What dog?" Mallory and Katelyn asked in unison.

Ma swiped at her eyes, and, instead of answering, sliced and cut a generous piece of pie for Mallory. She managed to put the plate down before covering her mouth again to prevent a peal of laughter.

Maegan took up the story. "Ranger—he was a collie. Beautiful old fella that Dad just adored. Every night when Dad got home, he'd brush out Ranger's coat. Of course, Ranger was actually our dog, and we were supposed to be the ones feeding him and training him and brushing him. You know how kids are." She giggled again.

Ma put her face in her hands and shook her head. "The look on your father's face—"

"Wait, wait, let me tell it!" Maegan insisted. "See, Dad was big on chores. Every one of us had something we were supposed to do. Andrew—he was about four at the time—Andrew was supposed to brush Ranger every day."

"I'm guessing he didn't?" Mallory asked. She brought a forkful of the coconut pie into her mouth and instantly realized why Katelyn had been gobbling it down.

"Nope," Maegan said. "He'd brush the top of Ranger's coat, enough to smooth it out, and if you know anything about a collie's hair, you know it will mat up like nobody's business. It took about four days before Dad actually realized what was happening and found all the tangles in Ranger's undercoat, and, boy, was Dad hot! He told Andrew that under no condition was he to come home from work to find one single tangle in Ranger's hair…"

Mallory closed her eyes, but still she could visualize the disaster in the making. Scissors plus tangles plus a deadline to remove the latter? She could visualize Katelyn's solution to such a problem. "Oh, no. Tell me he didn't. Now I know what happened to Ranger."

"Oh, gracious—that dog looked scalped!" Ma said. "I was angry, believe you me, but Andrew's dad was even madder, especially after Andrew told him—" Tears of mirth rolled down her cheeks.

Maegan got out what Ma couldn't manage. "Andrew laid Ma's best scissors down on the porch, put his hands on his hips, and said, 'But, Dad, you didn't say I had to *brush* the tangles out!'"

Behind Mallory came Andrew's groan. Apparently their laughter had masked the sounds of his arrival. "Please, isn't there some statute of limitations on embarrassing-kid stories?"

He leaned over Mallory's shoulder and

scooped up a piece of the pie. She glanced up at him. "What happened? Obviously you survived to tell the tale."

Andrew shrugged his shoulders. "Only because my parents had some sense of mercy."

"They let you off?" she gasped.

"Not on your life! I said mercy, not leniency." He shook his head. "It took me three months to earn enough allowance to buy Ma a new pair of scissors, and about that long for Ranger's hair to grow back out. To make matters worse, it was the middle of the winter, and the poor old mutt didn't have a hair that was more than a quarter-inch long after I finished up with him. Dad made me go out every night before bed to the barn where the dog slept and put a blanket on Ranger. Dad would stand on the back porch with the porch light on, hand me a flashlight and tell me, 'You were big enough to come up with your own solution to Ranger's tangles, so you're big enough to do this. I'll be right here when you get back.'" Andrew shuddered at the memory.

Mallory could picture the scene, the dark-haired kid with the cowlick traipsing slowly out across the dim yard to the barn that must have seemed a million miles away. It sounded like something her own dad would have done. "I take it you learned your lesson?" she asked.

He scooped another piece of pie and nodded. "After that, I was *crystal* clear on how to get tangles out of a collie's coat."

Ma agreed. "Andrew became a stickler for the rules and regs, as his dad used to call them."

A thought popped into Mallory's head before she could stop it. *He learned that lesson too well.*

CHAPTER SIXTEEN

THE WORST THING about a firefighter's job, Andrew decided, was the waiting. With his pocketknife, he whittled on a single piece of wood, making a ball and cage and chain.

Jackson looked up from his video game. "How do you *do* that? You've got that ball almost perfectly round."

"You should try it," Andrew urged him. "It gives me time to think, you know?"

"And what have you got to think about, huh? Got a girl we don't know about? Man, you get the best-looking girls. How do you manage that anyway?"

Mallory's perfect features and glossy hair and understated but polished looks instantly filled Andrew's mind. "I'm giving dating a rest right now. And I'm trying not to date the glamour-girl types anymore."

Jackson let out a bellow of laughter. "You with a plain Jane? This I gotta see."

Andrew stood up and dusted off the wood

shavings that had collected on his navy blue uniform pants into the trash can he'd been using to catch the shavings as he carved. "You won't see me with anybody for a while. Besides, take it from me, the really pretty ones tend to be superficial and self-absorbed."

"It's because you go for the looks, man." Jackson stretched out his arms, the video controller still in his hand. "You don't trouble yourself to see if you have anything in common with them. That last one you dated— whenever she came around here, it was obvious she was too good for a blue-collar kind of guy."

This was exactly the conversation he didn't want to get into, especially with Jackson, who'd been dating a great girl for the past three years. Maybe he was right. But Andrew didn't want to stir around the ashes of his past mistakes.

Especially when it looked as though he was falling right back into the same trap with Mallory.

To his relief, Daniel came trotting through the fire station. "Hey!" he said. "About that idea you had, for the spring coat collection."

Andrew waited for his big brother to trash-talk the idea, which was to gather coats for

next winter's coat drive as people were clear-
ing out their closets for the spring and summer.

"Yeah?" he asked.

"I got permission for us to use the county
shop as a storage place, but you've got to set
up the collection points."

Relieved to have something to do, Andrew
sprang from the saggy chair in the station's
rec room. "I'll get started on it now. It's so—"

"Don't say it!" Both Jackson and Daniel
spoke at the same time, alluding to the su-
perstition that if any firefighter commented
on how quiet it was, it would let loose a tor-
rent of terrible call-outs.

"I nearly did say it," Andrew conceded.
"What I meant to say was that I'll go around
to different businesses and see what support
I can drum up."

"Yeah, but before you do, you need to go
by Dutch's office and get official clearance
from legal," Daniel warned.

"For a coat drive?" Andrew scoffed.

"Hey, that's what the county manager said.
We clear everything through legal, that's the
rule."

Andrew knew better than to keep grum-
bling. He put away the carving he'd been

making, grabbed a radio in case he was paged out for a fire and headed for his truck.

Dutch was buried in about a thousand pages of contracts when Andrew showed up at his door. "Enter at your own risk," his buddy told him. "If you knew anything about law, I'd shove a couple of these at you to review. What's up?"

Andrew moved aside a stack of folders from one of Dutch's office chairs. "I need clearance on a coat drive." Briefly he described the plan and produced the form he'd filled out while he waited for Dutch to get off the phone.

Dutch listened to Andrew's spiel, then scribbled a signature onto the form and handed it back. "Sounds good to me—except make sure that the coats are dry-cleaned before they go into storage."

"Why?" Andrew asked, bewildered.

"Liability issues. Any chemicals or pests on them could create a hazard and liability for the county. If we store coats with any sort of infestation or toxic substances, we're on the hook for liability and workers' comp issues from county employees."

Andrew goggled at him. "Do they *teach* you to think this cynically in law school?"

Dutch grinned. "I learned the upside of pessimism when I was catching your pitches, buddy." He shook his head. "You get used to it, you know? Thinking through the worst-case scenario? Don't you have a dry cleaner that partners up with you in the fall for the winter coat drive?"

"Sure, that's not a problem. It blows my mind, that's all, that *your* mind would even go there."

"It blows my mind that you actually want to go running into a burning building. Hey, to each his own, right?" Dutch lifted his palm for a high five.

Andrew reached over and slapped palms with him. "Beats sitting around reading contracts all day. Thanks, man." He turned to go, then hesitated. "You heard anything more on that possible lawsuit?"

"You mean the Blair gal?" Dutch was focused on the contract he had in his hand. He scribbled something in the margin, then looked back up at Andrew. "No papers filed yet, if that's what you're asking. But…"

"But what?" Andrew prompted.

"I got some more dirt on the lawyer."

"Yeah?"

"Guess I should have told you already,

given you a heads-up, but they landed all this—" he waved a hand to encompass the file folders "—on my desk and needed it yesterday."

"What is it with the lawyer?" Andrew asked.

"Be careful what you say on the phone or put in an email. This lawyer usually hires a PI that engages in some pretty shady practices. Hacking into people's email accounts and tapping phones."

"That's illegal!"

"Sure, but for this Chad fellow, it gets him dirt. And dirt's what he needs to force a defendant to settle. He may not be able to use what he gets in court—fruit of the poisoned tree and all—but he doesn't need that. He needs leverage."

"That's blackmail," protested Andrew.

"I agree, and if anybody can catch the slippery scumbag, that'll be the icing on the cake, not to mention one less ambulance chaser to have to contend with. Still, until somebody does, change your passwords, and don't put anything in an email or say anything on the phone that you wouldn't want broadcast in public."

"I can't believe Mallory would hire someone as sleazy as that."

"Mallory, huh?" Dutch twirled his pen in his fingers and regarded Andrew for a long moment. "When I did her background check, I saw her driver's license head shot. She looks to be exactly your type."

"We're not dating."

"You're keeping your distance like a good little professional firefighter would? No? Listen, buddy, cynical or not, I can see this two ways. She's either out to charm you into rolling over on the lawsuit and pushing us to settle—and if you admit you were at fault, she'll have us for breakfast. Or she's an innocent angel who loves everybody and has no clue about the junkyard dog she's hired."

A sour taste filled Andrew's mouth. It wasn't anything he hadn't already thought of himself, but hearing it from Dutch made it seem more real and harder to ignore. "I take it that you don't subscribe to the theory of Mallory, pure as the driven snow?"

Dutch flipped his palms upward. "Hey, I'm paid to think the worst of everybody. You're paid to think everybody deserves to be rescued, regardless of whether it was a guy's own stupidity that led to the infinitely mind-boggling decision to fry a turkey in a propane deep fryer that subsequently results in him burning his house down."

"But you're pretty certain. About Mallory."

"Because I hear the doubts in your voice, buddy. If you were more at ease about her, I might be inclined to give her the benefit of the doubt. The way you describe her—you've mentioned one or two times she's a fashion plate, and heck, I can see that even from her driver's license. High-fashion clothes don't come cheap."

"She does seem to be focused on money," Andrew admitted.

Dutch pointed the pen at him. "Bingo. You of all people know better than to play with fire."

MALLORY SCURRIED AROUND the apartment, pitching clutter into drawers, yanking up the multitude of plates Katelyn had scattered on their coffee table. It was Friday night, when Kimberly and Ma and the rest of the Monroe women were supposed to see the muslin.

Mallory had already been nervous about them coming to her apartment, but there was no help for it. All her tools were here, and it would have been too cumbersome to load up the muslin and her sewing paraphernalia for a couple of hours at Ma's, only to have to load everything again and haul it back here.

If the apartment were cramped and tiny and filled with furnishings that would mortify a college student, it could still be clean and neat. Poor but proud, that was Mallory's motto. Nobody need know a person was struggling to make ends meet if you were clever enough to cover up the fact.

She had even made snacks for them. Ma had asked her to fix some of those "fluffy balls you were talking about," so Mallory had done her best to turn out a perfect batch of falafels and a tasty yogurt sauce for dipping. She'd even splurged on fresh cilantro for decorating the plate.

"Why are you so bent out of shape about them coming, Mal?" Katelyn asked, not even bothering to look up from her cell phone. "I mean, it's just Ma and Kimberly. Why do you, like, have to be so perfect? You put on this act."

Mallory ground her teeth. "Katelyn, I wouldn't be bent out of shape if you straightened up the place while I was at work."

Katelyn rolled her eyes. "Maybe because I'm in a wheelchair?" she retorted.

That was it, the straw. "Plenty of people get

around in wheelchairs, Katelyn! Even those with paralyzed legs or no legs at all. You saw people at the burn center who were much worse off than you—"

"Oh, sheesh, don't start on that again. I'm trying, okay? So I didn't clean up to suit you—"

"You didn't clean up at all, Katelyn—in fact, it was worse when I got home than when I left. And that was the deal, right? I could stay at work for Eleanor, she could go to her doctor's appointment and you'd clean up and drive yourself to therapy and back."

"Well, hey, I drove myself to therapy." Katelyn bent back over her phone. Then, as an afterthought, she muttered, "Oh, by the way, you're on empty."

Mallory groaned. Even short trips seemed to eat through a tank of gas. "I gave you money for gas... You know, if you honk the horn, the folks at Temple's have said they'd come out and pump the gas for you."

"Yeah, but I was hungry. I needed a little pick-me-up before I went out to therapy, so I used that to go through the drive-through for a shake."

That was why the gas in the tank hadn't gone as far as Mallory had thought it should.

Katelyn had spent it parked in a drive-through line smack dab in the middle of the after-school rush.

Mallory clasped her hands to her head in frustration. "Katelyn," she got out in as calm a voice as she could manage. How had Mom and Dad not completely lost it when *she'd* been the one to make harebrained decisions?

She never remembered her dad being anything but calm with her, refusing to get riled. Her mom had been the same—and even though she recalled Katelyn testing her mom's patience to the nth degree, not even then did her mother raise her voice.

"Oh, good grief, Mallory! A shake! A two-dollar shake! I'll give you back the blasted change! You're like, rad about pinching pennies. Just once, can't I buy a shake at a drive-through without getting the third degree? I mean, I could have not even been here—bet you would have liked that better, huh? If I died, you wouldn't have to worry about what it costs to feed me?"

Katelyn yanked the chair around so hard that it tottered on one wheel, then she raced to her bedroom and slammed the door. Mallory collapsed on the futon and dropped her head into her hands.

She had never meant for Katelyn to feel as though she were a burden. Maybe Katelyn *was* worried about money. Maybe Mallory's obsession with penny-pinching was causing her sister to feel that if she weren't around...

Mallory crept to Katelyn's door and listened. Inside, Katelyn was crying, great, heaving sobs. It was always like this after a blow-up.

She tapped on the door. "Katelyn?"

Her sister said something in response that Mallory chose to interpret as "Come in," so she pushed open the door. Sure enough, Katelyn had thrown herself on the bed, her yoga pants riding up to expose her scarred calves.

Now it was Mallory who felt tears threaten. She bit them back. Tears never helped. "Katie-bug..."

Katelyn scrambled up to a sitting position and held out her arms. Mallory dropped down to the bed and pulled her close. "You are not a burden, do you hear? I'm so glad you're here with me, and I know how close I came to losing you, okay?"

"I'm such a beast sometimes, Mal. I'm sorry. I knew I shouldn't have wasted the money on the shake, but...I'm so tired of being poor. I wanted to pretend."

"I make a big deal out of it, I know. It was two bucks. I'll bet we could scrounge around and find eight quarters under the futon cushion," Mallory joked.

"I'm sorry I didn't clean up and I made a mess. I'll do better, okay? Tomorrow you'll come in from work, and I'll have the place all magazine clean, and you'll be like, 'Wow, is this the right apartment?'"

Mallory stroked Katelyn's hair. "It's hard for you, I know. I can't imagine everything you've been through, even though I've seen it. You're tough, Katelyn. You really are. I'm proud of you for all that you've accomplished." Mallory bit her lip and sat back. Something about the mention of the futon niggled at her memory. "Oh! The other day I found a phone number you'd scribbled down. I think it got caught in the creases of the futon cushion. I meant to give it you."

Katelyn frowned. "What number?"

"I can't remember the number, but you'd written it in hot pink on a corner newspaper. There wasn't a name with it. You need to—"

Her sister tossed her head. "Oh, that. I've saved it in my phone contacts. You can toss it. And I know. Write the name and the number... I'm not an idiot. It was my legs that were messed up, not my brain."

Then use that lump in between your ears sometimes, Mallory was tempted to say.

A knock at the door serendipitously interrupted her before she could give voice to her gripe. Mallory stood up, called out a "Coming!" and smiled down at her sister. "I've got a delish batch of fluffy balls, as Ma calls 'em. Don't you want some?"

"Ma can have my share, thanks. I'm gonna chill out here, okay? And I won't be, like, in your way."

Mallory brushed her sister's cheek with her palm. "You are not ever in my way, Katie-bug. I love you."

"I love you, too, Mal. I can be a colossal brat, I know that. Thanks for putting up with me. Lots of sisters wouldn't. They'd have just dumped me in some foster family."

Mallory swallowed hard and turned to answer the door. Time to be the big sister and see if she could earn her way to an emergency fund for her and Katelyn. Maybe that way, she wouldn't feel so stressed and blow her top over a two-buck shake.

CHAPTER SEVENTEEN

Two HOURS LATER, Mallory was again ready
to pull out her hair. The logistics of cram-
ming Kimberly, Ma, Cara, DeeDee, Maegan
and the wedding dress muslin into the living
room seemed impossible.

"This is like one of those old jokes about
how many clowns can you fit into a VW
bug," Ma remarked finally as Mallory had
to resort to letting Kimberly stand up on the
coffee table for them to all get a good look
at the bride.

"I am sorry. I should have packed everything up and taken it out to the farm," Mallory muttered around a pair of pins she had
tucked into her mouth. Slipping one out and
adjusting the fit of the bodice with it, she
stepped back—and onto DeeDee's toe.

Only her good balance saved her from falling into the woman's lap. "Let me up, and you
sit here," DeeDee suggested. "You've been

on your feet all day, I know. I've worked retail before."

"Oh, no, you're the client—" Mallory insisted.

"Well, this client wants some more of those
falafels. Delish! I want the recipe!" DeeDee
wandered into the kitchen.

Mallory surrendered to the impulse to take
DeeDee's seat. She looked up at Kimberly
perched on the coffee table, dressed in the
muslin she'd made to guide the final sewing
of Kimberly's dress.

"Well, what do you ladies think of it so
far? Kimberly?" Mallory's stomach fluttered
with nerves. What if Kimberly hated it and
she had wasted all this time on something
that wouldn't do?

Kimberly smoothed the muslin underskirt
with her palms and preened. "I feel bridal,
even in this. It's beautiful, Mallory! The fit is
perfect. Are you sure I'm paying you enough?
Because if I were to pay for a custom dress
in Atlanta, it would be way more."

Mallory exhaled with considerable relief. "Pshew! I'm on the right track, then.
No, Kimberly, I'm fine with our bargain if
you are. My only worry is actually finding
enough room to sew everything once I start

in on the tulle. Because that tulle takes up a lot of space."

"That, I can fix," Ma said. "I've got a great big sewing room out at the farm. You bring that fancy machine of yours and all your gadgets out there, and you set up shop."

For a moment, Mallory was tempted to blurt, "Yes!" to Ma. She'd seen that space before, with its long counter and built-in sewing machine below the shelves of neatly arranged storage bins and a peg-board full of sewing items. To have a space like that would be heaven.

But...that would mean dealing with Andrew.

Andrew, who had gone cold on her again in the past few days. He practically ran from her whenever she picked up Katelyn.

"Oh, that's okay—"

"Nope, I insist. It'll be nice to have some company."

Kimberly bent down and took Mallory's hands in hers. "This battle is lost, trust me. Ma has adopted you and Katelyn. She's decided you need the space, and that's that."

DeeDee, Cara and Maegan bobbed their heads. "Saying no to Ma is as pointless as telling the rain to stop," DeeDee said.

"And to sweeten the pot," Ma tacked on, "I'll cook supper for you while you sew. I know how it is trying to cook in the middle of a sewing project. I'll even try my hands at your fluffy balls if that's what you want."

"Ma, your cooking is divine—"

Ma sat back, pleased with herself. "Well, then, it's settled. You need me to send Andrew here tomorrow to help you pack up everything? I'd tell you to move out there with everything and give up this rinky-dink place, but our bathrooms won't work for Katelyn. As soon as she gets shed of that wheelchair, though, the offer stands."

Mallory had no chance to respond, because Ma stood up, gave her a kiss on the cheek and a quick hug and said, "Girls, somebody needs to run this old gal home."

Cara and DeeDee offered, leaving Maegan to wait for Kimberly to change. While Kimberly used Mallory's bedroom to take off the muslin, Maegan followed Mallory's lead and began toting glasses and plates into the tiny kitchen.

"Where's Katelyn? I haven't heard a peep out of her," Maegan commented.

"She's in her room. I *hope* she's been using the time to work on her homework."

"She still in that accelerated program? The one where she takes college-level courses?" Maegan set the plates in the sink. "Where's your sponge, and I'll start washing?" she offered.

"Oh, that's—"

"Hey, you might as well take me up on it, because as soon as Kimberly gets through, your free help is gone, sister." Maegan grinned.

"Under the sink, then, if you're so willing to do someone else's dishes. I'll rinse and dry."

"Now, how'd you know I hated that part? I used to con Andrew into doing that for me when it was my turn to do the dishes. Rob and Daniel were too savvy to fall for my tricks, though."

A flutter went through Mallory at the mention of Andrew's name. "Speaking of MIAs, I haven't seen too much of Andrew lately," she said casually.

"Daniel's kept him busy with some spring coat drive—the fire department's collecting everybody's outgrown winter coats before people pack them up. That way, the department will have them on hand before folks need them. You wouldn't believe how many people can't afford a good winter coat," Maegan said.

Oh, wouldn't I? That would be me. I'm so glad the weather warmed up to the point I can do without. "He's been busy, huh?" Mallory asked instead.

"Between work and helping me and training Joker—yep, I hardly see him myself. I can tell him you were asking after him, if you'd like."

"No!" Mallory nearly dropped the glass she was drying.

Was Maegan chuckling? She was. Blast it.

"I just mean...it's not important...or anything. Conversation, that's all." Even to Mallory's ears, her words sounded unconvincing.

"You and Andrew... If you guys could get over being so prickly around each other, you'd be a good match. You're exactly his type, but at the same time—"

"Everybody keeps telling me that I'm Andrew's *type*. But that doesn't make any sense." Mallory gave the plate an extrazealous rub. She set it down and reached for the next one.

"You're pretty as a picture. Listen, my brother has excellent taste," Maegan said.

"And you fit the bill. Always so polished. I need you to give me a fashion makeover."

"You don't need it," Mallory countered.

"I do whenever I have to get gussied up to go somewhere. I never know what goes with what. If I do have to attend something fancy, will you help?"

"Sure! I love doing that. We'll go through your closet, see what you have—"

"Ooh, really?" Maegan clapped her damp hands, making water and suds spray everywhere. "Yay! See? That's what I mean, that you're his type, but you're *not* his type."

Mallory frowned. "What's that supposed to mean? Either I am or I'm not."

"On the outside? You're it, buddy. On the inside? You're nothing like the gals he's brought home. To be charitable, they weren't awful, but you could tell they wanted to be anywhere but on a farm."

"How..." Asking how she was an improved version of Andrew's type seemed to border on fishing with a net for a compliment.

"It's awful when they dump him, of course," Maegan allowed. She handed the last plate to Mallory and yanked out the sink stopper. "He mopes around for months. And then, wouldn't you know, he gets one as bad or worse. Honestly, I was a bit snippy with you when you first showed up, because I was sure you'd be another one. And if you'd broken my brother's heart, you would have had me to answer to."

Mallory's mouth went dry. She hadn't a clue what to say. "I don't think that will be a problem, because I don't think Andrew thinks of me that way."

Maegan arched a brow. "I'd say I was pretty much an authority on the subject of Andrew Monroe... I wouldn't be surprised if he does ask you out, though why he's waited this long beats me. If he does... Just remember. You don't know mad until you've seen a Monroe mad, so if you don't feel the same interest in him that he seems to in you...don't lead him on. Or else, be prepared to face me."

Kimberly's arrival back in the living room saved Mallory from having to make an answer one way or the other. How disappointed would Maegan—all of the Monroes, really—be if they knew she was planning to sue the county for Katelyn's medical expenses?

CHAPTER EIGHTEEN

"MA, I— THIS IS not a good idea. Have you talked to Daniel about this?" Andrew asked into his cell phone. He ran his other hand through his hair, realized that it was getting longer and that he needed to get it cut.

"Andrew! This *is* for Daniel—for Kimberly, anyway, and besides, why do I need permission to invite someone to use my old sewing room? Is Daniel suddenly going to take up sewing?"

What could he say? *Uh, the lady you trust so much may be more interested in suing than sewing?* Daniel and Dutch had ordered him not to speak to anybody about the suit, lest others' reactions might irritate Mallory into suing when she'd decided against it. As Dutch had said, "No need to go poking a bear."

Not that Mallory was a bear.

He sighed. "I'd feel more comfortable about this if you would talk to Daniel—"

"Andrew Monroe. I've invited her and

that's it. Unless you know something definite about this woman that means she isn't fit company, and if you do, you sure don't act like it when she's around."

"This isn't some elaborate matchmaking scheme, is it? Sending me by to get her things, moving her sewing machine—"

Ma sniffed. "First time I ever heard you might need help in that department, Andrew. Seems to me you can land any girl you set your mind to, but my advice has always been don't settle for just a pretty face."

That advice, sage and familiar, made Andrew relax. If Daniel had thought the suit threat was serious, he'd have warned Ma and Maegan earlier. "My shift ends in a few minutes, so I'll go by there and pick up her stuff."

"You call her and tell her you're on your way, then, because I said it might be the afternoon."

They rang off and Andrew dialed Mallory's cell phone. She answered, breathless. For a nanosecond, Andrew allowed himself to believe that she'd known it was him and raced to answer.

That wishful thinking died an early death with her confused "Andrew?"

Who had she been hoping it would be?

He recapped Ma's plans, which seemed to cause her to be even more flustered. "I— well, *now*?" Mallory asked. "It was nice of her to offer, but…"

Inexplicably he was disappointed in her answer. Yes, rationally, it was better for him that she didn't move her dressmaking operation out to the farm. He found it was hard enough to avoid her these days when she came out to drop off or pick up Katelyn. Avoiding her when she was in their actual house? Impossible. Dutch would be thrilled at how neatly this had turned out.

Why did Andrew feel as letdown as a kid expecting a bike for Christmas and not getting one?

"Ma was pretty insistent. She's got it all worked out." He kicked himself. He should have said, "I'll let Ma know."

"She won't be—offended? Will she?" The doubt was almost palpable in her voice. Andrew could sense he could push her either way.

He didn't want to manipulate Mallory into changing her mind.

"She won't be offended," he assured her, sticking to the truth. "She'd be disappointed. We all would."

Again he gave himself a virtual slap upside the head. That last confession was taking truth-telling a step too far. He rushed to temper the remark with, "She would definitely understand that you know best about these things."

Silence reigned as Mallory apparently weighed the pros and cons. "It *would* be nice to have more space," she confessed. "Still, I don't want to intrude."

Andrew's disappointment lifted like an early-morning fog burned off by the sun. "She wouldn't have offered if she'd considered it an intrusion. Trust me, she does this sort of thing all the time. That's why half the county calls her Ma."

"She is *so* nice—all of you are," Mallory blurted out.

"I can come by, then? Grab your gear?"

"Can you give me a few minutes? I was getting ready for work."

Right. The request brought Andrew back down to earth and to the real world. No matter how easygoing she sounded on the phone, appearances still mattered the most to her. A woman like Mallory would definitely devote a good chunk of the morning to apply her war paint.

Was it that she had to get so gussied up to do her job? Or did she choose the job because it gave her an excuse to dress so fancy?

He agreed to wait, then loaded his own gear into his truck.

He'd picked up coffee while he waited, and sure enough, when he showed up at Mallory's door, she was picture perfect in her usual skirt and blouse and heels and all the accessories from the fine gold chain at her throat to the jangly bracelets on her wrist.

Now he realized he'd wanted to catch her without her makeup on—in jeans and a T-shirt. He could pretend, then, that she wasn't like all the other girls he'd dated.

But this polished perfection? She must have gotten up before dawn to get dressed. Something about a person stressing about her looks that much irritated him.

She took the coffee and thanked him. "I haven't gathered all my things up—"

"No problem. I can wait. I just got off work, so I don't have anywhere pressing to be."

Mallory's guilty expression deepened. "Oh, no! This could have waited—"

"Actually, it saves me a trip."

He could tell she hadn't expected his curtness. Andrew tried to dial his irritation back a notch. "If you need me to come back, I can," he offered. "It's only that I was leaving the fire station and I told Ma I'd stop off and get your things as I was heading out to the farm."

"No, no need for you to make two trips, not with the price of gas as high as it is," she said. "Your truck can't get more than fifteen miles to the gallon, and it's seven miles out to the farm. A round trip would take almost a whole gallon of gas."

Money again, he thought. *The woman counts every nickel and dime.*

"That's right. Gotta save some for the shoe fund, huh?" he asked, allowing the sarcasm to needle through.

She pressed her lips together, the corners of her mouth pulling down. "Gotta save some for the shoe fund."

Andrew wondered why it always seemed to come down to this: the thing that attracted him to her was the thing that irritated him.

"Let me get everything together for you," Mallory said suddenly, and bustled off toward the living room.

As he came into the apartment proper, he realized why Ma had offered her space. Almost every inch of the previously neat area was covered with cloth, patterns, lace or some sewing apparatus he dimly recognized. Everything was neatly stacked—but even an idiot could see they had no room to wiggle in the apartment without knocking something over.

Mallory had bent over to tuck things into a beautifully quilted sewing box that looked as though it cost big bucks. Yep, beans for supper, skip the winter coats because they spoiled the outfit and choke on the price of a gallon of gas—because appearances were most important.

"It matters how things look to you, huh?" he found himself asking.

His question must have startled him— or maybe his tone—because she wound up whirling around and dropping all the implements she held in her hands.

"Oh, shoot!" Now she was kneeling down, mindless of her skirt, her knees on the bare floor, which looked as though it had seen better days. Some of the items had rolled under the edge of the cheap futon.

Hmm. Guess futons don't have to meet a certain standard, because that's the ugliest one I've ever seen.

She was mumbling invectives to herself,

and he picked up a host of not-so-kind self-critiques. A twinge of shame coursed through him. He joined her on the floor and reached for the items that were escaping her reach.

She was close to him now, her hair smelling sweetly of the strawberries that Joker had liked. Andrew had to admit, he liked them, too, on her. A slim locket dangled from the thin gold chain at her throat as she tried to rescue her tools, and when she leaned forward, it got caught in the metal frame of the futon.

"No, wait— Don't—" Andrew placed a hand on her shoulder as she started to jerk back, unaware. "Your locket is caught in the—"

"Oh! I don't want to break it or the chain—"

"Easy, easy—" Suddenly, Andrew felt as though he were calming a nervous horse early in its training. "Let me try."

She was impossibly close as he worked to free the short length of chain and the locket. Her proximity assaulted his senses—the warmth of her body, the way her huge green eyes were filled with worry that the jewelry would be ruined, the scent of those strawberries. Even at this close distance, her skin was perfect.

She's pretty enough to have anybody she

wants. Why on earth would she stick with some blue-collar type like you? Haven't you learned anything?

"Should I try to take off the necklace?" Mallory asked.

Andrew tore his focus away from her and forced it back to the task at hand. The locket itself was free, but the chain was still snagged. Andrew conceded, no engineer in his right mind would have ever dreamed of the possibility of some woman getting a necklace caught in his design.

He examined the nape of her neck—pale and smooth, her hair swept up in a careless-looking bun that he figured took her hours to do. The chain dug into the soft flesh of her nape, and when he tried to unfasten it, he found there wasn't enough slack.

"No, you've caught the chain too close—you don't have enough room to lean forward so I can slip my finger under the fastener. I'm going to have to work it loose where it's caught, I think."

"Can you get it? Without breaking it, I mean?" Her words were filled with worry, and he saw her clench her fingers into white-knuckled fists.

"I'm trying— Wait, no, thought I had it—"

He didn't dare to tug too hard. "Is this real gold?"

"Yeah. It's twenty-two karat."

Andrew swore softly. "That means it's soft, right?"

"Yes. The higher the number, the purer the gold."

Leave it to Mallory to wear only the best. He was probably handling a two- or three-hundred-dollar chain—maybe more, because he had no clue how much something this fine and delicate would cost. And the locket, which was heavy and ornate with deeply carved roses, probably cost another arm and a leg.

Finally, with a clink of the locket, the chain slipped free—so quick that he wasn't sure whether he'd managed to do it without breaking it. He grabbed it before it could get snagged again.

"Pshew! It's pretty much unharmed—though I have to tell you one of the links has a tiny dent in it," Andrew said, releasing the length of chain.

She touched the locket reassuringly, and then unexpectedly wrapped him in a hug. "Thank you, thank you so much."

This much fuss over a silly piece of jewelry? So he kind of liked having her throw herself at him as though he'd just rescued her kitten from a tree, but…jewelry? Really?

Now Mallory sat back again on her heels. She held the locket and stared down at it, rubbing her fingers along the mellow finish. "It was my mom's," she whispered.

Slipping the chain from her neck, she pried the locket open with a perfectly pink nail and handed it to him.

Two redheaded babies stared back at him. Even in their baby plumpness, he could recognize that one was Mallory and the other Katelyn. "Dad gave this to her when I was born. She always wore it," Mallory explained. "She was wearing it the day she died. I wear it now. To keep her close."

His breath caught in his throat. Not some silly necklace after all, not an expensive bauble. It hadn't been the money that had panicked Mallory, but the sentimental value.

Thinking of how important Ma was to him—to all of the Monroe children—made him realize he couldn't imagine not having a mother. Sure, he'd lost his dad…but so had Mallory. In one fell swoop, she'd lost both parents.

And he'd nearly cost her the last family member she'd had.

Her eyes were shining with tears that threatened to spill over. For a moment, he thought she'd lose it. Instead, she lifted her chin, closed her eyes and seemed to will herself into control. Somehow that moved him more than if she'd dissolved into a puddle of tears.

"Mal—I am so sorry—" he started.

Then Dutch's warning came back. No apologies about Katelyn, which was where he'd been headed.

He clamped down on his words. Held back, they felt as though they were live animals, desperate to force their way free, out into the world. When she reached up and clasped his hand, stared at him with grateful, wet eyes, Andrew found it even harder to bite his tongue.

"It's okay. I know this thing—it's just metal and screws, and if we sold it, it could feed us for a month, but…" She pressed the locket to her lips. "I can't. There are things I simply can't let go of."

"Nobody's asking you to," he assured her. "It's safe and sound."

"Thanks to you. Guess it's handy to know a firefighter, huh?"

"Cats from trees, dogs out of drainage pipes, necklaces out of futons. All in a day's work, and it's been a pleasure to be of service, ma'am." He doffed an imaginary cap at her.

"Well, now that I've completely ruined my makeup and look a fright, I'd better double-time it, get this stuff packed up and get to the shop. Otherwise, Eleanor will wonder where on earth I am."

Andrew saw that her knees were trembling as she stood.

"Oh, no! I forgot the rest of the things that fell!" Mallory said. "Uh, can you press into service some more of those firefighter skills and move that futon so we can get whatever else slid under there?" she asked.

"Yep." With one hand, he flipped up the futon and with the other hand grabbed the single item remaining: a pair of scissors. He held them up for her inspection. "Think you should trust me with these?" he joked.

Mallory's eyes crinkled at the corners, and real humor lightened her expression. "Sure, since I don't have a collie for you to brush. Did you really—"

"It was worse than they said. That poor mutt looked as though he'd been caught in a shredder by the time I got finished with him. Even as a kid, I knew I was in hot water."

"But you couldn't admit it?"

"Hey," he said, shrugging his shoulders. "I'm a guy—and a Monroe at that. It takes us a while to admit mistakes. It's in our DNA."

Pain and resignation flickered in those shiny green eyes at his confession. He realized that he could try to set things right, figured he might even head off that lawsuit, if he just had permission to apologize about his decision to leave Katelyn.

But he had followed the rules in that confusing, smoke-filled house, and the rules—as Dad had always hammered into his head—were there for a reason. They'd kept him safe. They'd kept Eric alive.

Maybe it had been a bad outcome, but what Mallory couldn't understand—didn't seem to want to understand—was that it could have been so much worse.

CHAPTER NINETEEN

MALLORY PUSHED ASIDE a paisley muumuu that Katelyn wouldn't be caught dead in, a striped seersucker jacket…ditto. Hangers scraped along the metal bar, rattling against each other as she flipped through her choices. Hmm… This thrift-store shopping trip wasn't going well.

The next item had some hope. It was an aqua colored dress big enough that it could have swallowed Joker, if the horse had stood still for it. The fabric was good, though, soft cotton that hadn't faded, and the print had a retro vibe with its white bubble circles and a contrasting banded hem. It still felt contemporary enough, and instinctively, Mallory knew that Katelyn would love it. She held it up to her for sizing. Yes…it would do.

"Mallory! What the heck—"

She looked up to see Andrew gaping in astonishment at her and gripping a stack of handouts. Mortification at being caught in a thrift store suffused her.

That'll teach me to start shopping near the door, she thought grimly.

"What are you looking for? Some sort of costume? Because that would fit three or four of you," he said.

Mallory drew in a deep breath. So what if he had found out her secret? Shopping here was nothing to be ashamed of. Besides…he had a point. She frowned, looked down at the dress and realized that it would indeed have enough fabric to make an outfit for both Katelyn and her.

"I'm using it for the fabric," she explained. "Katelyn needs some cooler clothes now that the weather is beginning to warm up. Her skin grafts don't allow for proper temperature regulation…and, well…I can cannibalize this dress and make her a long skirt that will be cooler than pants, or I can whip up some palazzo pants."

"That—that thing doesn't look the least bit like Katelyn," he protested.

Now she laughed. "It's there. Trust me."

He wrinkled his forehead. "Sorry…for the life of me, I can't see how you could make anything remotely wearable out of that thing. It looks like a bedsheet."

An urge to show him, to convince him, came over her. She folded up the dress into a skirt-like dimension, with the broad striped hem forming a decorative band along the bottom. She held it up against her. "See it now?"

"I do. You're good! I wouldn't have used that thing for washing my truck." He shifted the flyers he held to his other hand and reached over to stroke the fabric. "That's pretty cool."

"New fabric costs a bunch—and so do the zippers and the buttons," Mallory told him. "I look here to see if I can find raw materials."

"You *make* your clothes?" Now Andrew did look gob-smacked. She realized in an instant that he'd assumed she bought her wardrobe new. His admiration overcame her mortification at being caught.

"Sure. I can buy a pair of men's slacks here for five bucks—nice suiting out of summer-weight wool—and turn them into a skirt for work, easy peasy. And those shoes you're always teasing me about?"

"Don't tell me you're a closet cobbler who has elves lined up to make shoes," he joked.

She shook her head, leaned down and

pulled off one of her heels. Perching on one leg, she handed the shoe to him. "See? I buy cheap shoes and recover them to match my outfits. All it takes is a lot of fabric glue, some scraps of coordinating fabric and patience."

Andrew tucked the handouts under his arm and took the shoe she'd offered. He turned it over, inspecting her workmanship.

"That's pretty neat," he allowed. "I'll have to tell Cara and DeeDee about that."

Panic swamped her at the thought of her secret going beyond Andrew. "Er—can you keep it under your hat? I don't advertise the fact that I make my own clothes from thrift-store items," she said.

He drew his brows together. "Why not?"

Other shoppers were beginning to stare at her. And why shouldn't they gawk at a woman impersonating a pelican? "Can I have my shoe back? We're attracting attention."

If she'd expected Andrew to simply hand her shoe back to her, he didn't. Instead, he knelt down, much as Prince Charming would have before Cinderella, and offered it to her.

His work-roughened fingers skimmed the sensitive skin along the top of her foot as he guided the shoe on. Did they linger a half second longer than they should have? He gazed up at her, his eyes alight with merriment, his mouth in a quirky I-know-your-secret smile. She couldn't help smiling back as she lowered her foot to the floor.

Would that one day she could find her real Prince Charming. But could it ever be Andrew?

Would she *want* it to be Andrew?

He rose to his feet and repeated his question. "Why don't you like to tell people how you remake clothes?"

People were still staring at them. Mallory felt her insides quiver as though she were under a magnifying glass.

"I work in retail, for one thing," she explained. "If the women who came into BASH knew I didn't actually buy my clothes new, maybe they wouldn't buy them new, either. You're kind of expected to support the shop you work for. As much as I love Eleanor and her taste in clothes…she can't afford to pay me enough to be able to buy her merchandise."

"I can see that. But DeeDee and Cara don't shop at BASH anyway. It's too expensive. You wouldn't be scaring off customers if you told my sisters."

Mallory hated the way embarrassment made her squirm. "They're always complimenting me on my clothes," she muttered, avoiding Andrew's way-too-intense gaze. "They might feel like I'd lied if they found out they were homemade."

Andrew's guffaw drew her attention back to him. "Are you kidding me? They'd be even more impressed than I am. Neither one of my sisters can so much as sew on a button, or so Ma says, despite her trying to teach them. They'd probably hire you to sew stuff for them. And homemade? Not a chance. You always look like a million bucks."

His praise boosted her spirits and gave her a burst of pleasure. "Yeah? You think so?"

Andrew reached out to touch her, seemed to realize where they were and pulled back. He exhaled sharply, staring at her as though she were missing an important point.

"What?" she asked. "Say it, whatever it is."

"You *know* you look good, Mallory. Don't you? I mean, you spend hours on making sure you look good. You don't need me to tell you that. Plenty of guys would."

I don't want plenty of guys to tell me that, she thought. *I want* you *to tell me.*

Somehow being honest with him, especially after he'd tumbled onto how she afforded clothes to begin with, felt too risky. She dropped her focus to the aqua-colored tent in her hands and smoothed out a wrinkle. "It's nice to be told" was all she said.

"Consider yourself informed, then. And, uh, I won't tell DeeDee or Cara, but believe me, if you think they'd look down their noses at it, you're wrong."

He pushed past the racks of clothes and headed for the counter. She watched him as he talked with the salesclerk, and then the thrift-store manager. He had them eating out of his hand—the manager was sending out all the signals, the touch to the throat, the flutter of hands on her hair, the sideways glance.

No wonder Andrew always seemed to know what to say to make her feel better about herself. He'd had quite a bit of practice.

She started to shove the dress she'd chosen back on the rack, then changed her mind. No. It didn't matter that she'd think of Andrew no matter whatever creation she fashioned out of it; she was going ahead with it.

Maybe if you're honest with yourself, you're buying it because *you'll think of Andrew every time you wear it.*

With that, she melted into the racks, determined to forget all about impressing Andrew Monroe and focus instead on making her dollars stretch.

He hadn't realized she and Katelyn were so broke that this was the only way they could afford to put clothes on their backs.

A sour note spoiled the pleasure she'd felt earlier as she realized that Andrew was one of the reasons they were struggling financially.

BTA—before the accident—Mallory had been in the best financial shape she'd experienced since her parents' death. She'd had a job she'd enjoyed, a decent apartment, no worries about buying groceries or paying the rent and Katelyn was going to college early on the state's dime except for books and supplies.

Back then, Mallory could afford to splurge now and again on small treats for herself: a mani-pedi maybe, or a dinner out with friends, or a dress she'd found on the clearance rack. She'd even considered enrolling in some business classes in a community college to work on her abandoned degree. She'd trolled thrift stores mainly to satisfy her need for creativity.

ATA—after the accident—the thrift shop

was a matter of self-defense. She had all these bills, including the sizable co-pays that went to Maegan for Katelyn's therapy. But she still had to feed and clothe her and Katelyn, and thrift stores, plus some time and patience and an eye for design and color, made that possible.

It was a slow and painful way to live, but ATA, there was no other choice.

ATA… Now she could think of it another way.

After there was Andrew.

CHAPTER TWENTY

ANDREW STOOD ANKLE-DEEP in water and fished the mewing cat off the top of the water heater. He tried to be gentle with the critter—it was a cutie-pie gray-and-white tuxedo cat that brought to mind, of all things, the old Batman comics.

The cat, however, didn't want to be gentle with him. Instantly all claws came out, its mouth yawned wide in a ferocious hiss, and the thing tried to bite him.

"I don't think that animal likes you," Eric told him.

"Feel free to jump in anytime, buddy," Andrew shot back. "If he bites me, you'd better be prepared to catch if I accidentally toss him."

Fortunately, this was not Andrew's first time herding cats. He scooped the feline up against his turnout gear and splashed out of the utility room, Eric trailing behind. Outside, the homeowner, a little old lady stretched out her arms. Andrew gratefully surrendered the hissing, spitting creature.

"Mr. Kitty!" she crooned. "Oh, did that big, bad firefighter scare my Mr. Kitty?" And darned if she didn't kiss the cat square on its gunmetal-gray head.

"Ma'am, your water heater has sprung a huge leak," Andrew informed her. "We've turned off the supply line, and my partner here has switched off the breaker that provides power to the unit, but you'll need to call a plumber."

She looked up from comforting Mr. Kitty. "You can't fix it? You're a firefighter. I thought all you firemen knew how to handle pipes and water and such."

I will not groan. I will not roll my eyes. I will not look at Eric, or I will burst out laughing. Instead of giving into temptations best avoided, Andrew shook his head. "No, ma'am. City ordinances state that you need a licensed plumber to repair a water heater."

She twisted her lips, carelessly covered in hot pink lipstick, into a pout. She even batted her eyes. Laying a hand on his sleeve, she wheedled, "But you're here, and I won't tell. Besides. You've seen how I have water in my kitchen. That's where my phone is. A woman my age shouldn't be tramping around in water, or she's liable to fall and break a hip, and then you'll be right back out here, helping me again."

I will not groan, he ordered himself again. It didn't help that Eric was barely containing a snicker.

"Ma'am, I agree with you that you shouldn't venture into your home until the water has been cleared out," Andrew said stiffly. Diving a gloved hand into one of his pockets, he came out with a list he'd printed. He saw a neighbor gawking across the hedge and waved her over.

As the woman approached, he said to the cat lady, "I'm sure your neighbor here will allow you to use her phone. This is a list of all licensed plumbers and cleanup businesses in the city limits, as well as their contact info. If you tell any of them what happened and that we came out, along with this code," he pointed a gloved finger toward the number at the bottom, "they've agreed to give you a ten percent discount."

The cat lady's glower turned into a sunshiny smile. "Well, thank you, sonny! You're a most helpful young man!"

With that, Andrew doffed his hat and

walked briskly for the rig and the guys already loaded up on it. Eric caught up with him and asked, "Where'd you get that list?"

"What? You mean you didn't learn from the last time you got hornswaggled into doing some on-the-scene plumbing for a homeowner? Never get out of the rig without a tool in your hand, and never forget to put something useful in your pocket."

Eric ignored him and said, "I want one of those to make copies of."

"Nuts. You could have come up with your own. Besides, you didn't offer to help me out with Mr. Kitty."

"Nuts yourself. You afraid of a wittle bitty kitty cat?" Eric jostled him by the arm and stole his hat. Andrew nabbed it back, the two roughhousing all the way to the rig.

"You two ever gonna grow up past ten?" Captain groused as he leaned out the open window. "C'mon. We've got reports to write, not to mention training to get through, and you guys are goofing off."

"Aw, Cap, it was him who was fooling around with the cat," Eric told him.

"Like I said," the captain reminded while the rig was pulling out into the street, "I'm waiting for the two of you to get past ten."

They bounced back toward the fire station through a leafy green residential section of town. The radio crackled to life with a call for Andrew to report to a meeting with the chief.

Eric waggled his eyebrows. "Been pulling your sister's pigtails?"

Only Eric could get away with mentioning that Daniel was Andrew's brother. Andrew had been a probationary firefighter when Daniel was promoted.

Truth was, Daniel was a terrific chief and harder on Andrew and Rob than he ever dreamed of being with any other firefighter. Still, Andrew never liked people to bring up the fact that his big brother was the chief. And he didn't like Daniel calling him on the carpet; that was what his supervising officer was for. Daniel knew well enough that Andrew hated it whenever his big brother got his head-of-the-family and head-of-the-department wires crossed.

Back at the station, he left the crew replenishing the rig, which netted him more than a few you-planned-this-to-get-out-of-work jabs, and ditched his turnout gear. He took off across town to the station house, where Daniel had his office.

"Hey, he went out with the crew that got

paged out to that car fire on the interstate," one of the guys told him. "He said to check in with Dutch."

Cats and confused calls, that was how this day was shaping up, Andrew thought. He trudged back to his truck. Should he take the time to check in with Dutch? Or head back before his buddies took it upon themselves to short-sheet his bunk in retaliation for leaving them holding the bag?

Aw, shoot. They're going to short-sheet the bunk anyway. Might as well go and see what Dutch has on his mind.

Dutch was in his office, surrounded by the usual piles of papers and file folders, tossing a baseball in the air. He leaned back in his desk chair, a thoughtful expression on his face, lobbing the ball straight up and catching it with the same hand. He snapped forward in his seat, not missing the ball, when Andrew tapped on the doorjamb.

"Daniel said to check with you?" Andrew asked.

"Oh, yeah. It's about the Blair thing."

Andrew tensed. Would Dutch tell him that the suit had been filed after all?

"Okay. So..." Andrew waited, but Dutch leaned back and began tossing the ball again.

"You're off tomorrow, right?" Dutch asked in an idle tone.

"Yeah. C'mon, Dutch. I left the guys pulling my share of the work at the station, and I'll bet they've already short-sheeted my bunk and traded out the ketchup for hot sauce."

"I'm just wondering if you come in on your off-time for a meeting, does it count against your regular hours if we don't give you overtime?"

"Oh, man, Dutch! Can you quit with the lawyer crap for even thirty seconds? If I need to come in for the Blair case, I will. For free."

Dutch frowned, stared at the ceiling, tossed the ball a couple of more times and nodded with evident satisfaction. "You're volunteering, right? And you realize it's off the clock? That should take care of the county's end."

Andrew ground his teeth. "Spit it out. What do you need?"

"I want to do a run-through, in case the lawsuit gets filed. A reporter buddy of mine called me from Macon, asking some mighty pointed questions. Something is coming down the pike sooner rather than later."

A metallic sourness filled Andrew's mouth. He tapped his knuckles against the doorjamb again as he thought of what he should say.

"Why can't I ask her, Dutch? Enough of this cloak-and-dagger business, waiting for a trap to be sprung. She seems happy enough with Maegan's therapy—and Katelyn's walking more now. She's able to actually take a few steps on her own with a set of crutches. Maybe Mallory won't sue after all, and if I ask her, we can be done with this."

Dutch's eyebrows went skyward. "No, no, no. I can think of about five thousand ways that could go south. Answer these questions. Do you have a law degree?"

"No."

"Are you aware of the various ways your actions could increase the county's or yours or Daniel's liability?"

Andrew blew out a long sigh of exasperation. "If you're asking if I'm as much of a doomsdayer as you are, then no, not in this lifetime."

Dutch fired off another question. "Have you been hired to represent the county in any sort of legal capacity?"

"You mean besides being a firefighter and talking to preschoolers about not hiding from a guy in turnout gear? Nope."

"Then, buddy, I'd say leave it to the professional. And the professional needs you here when you get off shift tomorrow morning so that you, me, Rob and Daniel can go through what happened that day step by step."

"Sure. After I have a wonderful, restful night's sleep during which the guys have short-sheeted my bed, put shaving cream on my hands and tied my shoelaces together. I'll be as energetic as a sloth."

Dutch scoffed at him. "What's the county paying for? A fire department or summer camp?"

"Well, not everyone can grow up to be a big bad lawyer who understands the, what did you say? The various ways his actions could result in liability for county employees? Some of us have got to be trained to put out the fires lawyers like that start with all their hot air."

Andrew ducked and ran before the baseball that Dutch threw at him could tag him on the shoulder.

MALLORY SMILED AS she finished ringing up the sale for her current customer, grateful that it was big enough to give her a bonus commission. If her week kept going like it had started off, she'd have some extra tucked away.

Eleanor grinned at her from across the

shop as she wrestled a dress onto a headless mannequin. "You're on a streak today!"

"It's all because *someone*," she winked at Eleanor, "has excellent taste when it comes to picking out merchandise. These clothes practically sell themselves."

"Don't sell yourself short, Mallory. You have a talent for helping these women put things together, see what looks good on them. I was smart to hire you."

Mallory beamed, her boss's praise warming her. Maybe Andrew hadn't been full of empty charm. Maybe he'd actually meant what he'd said.

Her cell phone buzzed, and she glanced down to see that it was the number to Happy Acres. "Uh, Eleanor, this is Katelyn's therapist. Do you mind if I—"

Eleanor waved her hand. "After that sale? Honey, take a well-deserved break." She went back to her task of scooching the dress down the mannequin's unforgiving form.

Mallory answered the phone to hear Maegan's voice on the other end of the line. "Don't worry—nobody's hurt," Maegan assured her. "We do have a bit of a problem."

Her mouth went dry. What had Katelyn

done now? She walked back to the storeroom. "What is it?" Mallory asked.

"Well…you know I have to get preapproval for Katelyn's therapy sessions."

"Yeees." Mallory leaned against a unit of storage shelves and crossed her fingers in hopes that the doctor wasn't refusing to authorize more sessions.

"Katelyn's orthopedic surgeon sent me the orders back pronto and was excited about my last progress notes. She's very pleased, Mallory."

Mallory's breath eased, then she realized that if the doctor wasn't the problem, Maegan hadn't gotten around to the part that was. "That's all you need, right?"

"Eh…no. Your insurance. The company refused to pay for any more visits."

"What? The insurance company assured me that as long as the doctor ordered it and it was medically necessary, Katelyn could get therapy until she no longer needed it."

"I know, I know. This stinks," Maegan said. "Their justification is that it's actually *not* medically necessary. According to the insurance company, Katelyn has reached her goals. They say she isn't going to improve enough to warrant the cost of more therapy."

"You mean it's a bean counter sort of thing? Can I appeal the decision? Surely there's got to be a way for me to show them that she is improving, but still needs more sessions." Mallory's fingers gripped the edge of a metal shelf to the point where it dug into her palm. She forced herself to let go and pulled her hand away to see it gray with dust.

"Once they send you an official denial, sure, you can appeal it. Sometimes it works. I did manage to get the doctor back on the phone, and she called the insurance company personally to tell them she'd wanted two more months of therapy. She told me she gave them a good piece of her mind."

"Did it help?" Mallory asked.

"Kinda, sorta. The lady with the insurance company was kind, and very sorry she had to take such a hard line. She worked her best to get us any little bit of flex. She's given me a compromise deal: three more weeks of visits, but then it has to go before their medical review board."

"Will the review board see reason? Katelyn's come so *far*," Mallory said wistfully.

"She has—much further than I thought she would. I think with another three months of uninterrupted therapy, she'd be completely out of the wheelchair and using a quad cane."

"How much would therapy cost? If I had to pay for an entire visit myself?"

"Oh, sweetie…" In the background, Mallory heard the staccato sound of a calculator's printer. "My usual rate is three hundred and fifty dollars a session, and my usual self-pay discount is twenty-five percent off that or two hundred and eighty dollars for the visit. Katelyn's doing so *well*. If the insurance covers the next three weeks, maybe…half off? That would be one hundred and seventy-five dollars a session. I wish I could go lower, but I have to take care of the horses, and you would not believe how much they eat. Could you see your way to paying one hundred and seventy-five dollars a session?"

It might as well be the moon, Mallory thought. "I— I'd appreciate that. I don't know how I'll swing it, but—"

"Well, about that. I was talking with Ma—I hope you don't mind. She suggested mentioning an idea that Cara and DeeDee had after they saw your progress on Kimberly's dress. They were thinking—we were all thinking, actually, that maybe you could sew our bridesmaid's dresses. I know, you're swamped with work and taking care of Katelyn and sewing the wedding dress. Kimberly's open to something simple, like a sheath. Ma says she's going to buy that dress you suggested from BASH, so we won't be cutting Eleanor out of that sale."

Mallory slapped her hand to her mouth to keep from crying. She'd had many small kindnesses extended to her over the years, but none this big.

"Oh, Maegan...are you suggesting a barter?"

"Eh, I can't do that, as much as I'd like," Maegan said with a rueful chuckle. "After all, we're looking at four sessions a week for eight weeks, and even at half price, that adds up to over five grand. I hope your bridesmaid's dresses don't set us back that much, or else we'll have to shop somewhere else."

"Oh, gracious, no," Mallory told her. "If it's as simple as a sheath dress, even with a lining and shantung silk for the fabric, I'd be surprised if it cost more than fifty bucks a dress for the material, and I could sew a sheath in my sleep. Hmm, maybe since I'd be doing, what, three?"

"No, four, because Kari's going to be a

bridesmaid, too. We're pitching in and buying her dress since she's supplying the cake."

Four dresses, *plus* the wedding dress. If it hadn't been for the bad news from the insurance company, Mallory would have been dancing a jig. "How about seventy-five dollars a piece, then? If you go with the silk. Less, of course, if you go with an easier-to-sew fabric."

"Wow! That sounds like a deal! For us anyway…" Maegan trailed off. "For you, it won't pay for Katelyn's therapy."

Mallory squared her shoulders and focused on the positive. "Maybe not, but it would help pay for several sessions, wouldn't it? And you're being so generous with your discount already."

"Hey, we need the dresses, and Katelyn needs the therapy. Plus, we've got Kari's wedding coming up next year, so…if you're still around…"

To be around a year from now. To still be a part of the Monroe family, surrounded with people who honestly seemed to care for her and for Katelyn.

Maybe by then, even Andrew would have decided she wasn't all about glitz and glamour, and maybe she wouldn't mind him knowing that about her.

But after she sued the county—and she'd have to now. She couldn't pile the extra therapy charges on top of the money she already owed without having some way to pay.

No, Mallory feared, after she sued the county, none of the Monroes were likely to speak to her again. Most of all Andrew.

CHAPTER TWENTY-ONE

"OH, MAN, I need coffee," Andrew announced as he stumbled through the door of Dutch's conference room. "Give me a java jolt if you expect me to make any sort of intelligent conversation."

Daniel and Rob, looking entirely too well rested to suit Andrew, didn't bother to hide their amusement.

"I heard that somebody got the ol' chain saw trick pulled on them this morning," Daniel commented, stretching his hands behind his neck as he leaned back in his chair.

"Bounced up like a rubber ball, the way I heard it," Rob added with a smirk. "If they'd asked me, I would have told them that was the only way to get you out of bed in the first place."

Andrew growled in sleep-deprived frustration. "You think it's funny, you should get the whole deal thrown at you—all the pranks at one time. Not to mention that I had to respond to a call-out on the interstate at 3:00 a.m. So I wasn't awake enough at five thirty in the morning not to jump out of my skin when somebody came at me with a chain saw. Big deal."

"Aww, poor baby," Rob said. "Was he scared of a chain saw without its chain? Did the big, bad noise terrify him?"

Andrew didn't dignify the tease with anything but silence. He fixed himself a cup of Dutch's coffee. A swallow told him that his buddy still made his coffee strong enough to stand up and walk on its own. Another swallow convinced him that perhaps he might survive the morning after all.

He sat down at the table and gave Daniel a pointed stare. In a mock serious tone, he posed the question, "As chief, don't you think such foolishness is inefficient? You're always telling us not to waste time on nonessentials. Priorities, isn't that your watchword?" He raised an eyebrow along with his coffee cup.

"The way I see it…" Daniel rubbed his chin thoughtfully. "A good firefighter is proactive. I'm surprised you didn't think about all those possibilities and prepare for them in advance." He winked at his brother. "After all, you've been pranked by the best."

Andrew nearly choked on his coffee. "I haven't been pranked like that since I was a probie. You just wait. I *was* taught by the best, and I can still teach the teachers a thing or two, since you two have zero sympathy." He yawned again. "Where's Dutch?"

"Oh, he's coming. You know him. He's probably calculating the odds of something catastrophic happening to all of us as we sit here on our own dime," Daniel remarked.

"Wouldn't doubt that a bit," Andrew agreed. "Besides the reporter nosing around, is there anything else that's worrying Dutch?"

Rob snickered. "Who? Dutch? Worry? You don't say. When someone in the department sneezes, he thinks we're all about to wind up with pneumonia."

"I meant real worry, not baseless Chicken Little stuff that means the department is in for another four hundred gajillion new policies and procedures," Andrew replied. He fidgeted with his cup, antsy as he waited for Dutch to come in and say whatever Dutch had to say. For all their teasing, everyone in the room knew the lawyer was good at his job and could spot trouble a mile away.

"You poking fun at me?" Dutch asked as he finally joined the party. "I'm only trying to keep everybody happy and safe. If we'll all learn to color *inside* the lines, I wouldn't have to run around and scream about the sky falling. Because just as sure as if I don't warn you, a big old piece of blue horizon will come crashing down."

He came around the conference table and claimed a chair, spreading out files, papers, two legal pads, four markers, three pens, plus a mechanical pencil and a stack of sticky notes.

"Sheesh, Dutch," Rob said. "Give you ten minutes and you could clutter up an empty warehouse."

Dutch didn't pay Rob any mind, just cracked his knuckles and picked up one of his three pens. He stared at each of them in turn. "You know why you're here."

"Actually…" Andrew cleared his throat. "What I want to know is why I'm here and Eric and Jackson aren't. They were on the scene that day. Oh, and the captain. Why isn't he here?"

"Good question. First of all, you guys are the three musketeers. I know you won't talk out of turn about what we're discussing today.

Also, Daniel's here in his capacity as chief, and Rob investigated the cause of the fire—"

"No, I didn't, not to my satisfaction—the case is still open," Rob interjected. "There wasn't a whole lot left in the way of evidence, and the landlord wasn't the most cooperative."

"Duly noted," Dutch conceded. "However, you have looked at the cause of the fire, so you'd be called to testify in the event of a jury trial."

The thought of both his brothers being dragged into a courtroom to testify in a case that he was the center of wigged Andrew out. He didn't want to contemplate Maegan's reaction if she were subpoenaed.

"But Eric and Jackson were there," he protested. "They can back me up, right? Corroborate the events."

"Eric can't. Due to the head trauma, he's not clear on the events of the day. And Jackson didn't come in the structure with you until after Katelyn Blair was down for the count. As for the captain on the scene, all he can do is relay what *you* told *him*."

Andrew folded his arms across his chest. "Why do I feel as if I'm defendant in a criminal case here? I followed the regulations—

regulations *you* helped Daniel and Rob write, Dutch."

Dutch nodded. "Stinks, doesn't it? But the sooner you get your mind wrapped around the question of liability, the sooner you can approach this thing with an eye to helping us all out. The plaintiff is going to have to blame someone, Andrew. And I'm afraid that someone is you."

Andrew grimaced. He took another sip of his coffee in an effort to cover up how shaken he was at the prospect of Mallory pointing a finger at him in open court. She wouldn't do that, would she? True, she'd been plenty angry that first night, and super fired up the day she'd realized he'd been the one to suggest Happy Acres to Katelyn.

Since then? The sharpest edges of her anger had been worn off by time.

Or it seemed as though that were the case. Was Mallory's cooling off simply an act? Something she was doing to sandbag them into believing she wouldn't sue?

Now Dutch was going over the timeline in detail. He'd sprung up and stood in front of the conference room's whiteboard, which was mottled with a rainbow's worth of traces from past meetings. A dry-erase marker squeaked across the hard surface as he listed the events along a not-so-straight line that extended the width of the piebald board.

Each point in the call was listed with a to-the-minute time attached to it, from the original 911 call by a neighbor at 6:09 a.m. to the time the fire was fully contained and controlled with not a hotspot in sight, at 10:26 a.m. In between…

In between was Katelyn.

Andrew realized he didn't want to talk about that day because he didn't want to think about his actions. They were what had put Katelyn in that wheelchair. He didn't want to think that his choices were what had caused a bad fire to become a near tragedy.

Dutch consulted his legal pad. "According to the tape transcript and the interviews I've done, by 6:15 a.m., the first engine had arrived on scene. You and Eric were on the second rig, right?"

"Yeah. House went up in flames like a chimney stuffed with newspaper," Andrew remembered. "They called in the second engine when they got on scene and realized how bad it was. We were there by…what, Daniel? 6:19?"

Daniel consulted his notes. "I've got that,

yeah. By then, I'd gotten paged out as well, because the captain on the scene had been informed there were possible entrapments."

Entrapments. For the first time, Andrew realized that the purpose of firefighter jargon might well be to distance those on the job from the horror that it could hold.

"Here's what I want to know," Dutch said. He scratched his head with the capped end of the marker as he studied the board. "You've got two calls to the power company, one before Andrew went in and one after. Why?"

Andrew spoke up, "That has to be a mistake. Right, Daniel? I remember when we got on the scene, the first rig had already checked and there was no power to the structure. So... that second call, it didn't happen then."

Daniel and Rob exchanged glances. Something about their silence sent an alarm through him. "Right?" he prodded. "There was no power to the structure."

Dutch asked. "Is Andrew right?"

"That's the thing," Rob finally said, his index finger tracing a circle on the dark finish of the conference table. "One reason I can't close out the investigation is that, in my opinion, the cause of that fire was electrical in nature."

"That's crazy, Rob!" Andrew insisted. "I was there, and you weren't. You didn't begin your investigation until the next day."

"I know, and, like I said, there wasn't much of the house left standing. But there is a discrepancy. The power company told the first unit that the power had been cut off for non-payment. The meter had been pulled. Since the house was fully engulfed where the meter would have been, the guys on the scene couldn't verify that no meter was there, not at first. They knocked down the fire, and two guys say there was no meter. When I investigated, I found no trace of a meter in the debris."

"See?" Andrew said. "There you go. No meter, no power."

"Not so fast, little brother. One of the guys laying down suppression on the basement said he could have sworn there was a light on upstairs. And a neighbor that I talked with— a woman who lived down the street—said she saw lights on early that morning before she went to work."

A pool of acid began to form in Andrew's gut. Had they missed something after all?

"It was pitch-black when I went in there," he insisted. "Granted, it's pitch-black in any fire, but I didn't see anything that would have signaled power still connected to the house."

Rob shrugged his shoulders. "Well, the log shows that the guy in the backyard, the one who saw the light on upstairs? He alerted the captain, who called back into the power company, and to be certain, they cut the power at the transformer."

"I'd remember that, though," Andrew said. He frowned, trying to recall if he'd seen a bucket truck at the scene.

Dutch looked back over the times and then his notes on a legal pad before he answered. "You would have been inside with Eric at the time. And the captain had to get the power company to move their truck in order to get the ambulance in for Eric and for the—"

"Katelyn," Andrew interjected. "We all know it was Katelyn."

Dutch groaned. "See? *That's* what worries me. You're involved in this, Andrew. You've invested yourself into knowing these sisters."

"Of course I have! I want you to pull a half-charred body out of a burning building after you've nearly lost your partner, Dutch! I wouldn't be human if I didn't care."

"You get on that stand, and you start going

all weepy-eyed, and the jury is going to be-lieve that you feel guilty—"

"We all feel guilty, Dutch," Daniel said quietly. "We all wish we could have gotten Katelyn out before she was injured. We did what we were supposed to do. We followed the rules—we even did a redundant power check. Does it matter when the power was actually cut off? Because it seems to me that it wasn't our fault here. It may have been a mix-up on the power company's end."

"The power company's not the one they're going to sue, Daniel," Dutch pointed out. "Because at the end of the day? It wasn't a power company employee who chose to leave a girl in a burning building."

Andrew felt anger and shame and guilt burn through him. "I did my—"

"Job." Dutch's voice was flat. No trace of his usual humor lightened it. "I know. You did your job. Explain that to the jury. Explain why a civilian gets left behind and a trained firefighter doesn't—"

"Whoa, Dutch!" Rob rocked forward. "If Andrew hadn't pulled Eric out of that fire, you might be dealing with a grieving mama of a firefighter and have every newspaper in the state breathing down your neck. He *saved*

Eric. I may tease my little brother and prank him every chance I get, but he's good at his job. He follows orders. He does what he's supposed to do. And what he was supposed to do was pull Eric out of that fire."

"I *know* that." Dutch collapsed into his chair and threw the marker down in disgust. "Don't you see I get that? We make these regulations exactly for this purpose, so that firefighters don't have to think in situations like that. For the most part, it works out. A case like this comes down to whether a jury will understand why we make these rules and forgive us when someone—" He stared at Andrew. "When Katelyn falls through the cracks. They'll be asking you why it happened. And what will you say?"

Andrew dropped his gaze to his coffee cup. The liquid was as dark and murky as his thoughts. "What can I say? That it was an impossible choice. That I hate like hell that I had to leave anyone behind. But I did my job, Dutch. That meant leaving her to get Eric to safety, and only after that going back in and getting her out. *I did my job.* Nobody could expect me to do more."

CHAPTER TWENTY-TWO

MALLORY STOOD AT the records counter, striving for patience. The big round clock on the back wall of the office in City Hall declared that it was 9:25 a.m. She needed to be at BASH by ten.

She hadn't bargained on how long it would take to get the records she'd asked for. A sliver of paranoia curled through her. Had the county flagged the records pertaining to the fire as some sort of trip wire?

The evening before, she'd spent hours on the phone with the insurance company, begging them to please extend the therapy sessions for Katelyn. Her pleas hadn't exactly fallen on deaf ears—the customer service representative she'd first spoken with was extremely nice, but extremely firm, offering only to transfer Mallory to speak with a supervisor.

That had been the first of many transfers on a merry-go-round of customer relations specialists and health advocate liaisons and appeals management personnel. Up the chain she'd gone, only to be transferred to yet another department, and put on hold yet another time before working her way up to yet another supervisor and repeating the whole process. They were all polite, all businesslike and professional, and had all been trained to say no fifty different ways.

Mallory was clear on one thing. A snowball had a better chance of surviving a summer day than she did of getting that insurance company to pay for the extra two months' worth of visits.

Discouraged and frustrated, she'd picked up her phone again and dialed the attorney. Maybe Chad knew of a way to get the insurance company to play ball.

Amazingly he'd answered himself. His solution? Forget the insurance company and sue the county. "Make them pick up the tab."

It did no good to explain to him that there was no way the county would settle before Katelyn ran out of paid therapy sessions.

"You don't know that," he insisted. "You get the right kind of ammunition, they'll settle quick. You just have to find the dirt they're covering up—pull back that rug, Mallory, and expose the dirt. Believe me, I've filed a lawsuit on one day and had them begging for a settlement the next."

"That's great," she responded in what she hoped was a hearty tone brimming with optimism and patience. "But your investigator has yet to get started, so when do you think he might?"

"Well…" The audible shuffle of papers filtered through the line. "It looks like you haven't signed all the paperwork we need on our end. I don't see a signed contract in your file designating us as your legal counsel and authorizing us to start legal action on your behalf. Did we send that to you?"

"Yes, but you said that wouldn't delay us with the initial investigation. Remember? You said your investigator would help you to see if we should even pursue legal action. Besides…the agreement sounded so…" What was the word she wanted? She'd read the legal contract carefully, and it seemed too gung-ho about legal action to suit her. "The part about allowing you to use your best judgment on legal strategy without consulting the client made me…uncomfortable."

He chuckled expansively and assured her that the clause was strictly boilerplate and allowed him to negotiate a quick settlement if it came to that. "You don't want me having to say to them, 'Uh, hold on, I don't know if my client wants to settle.'"

What he said made sense, but still, ceding that control gave Mallory pause. "I'll look over it tonight and try to get it back to you as soon as possible."

He rang off after urging her to get the paperwork in and the timeline nailed down with as many official reports as she could turn up.

Now, in the bright sunshiny office, she waited for a clerk to print out records of the fire. Mallory had first called the fire station, afraid Andrew or Rob or Daniel might answer the phone. But, no, a cheerful secretary had explained that all records requests were handled in the municipal building.

"It's all electronic, and they took it over so that people would have one centralized location—not have to figure out which fire station to go to. Go ask for Pam," the secretary had told her.

Pam now looked up from the computer terminal. "Wait, do you need the police incident report or the fire department's? Or the EMS report?"

Wow, this was an embarrassment of riches.

"Uh…" Mallory shrugged her shoulders. "I'm not sure. Can you give me all three?"

"The fire and police are public records, so I can give them to anybody. The EMS report is considered medical records, so I can only release that to the individual or, in the case of a minor, a legal guardian."

Mallory smiled, a huge weight lifting off her shoulders. "I'm my sister's legal guardian. Here, I have a copy of the court order." Thank goodness she'd tucked that piece of paper into her bag before she'd left for the morning.

"Well, then, let me get this printed out for you. It's twenty-five cents a page, though. That okay?"

It's worth it if it means Chad can get those medical bills paid for me. "Lucky for me," Mallory said with an even wider grin, "I scrounged under the couch cushions for some change."

"It's amazing what falls under there." Pam chuckled. "Now, if only the couch would pay interest!"

A few minutes later, Mallory exchanged a handful of quarters that she had indeed scrounged from under her futon cushion for copies of the reports.

Outside the office, she glanced at her watch. She had a few minutes left to peek through the pages before she had to head over to BASH. Mindless of her skirt, she plopped down on the bottom step of the municipal building's main stairwell and began skimming through the fire department's report. It should have the timeline that Chad was most interested in.

It did have a rough chronology of the main events: the 911 call, the dispatch of the first unit to the scene and then…

Oh, my word. It took three fire engines to put out that fire. It's a miracle that Katelyn even survived.

She uttered a silent prayer of thanks that Andrew was able to rescue Katelyn and kept reading. The strange and unfamiliar jargon was hard to understand. If only she dared ask him to translate the report for her.

Now, that was silly. How would she explain why she needed him to do that?

In the summary section, the captain had written a bare bones narrative of the events. Here, he mentioned Katelyn's rescue, and the injury to a crewmember. His description of the firefighter's injury chilled Mallory: concussion, collapsed lung, possible injury to his leg.

Andrew said it was no big deal, that the guy was released from the hospital, what? That night? The next day? Mallory couldn't remember anything but her anger that night in the trauma ICU waiting room. Chagrin filled her as she realized she'd never even bothered to ask how that firefighter had fared.

Wait—there it was, a mention of a request for the power to be turned off. Andrew had been right about no power connected to the house. How had Katelyn suffered an electrical burn? That was what had knocked her out. That was what had rendered her unable to escape.

Mallory's index finger slid along the tiny print of the narrative. What she read didn't make sense. The power was off—but it wasn't. Because at one point, the narrative stated that the captain had to call again and have the power cut off at the transformer.

She lifted her gaze and stared into the distance, trying to remember exactly what a transformer was. That was the canister on the utility pole, right? The one at the edge of the street that fed into the house? They had to cut the power off at the street?

Andrew had not told her the truth. There *had* been power turned on in that house.

When did they find out? And had Andrew known he'd left Katelyn in that house with not just smoke and fire but live electrical wires falling down around her?

If only I could ask him.

"Hey! What are you doing here?"

For a moment, Mallory was so lost in her thoughts that she thought she was imagining Andrew's voice, that she'd conjured him up out of thin air. But no, there he was, coming out of an office down the hall.

He didn't look especially thrilled to see her. Dressed in his uniform, he seemed to lack his usual verve. His face, as he closed the gap between them, was drawn and tired, as though he hadn't gotten enough rest.

She stood to greet him, fighting the urge to shove the papers behind her back. "I had to get some records," she said. Maybe if she kept it vague, he wouldn't press her. "What brings you here?"

Andrew came to stand near her, his thumbs latched into his belt loops. He didn't answer right away, but then allowed, "A meeting."

Hmm. He was cagey, too. She didn't ask for more details, only said, "You look tired."

"Yeah, I just got off my shift. It was…a long night, and then the meeting to boot."

Mallory lifted her hand to touch Andrew on the arm, an instinctive move to offer him comfort. He seemed so disconsolate, with an undercurrent of distinct unhappiness that was almost palpable.

Andrew stepped back.

For a moment, she froze, hand still in mid-air. Clearly he didn't want any physical contact with her, which was weird, because he'd never shied away from her before. Her cheeks flushed with the memory of that night in the truck, the way his hands had slid through her hair, his lips on hers.

"Sorry," Andrew mumbled. "I'm…really tired." He reached forward to give her an awkward pat, which caught her off guard and sent the pages in her hand flying.

She scrambled to retrieve them before he could see what they were.

"Oh, sheesh," he muttered. "Am I a klutz or what?" He knelt down beside her. "Let me see if I can— Hey. This is the report on Katelyn's…"

She cringed inwardly, but forced herself not to show any guilt. Quickly she gathered up the rest of the sheets. After all, she had a right to these records.

"Yeah, that's what I came to get." Mallory strived to keep her voice noncommittal. "Maegan called yesterday and told me that our insurance is cutting off our therapy visits. Katelyn's claim has got to go before a medical review board, so I'm trying to gather everything they could possibly want to prove Katelyn still needs more therapy." *A bit of a white lie, but the medical review board* might *need the reports.*

"Cutting off—" He sat back on his heels and rubbed both eyes. "How can they justify that?"

His outrage heartened her. She was glad to see that he was as upset as she'd been. "She's had the maximum number of visits allowed. They have a cap, and then they send the case to this review board..." She would have told him how slim the chances were, but then what would be her reason for wanting the reports?

Andrew stared down at the page he held in his hand. "What's she supposed to do? Continue therapy on her own? That's crazy! She needs that therapy. She's come so far."

"Yes, she has. I'm not going to give up. We've still got some time. Maegan and the orthopedic surgeon have gotten the company to agree to a dozen more visits, so that's three weeks. And Maegan has said she'll give me a discount if the insurance still refuses to pay. Like I said, I'm not giving up."

"Why do they need this? What could a medical review board possibly want with a fire department's incident report?" Andrew tapped the paper, looking confused.

Mallory's mouth went dry as she tried to figure out a plausible answer. She loathed the idea of confessing she was so desperate for money for Katelyn that she would sue the department.

It's not him I'm suing. It's not even the county. Chad said the county and the fire department would have insurance, so that they wouldn't have to pay a penny. And Katelyn needs this.

She again resorted to prevarication. "Who can tell? Maybe they won't. I have no clue what they might ask for. I'm trying to get my ducks in a row and…you know…bury them in paper. I was thinking that if they saw how bad the fire was…"

Andrew closed his eyes again, rubbed them even more fiercely than before, as if he was trying to rub out the memory of that fire. His shoulders, usually so straight and upright, drooped into a weary curve. Again, Mallory lifted her hand to stroke him.

This time, though, she stopped herself before he could jerk away.

He struggled to his feet, fatigue evident in the uncharacteristically sluggish way he moved. With fingers stretched out to her, he pulled her up as well, holding on to her hand for a moment before letting go.

It was a good one, that moment. His fingers were strong and warm and seemed like a buoy to cling to amidst a rough sea. In those few seconds, Mallory didn't feel alone anymore.

Andrew dropped her hand abruptly, shook his head. "I'd tell you to call me if you could think of any way I could help," he said. "But I'm afraid I'm no help at all."

With that, he turned on his heel and headed for the main exit, his boots echoing in the empty corridor, leaving Mallory to feel more alone than ever.

CHAPTER TWENTY-THREE

MALLORY WAS BENT over her sewing machine, concentrating on her work, when Katelyn shouted over the rhythmic clack of the machine. "Hey! Ma says supper's ready. I've called you, like, three times already."

Mallory looked up to see Katelyn in her wheelchair, a put-upon expression on her face. She was wearing an awful hoodie so ragged that it looked as though rats had gnawed holes in it.

"I've bought you better clothes than that—" Mallory began.

Katelyn held up her hand. "Don't start in on me. Just come on already. Ma's waiting."

"Katelyn, we can't keep eating supper out here. We have food at home." Mallory's stomach churned at the sense of betrayal she felt already, working on Kimberly's dress while contemplating suing the department her fiancé ran.

"Not like Ma's. Besides, you're doing work

for them. It's kind of like a bonus, right? A tip?"

Mallory flipped up the sewing machine's foot and pushed back her chair. Her neck ached from bending over the fabric, but she'd been hard at it since getting off work. She'd wanted to get as much done as possible and get the two of them out of there at a reasonable time. That had been the only drawback to moving the sewing out here.

Well, that, and the fact that you feel like a total heel.

"They are paying me, Katelyn," she pointed out. "And people don't get a tip or bonus until the work is done, and done better than it was expected to be. Face it, we're moochers."

Katelyn spun her chair around, shrugging her shoulders. "It's only mooching if they didn't offer to begin with. They like us, Mal. Can't you get over your stupid pride and just…" Her words caught. Her bravado failed her as she trailed off in a near whisper. "It's like a family. You know? Like when Mom and Dad were alive?"

Mallory sucked in a breath and had to brace herself against the sewing cabinet. Her sister was right: being at Ma's was such exquisite torture. Even while she lapped up the warmth and coziness, the friendly banter, the teasing, Mallory couldn't help knowing this was only temporary. She and Katelyn would go back to the apartment, where they would be orphans again, not belonging to anyone.

Plus, there was that nagging doubt... Wasn't the Monroe family a little too good to be true? Would they have extended the same generosity to anybody? Or was it a way to manipulate them?

It can't be. I'm a pretty good judge of character, and it just can't be.

Mallory touched Katelyn on the shoulder and realized her sister was weeping. She knelt down beside her and took her hands in hers. Not quite sure what to say, Mallory found herself focused on that starburst scar on Katelyn's hand.

"I miss them so much, Mal! If I hadn't been such a pain and tired them out, they wouldn't have needed that trip! It's my fault they're dead, mine!"

Mallory's heart broke at Katelyn's ragged confession. In all the years since their parents' death, Katelyn had never let on that she blamed herself. Now Mallory folded her into a hug and shushed her.

"No, honey, you can't think that way. It

wasn't your fault. Mom and Dad wanted that trip—not to get away from you, but to be with each other. If it was anybody's fault, it was that truck driver who T-boned them. You didn't— Please don't think you did anything wrong. That's like saying you getting hurt in that fire was your fault—" If Mallory had intended the words to comfort Katelyn, they had the exact opposite effect. The girl sobbed harder, shaking in Mallory's embrace.

Uncertain what to do, she held on tighter and waited for the storm to pass. It wasn't the first time Katelyn had suddenly dissolved into tears. Her doctors had warned Mallory that Katelyn would likely suffer serious bouts of depression. All she knew to do for her sister at times like this was hold her. Still, feeling Katelyn's thin shoulders through that tattered hoodie reminded her how close she'd come to losing her completely.

A few moments later, Katelyn had managed to rein in her emotions. She swiped at her eyes with the gray fleece sleeve. "Sorry. It's, like… I dunno."

"You're doing great, kiddo. Just think…by the summer you'll be walking. Maybe you can even take one of those summer session classes on campus. It will beat the online version you've been doing."

Katelyn fiddled with the threadbare cuff of her hoodie. "I don't think I wanna do summer classes, Mal. Maybe I could have a break, you know? Like, chill and have a little fun. I've been working so hard…"

A foreboding filled Mallory. "Katelyn, we talked about this. It was part of the agreement with the school that you'd use the summer to catch up so that you could go ahead and graduate."

"I've got enough credits already. You know, to get out with a regular diploma. That's good enough, right?" Katelyn asked, but it was not a question that invited any debate. "Nobody cares whether I took precalculus or general math as long as I can add."

"No! You need that college track diploma. You're going to college—you'll have ten credit hours by the time you graduate, and the summer session will allow you to finish up your foreign-language requirement. I know it's been hard but—"

"Since when do you get to decide what I want, huh?" Katelyn spat out. Her formerly limp frame was now rigid with anger. "Maybe I don't wanna go to college, Mal.

Maybe I don't want to be some dull stick-in-the-mud company drone who has to wear skirts and jackets to work. I was talking to my friend Dusty today, and she's making good money doing hair. I could do that. It wouldn't be some fancy college degree, not some lawyer or doctor like *you* want me to be, but I could do it. It would be fun. There's more to life than money. I could get a cosmetology diploma easy, but no, it's not good enough for you."

The blast of Katelyn's fury scorched Mallory. She found herself pulling back from her sister, hot words of defense bubbling up in her throat.

Drawing in a deep, cooling breath, Mallory tried to de-escalate the situation. "I never said that a cosmetology certificate wasn't good enough. I said…" Another breath to keep her own fury in check. "I said you needed to choose a career with good benefits, one that provides you with some stability. Retail is… fickle, Katelyn. Trust me, I know. Even if you have a good client base, one downturn in the economy, and poof! Suddenly people aren't spending money."

"Ha. People have always got to get their

hair cut," Katelyn scoffed. "See? It's infla-
tion proof."

Mallory pinched the bridge of her nose. No
need to point out to Katelyn that the last time
they'd needed a trim, they'd cut each other's
hair because they had to use the money for
groceries.

"Look—you said Ma was waiting on us.
Let's—let's put this on the back burner and
talk about it when we get home, okay?"

Katelyn raised her brows in surprise, as
though she'd expected to go another round
or two. "You're not, like, saying no?"

Mallory stood up. "We'll talk about it later.
It's rude to keep Ma waiting. If we're going
to mooch, let's not be even ruder about it."

"Wow. Andrew was right. He said to tell
you how I felt, and you'd understand."

Katelyn's words caught Mallory up short.
"What do you mean, Andrew was right?"

"He—" Katelyn snapped her mouth shut.
Her gaze flicked back and forth as though
she were searching for a means of escape. "I
talked with him about it. The other day. You
know. When you gave me the brochures for
signing up for summer classes."

That had been a couple of weeks before.
And he'd never mentioned a word of it to

her. Didn't he think Mallory should know that Katelyn was considering ditching her classes?

"Yeah? He thought it was all hunky-dory for you to quit school? Change your plans and get a cosmetology certificate?"

"Sure. He said he wasn't cut out for college. Some people aren't. Maybe I'm one of them." Katelyn flipped her hands palms up. "Who are you to talk anyway? You didn't finish up college. You dropped out."

Hot rage engulfed Mallory. "One day, Katelyn, maybe I will finish. Because I know how important that piece of paper is—"

"Later. You said we could talk about this later. Ma's waiting, right?" And with that, Katelyn rolled out of the room.

THAT NIGHT, MALLORY tossed and turned in bed, not able to sleep. Visions of all her bills kept chasing through her mind, and if she managed to banish them, the argument with Katelyn was standing by, ready to jump in their place.

Andrew hadn't been at supper. She'd planned on having it out with him, telling him in no uncertain times to leave academic advice to her.

As irritated as she was with him, she couldn't squelch the disappointment at not seeing him across from her at Ma's table. Her mind now took her to earlier in the day, when he'd jerked away from her as though she had some dread disease.

Of course it worked that way. Now that she was trying to reach out to him, he'd already moved on. Didn't she always tell Katelyn that sometimes opportunity only knocked once, so you'd better be at the door?

Throwing off the covers, she pulled on her robe and stuck her feet into her slippers. If she were going to be awake, she might as well do something. She could work on the sequins for the back of the lace bodice in Kimberly's dress.

Even with that tedious work done under the sallow greenish rays of the fluorescent light over the sink, she couldn't banish the thoughts. It was only 10:15... Maybe she should call him, get this irritation out in the open.

Or maybe it wouldn't help, because her anxious thoughts sprang from the idea of that lawsuit. She'd spoken with the lawyer earlier, and he'd been disappointed at the lack

of specifics about why the department had
requested the power be turned off twice.

"You need to talk with the power company,
get them to tell you," Chad had told her. "I
wouldn't even think about sending my investigator in for that one—just go in and smile
your smile and ask if they have the records."

"What if they won't give them to me? I'm
not anybody special," she pointed out.

"You find out where they are, and if they're
in a computer, we'll get them," he said confidently.

"Wait—you're not talking about anything
illegal, are you?" Mallory asked.

"No, no, of course not. That would be unethical. Do I look unethical? There's not anything illegal about you asking, and even if
you don't get them, you'll be confirming a
useful fact—they have something to hide.
We'll know what to look for, and where."

It had made sense at the time. Now, as she
used tweezers and fabric glue to attach one
sequin after another, Mallory wasn't so sure.
She thought of the papers she had yet to sign
to give the green light to Chad.

Sue?

Or not sue?

If only there was some way to pay her bills

without taking the county to court. Even if
the litigation wasn't targeted at the Monroes
personally, they practically were the fire department. Carole the librarian had said it
best—fighting fires was the Monroe family business.

Chad was right about one thing. It had been
a mistake to get to know the Monroes as well
as she had. The idea of suing the county had
been incredibly easy to go along with before
she'd learned how unfailingly *nice* they all
were.

Maybe the cause of her insomnia wasn't
anything more than the yawning distance
she'd felt spring up between her and Andrew
this morning. If he could be that distant with
her and not know she was suing…

What would he be like after she lodged the
case in court?

Dropping the delicate lace onto the scarred
laminate tabletop, Mallory retrieved the papers she'd gotten that morning.

The fire department had called the power
company twice.

Twice.

What if…

Her heart soared with hope. What if it
wasn't the department's fault? What if in-

stead it was a screw-up on the power company's end?

She might not have to sue the county. If the power company had been the one to make the mistake, perhaps they'd be willing to offer a low-ball settlement. Power companies made millions—what would twenty-five thousand dollars in medical bills be to a profitable company like that?

Invigorated, she folded the papers up and tucked them away. Tomorrow she'd try to get the power company's records—on what pretense she had no idea, but it surely couldn't hurt to ask.

And it might mean all the difference in the world.

CHAPTER TWENTY-FOUR

EVEN A RIG cleaned to a sparkling shine couldn't lift Andrew's spirits. Usually the morning labor of washing and prepping the fire trucks was enough to remind him how lucky he was to have this job. The gleam of a fire engine's red paint in the early-morning sun never failed to put him in mind of how many kids wanted to grow up and *be* Andrew.

Not this morning, though. He dropped his sponge into a bucket of suds, and it splatted like his own sour mood. Even after two days off, the meeting he'd had with Dutch and his brothers, not to mention seeing Mallory as he'd come out of it, still sat on him with the unmoving pressure of a sleeping elephant.

A jet of water shot his way. Eric and Jackson's raucous laughter showered over him as he jerked out of the path of the water. "Woo-hee!" Jackson yelled. "That boy can dance like a chicken on a hot tin plate! Do it again, Eric!"

Eric didn't have the chance. Andrew had closed the gap and snatched the hose out of his buddy's hand. He flung it on the ground, where a river of water ran between his legs and down the oil-stained concrete of the firehouse's drive. Afraid of what he might do or say if he hung around even a second longer, Andrew stalked into the engine bays.

A glance through the glass-paned door leading into the station told him that the rest of the crew had finished up with the indoor chores and had gathered together in the rec room. There'd be no peace in there. He walked farther into the bays, lowering himself down onto the bumper of the ladder truck.

The sound of boots—Eric by the way he was walking—echoed along the walls of the bay. Sure enough, his buddy came to stand alongside the front of the ladder truck. "What bear got you this morning?" Eric asked.

"Why does it have to be a bear? Why can't a guy simply not want to get hosed down first thing in the morning, huh?" Andrew stared at the scuffed toes of his boots, barely visible in the gloomy, unlit interior of the bay.

"Because your usual response is to return fire. If you're still ticked off with us for all the pranks, get over it already. You know how to hand it out to the rest of us, so suck it up and take it when it's your turn."

Andrew worked his jaw, tried to think what he should say to Eric. "It's not the jokes—well, heck, not all of it. Sure, I know I get rowdy sometimes, but not nearly as bad as Rob. You guys didn't mean anything by it, I got that."

"Shoot." Eric scuffed the concrete with his own boot and leaned a palm against the rig. "I was afraid of that."

Andrew turned full on to face him. "What do you mean, you were afraid of that?"

"That it wasn't the practical jokes, which meant I was gonna have to have one of *those* conversations with you."

"Those conversations? What conversations?" Despite his foul mood, Andrew couldn't help but chuckle at the contortions Eric's face was going through. The guy could have been a five-year-old presented with a whole plate of broccoli to eat.

"That's part of the reason we all pranked you like we did. You've been moping around here for the better part of two months, traipsing off into corners and sighing like a love-sick pup. It doesn't take a brain surgeon to know what's going on."

"There's nothing—"

Now Jackson had joined them, and he was vigorously nodding his head. "Not a thing, huh?" the firefighter asked. "When we hear that the kid you pulled out of that fire is having therapy at your sister's place, and that the kid's sister looks like a fashion model, that's not your usual recipe for disaster?"

"Mallory's not like that. Once you get to know her, she's actually nice—"

Jackson held out his hand. Eric swore, reached into his back pocket, pulled out his wallet and liberated a ten, which he slapped into Jackson's waiting palm. He shook his head in disgust. "I thought you had better sense. I even bet Jackson double or nothing that you weren't getting sucked into another diva disaster."

Jackson smirked. "And you're supposed to be his friend. Ha! Do I know him or what?"

"Wait a minute." Andrew stood up, looked from one to the other. "This whole 'concerned for you' crap was just an elaborate way of confirming a bet?"

Eric and Jackson swapped high fives. "Had you going, didn't we?"

With considerable effort, Andrew reined in a temper that was on a turbo-charged boil. On some level, he was impressed with Eric's acting skills. He could enjoy a good prank as well as the rest of the gang.

And Jackson had been so eager for his money that he'd horned in before Andrew could do what he'd been about to do. Five seconds more, and Andrew would have spilled out the entire story to Eric.

Sheesh. They would have had enough ammunition to tease him for weeks.

Andrew was an even better actor, when push came to shove, than Eric. And if it killed him, he wouldn't reveal a sliver of the truth.

"Jackson, you may need to repay Eric that dough," he said. "No diva disaster. I learned my lesson. What's got me in a foul mood is being called on the carpet by legal. They give you a medal and put you on the front page of the paper, and then six months later, they're telling you, 'Naughty, naughty, don't do that again.'"

"Dutch? You've been moaning and groaning because you're in hot water with Dutch?" With evident frustration, Jackson handed his winnings back to Eric, who took them with a broad grin. "That man is even screwing up my bets. Dang him and his policies and procedures. What are we, firefighters or a nursery school?"

Now it was Jackson who stalked off toward the open bay's doors, still muttering under his breath. Eric looked down at the ten-dollar bill in his hand, then slowly put it back in his wallet. As he tucked the wallet into his back pocket, he said, "It wasn't just for the bet, you know."

"Uh-uh. Fool me once, shame on you. Fool me twice—"

"No fooling. You all right?"

"I'm all right, Eric."

Eric toed the concrete as he had before. "You sure?"

"Sure."

"Because we *are* friends, you know, and if you ever—well, you know—"

"Shoot, Eric, we're not having one of *those* conversations, are we?" Andrew joked.

"Nah." He socked Andrew lightly on the shoulder. "Nah, we're not having one of those conversations."

In the awkward silence that followed, voices from outside floated back to them. Then the sound of footsteps echoed off the concrete again—Jackson's work boots and the tap-tap-tap of a woman's high heels.

Andrew peered around Eric to spy Jackson bearing a smug Cheshire-cat-size smile. In his wake came the source of the tap-tap-tap.

Mallory.

He hated the way his stomach lifted in the instant of recognition. Dutch had made the whole situation clear at the meeting, if he hadn't before. Even Daniel had come down on the lawyer's side.

Keep Mallory Blair at arms length.

It was hard to do when the very sight of her drew him. Eric and Jackson would swear that Mallory's looks were the draw, but they weren't.

In fact, her prettiness had been off-putting to him at first, too much akin to his previous… what had Eric called them? Diva disasters. It was only after he'd gotten to know her— little bits of her, like how she made her clothes out of thrift-shop discards, and that she liked to read the same authors he did—that he'd allowed himself to look past her physical appearance.

The guys would never believe him, though. She was a vision. High heels, a skirt in some billowy fabric that brushed her knee, a blazer that clung to her curves like a glove.

Her face, though… Her expression was purely professional. Pleasant enough, but devoid of even a degree of the warmth he'd come to know.

Jackson halted. "Hey, Monroe, you've got a visitor."

Mallory walked past Jackson, right up to Andrew.

"You've been ducking my calls," she said cheerfully.

It wasn't real cheer. It was that bonhomie hail-good-fellow type of humor that always rubbed Andrew the wrong way.

Not to mention the fact that he *had* been ducking her calls.

"Looks as if you need some privacy," Eric muttered. He melted away, joining Jackson. As they headed back to the front drive, he could see the silhouette of Eric handing Jackson what was presumably that ten-dollar bill.

"I've been busy," Andrew told Mallory.

"Not at the farm. I went out there two days running, trying to find you."

"Yeah, well." He didn't want to admit that he had been avoiding her. "I had stuff to do."

He could see she was primed to argue. He

knew from his previous girlfriends what was coming. They were always in his face about how he disappeared when they needed to "talk." A statement like he'd just uttered was practically all the ammunition LeeAnn had ever needed to go to DefCon 4 state of alert.

Andrew braced himself for the recriminations and accusations, prepared for her lashing out at him.

Only...

She didn't.

Mallory's shoulders rose as she drew in a breath. She ran a tongue over her lips, started to speak, stopped. "I guess it doesn't matter about that," she replied grudgingly. "I'm here now."

"Yes, you are." He blinked a few times, sure that any minute she was going to explode into LeeAnn-like shrieks. "Er—what was it that you needed to see me about?"

With LeeAnn, it hadn't ever been anything important, just that he wasn't willing to pick up the phone the sixteenth time she'd called him during a day.

But Mallory hadn't lost her temper over not being able to reach him.

"It's about Katelyn," she said. Now her shoulders squared, and her back went even straighter. There was a rehearsed air about the line, as if she had been primed to say this for two days.

He propped himself against the fire truck, his palm flat against the cool red paint, his whole being drawing strength from the contact. He might not ever get women right, but firefighting had never yet let him down. "What about Katelyn?"

"It's about her school. About you telling her it was okay to quit school."

He stumbled at her words. "Quit—I never said for her to quit."

For a moment, Mallory looked nonplussed. "You didn't?" she faltered.

"No. An education's an important thing."

"Oh," she replied. The battle readiness had evaporated, and she was left slightly drooping. "Wow. I'm sorry. Katelyn told me the other night that she didn't want to take summer classes, and that you said I'd understand if she wanted to go for a cosmetology certificate."

He lifted his shoulders in a shrug. "Sure. I told her that college wasn't for everybody. Take me for example. I get twitchy having to do an hour's worth of classroom training to keep up my certification. Maybe the Ivy League's not for her."

Mallory's face went slack with what he recognized was speechless anger. It was that same expression he'd seen the first night they'd met.

"You—you—" Her voice shook. She calmed herself with visible effort. "Do you realize that her college courses *are* what she needs to graduate from high school?"

"Huh? I thought it was extra. You know, for bonus points."

"No. In the spring of her junior year, she decided that high school was boring and dumb and that what she wanted to do was to go on to college. Like an *idiot*, I let her sign up for the precollege program. I thought it would be good for her, because she's smart as a whip."

Her eyes closed, and Andrew could see her carefully applied, flawless eye shadow. With a pang, he realized he liked her face better when it was bare and exposed and un- sophisticated.

Mallory was speaking again, and Andrew forced himself back to her words.

"—when she had the accident, everything was in jeopardy. She couldn't get credit for regular classes, because she hadn't taken them. And she was about to be booted out of the college classes. But I begged and pleaded, and I got them to give her independent studies in all of her classes."

Andrew wasn't sure what an independent study was, but he could tell it had been a huge concession. "What's me telling her she could get a cosmetology certificate take away from that? Hasn't she been doing the work?"

"Yes, but she's still got to take summer classes in order to finish. She couldn't handle but one course and therapy, too, this semester—and now you fill her head with ideas about quitting?"

"Whoa." Andrew held up a hand. "I agree that I should have laid off on the advice giving without asking you first. I didn't have a clue that her high school diploma hinged on her finishing classes during the summer. Still, I'm hearing something else under all this."

"You're hearing that I'm ticked—"

"You're disappointed she's not interested in pursuing a college degree."

"Disappointed? Are you kidding me? I'm not disappointed, because a cosmetology certificate is so not happening, Andrew Monroe.

I won't be disappointed because my sister *will* get over herself and get that degree."

Andrew couldn't stop his empty chuckle. "See? I knew it. You're an educational snob. *You* don't want your little sister to be blue collar."

Her eyes rounded with even more anger. "Blue collar? Andrew, I *am* blue collar. I'm in retail, probably lower than blue collar. A plumber or an electrician makes a good living and has job security."

"What's wrong with Katelyn wanting to do something besides being a doctor or a lawyer?" he asked.

She clamped her jaw shut, nothing coming out but a low groan of frustration. Her chest heaved with the effort she was using to keep her volcano-like temper within. He had to hand it to her; by now LeeAnn would have thrown something at him.

"So?" he prompted again.

"For someone so smart…" She exhaled, stared off into the distance. "Think about it, Andrew. Katelyn's in a *wheelchair*. She can't stand on her feet all day. When we swapped hair trims, I had to sit on the floor for her to do it."

"You let Katelyn cut your hair?" Another

amazing fact that proved she was not Lee-Ann. His ex-girlfriend would travel two hours to have her hair cut by a professional of the appropriate quality and caliber and pedigree, and heaven help the poor sap if it didn't turn out exactly as she'd wanted it.

"A trim, Andrew, a trim, but that's not the point. The *point* is that physically, right now, Katelyn can't do the job. The *point* is that she'll have ongoing medical bills for a long time, and she's going to need good insurance to help cover them. A college degree... A degree... Oh, if I'd just been able to get my degree before my parents died..."

A sob ripped through her. He was desperately afraid she was going to bawl on him right here, right now, and the only thing he'd want to do was pull her into his arms, hang Eric and Jackson.

Exactly as she had with her anger, Mallory hemmed up her emotions with the same skill he used to control Joker. She pulled herself together, calm and collected now, except for the way she clenched and unclenched her fists by her sides.

"It doesn't matter. You don't have to worry about my reasons, do you? Suffice it to say—" again, she adopted a slightly prissy tone "—I would appreciate it if you would leave the career advice to me and to her guidance counselor and her advisor, oh, and Maegan as her therapist."

"I should let the kid think it's okay to be desperately unhappy because she can't meet your expectations? And because you can't see her as anything but what she is now?" It wasn't fair, he knew it wasn't, but something about her snooty "leave it to the professionals" riled him.

"No, you should let me—"

Her words were cut off by the reverberating "ennh" of the alarm buzzing insistently, and the radios crackling to life. A call-out, and at the worst possible time.

"Hey, I gotta go—it's a structure fire. Stay back out of the way," he warned her, flying for his turnout gear.

"Right. Sure. Nice timing. Saved by the bell, huh?" she responded acidly. "Hey, how about *this* time, you actually manage to get the power turned off?"

Her words stopped him in his tracks. He turned around to face her. It didn't matter that he had to get going, that this was his job, that there were possibly lives on the line.

He wasn't comforted when he saw her

anger fade into a sick remorse. "Andrew—
I'm sorry— I—"

"No. You meant it. I can't talk about it now.
Maybe later, maybe never, but certainly not
now."

Then he turned back to the rush for his
gear and the fire to be put out.

He could handle that.

Because he had no clue what to do with a
woman who not only knew about the power
being left on in that house…but blamed him
for it, as well.

Who was he kidding? Mallory Blair was
never going to stop blaming him for what had
happened to her sister.

CHAPTER TWENTY-FIVE

Two days later, Andrew still didn't know what to say to Mallory.

Apparently, nothing was required, not on his part. She sat at the dining table next to him, sharing lunch with him, Ma, Maegan and Katelyn.

Oh, she was polite. One thing Mallory Blair never forgot was her pleases and thank-yous. Still, the sudden drop in temperature as she turned from her right, where Ma was sitting, to her left, where he sat, told him all he needed to know.

He hadn't expected to see her. In fact, he'd planned to head out for some made-up errand before Katelyn's therapy appointment. What he hadn't figured on was that blasted wedding dress.

Mallory had the afternoon off from BASH, so she and Katelyn had come early. And of course Ma had tempted them with food—this time leftovers from the night before, but

Ma's leftovers were better than most people's regular meals.

After he'd finished up with the structure fire and returned to the station, Andrew had tried to call her twice. His first idea was to explain more clearly why he thought maybe college and Katelyn weren't such a hot mix. Then, after a talk with Ma, who'd pointed out that he'd stuck his nose in business that didn't quite belong to him, he'd thought about calling to apologize.

He'd thought about calling simply to hear Mallory's voice.

Now he was hearing her voice, but it was pointedly not directed at him. She was bent on freezing him out, and she was doing a good job of it. The longer Andrew sat there and took it, the madder he got.

He couldn't help that he'd had to go when the alarm went off. He hadn't asked for that structure fire. He was a firefighter. Dropping everything was part of the job. She had to know that by now, what with all the time she'd been around his family.

And he couldn't have helped that the power somehow mysteriously came back on in that rattletrap heap that Katelyn had been living in. It had been his job to get in and get Katelyn out...and he'd done that. Maybe not as soon as everybody would have liked, but he'd done it.

He brooded over his lunch. The chatter between the four women at the table, along with the clink of silverware against Ma's second-best stoneware, washed over him. Andrew found himself retreating to some place deep within himself, where he could nurse his grievances and polish up his justifications.

He didn't like that. It was exactly the kind of behavior that had been the prelude to the final act of all his other relationships.

Was this thing with Mallory a relationship? Unless she totally swore off that lawsuit, was it even a possibility?

Her words of thanks and the scrape of her chair as she pushed it back brought him to the present. He'd spent the entire meal stewing over something he couldn't control— her reaction. That was like getting angry at a building for catching on fire instead of concentrating on putting the fire out.

A firefighter worked with what was in front of him. He didn't whine about wanting better conditions. He made his own opportunities.

And, above all else, Andrew was a fire-fighter.

She'd rinsed her plate, put it in the dish-washer and disappeared into Ma's sewing room by the time he'd pushed back his own chair. He thanked Ma, gathered up his dishes and headed for the sink.

As he was about to follow Mallory to the sewing room, Katelyn blocked his path with her wheelchair. "Can I—can I talk to you?" she asked.

Andrew guessed he owed her that much. He followed her down the hall to the living room, where she expertly twirled the chair around, braked it and folded her hands. This girl had grown so much since she'd first arrived at Happy Acres. Maybe Mallory couldn't see it, but he could.

That wasn't to say she didn't have some more growing up to do, but, hey, at seven-teen, he'd been a far cry from mature.

"What's on your mind, kiddo?" he asked Katelyn.

"I wanted to apologize."

"For what?" Andrew dropped into Daniel's easy chair so that he'd be at eye level with Katelyn and she wouldn't have to look up.

"I ratted you out. Mal's on the warpath

with you because I told her what you said. You know. About me quitting college."

He rubbed his eyes. "I got myself in hot water. I shouldn't have tried to give you advice when I didn't understand the situation."

"But you *do*. Mallory means well, but all she wants is for me to grow up and get a job and be boring like her. Work, work, work." Katelyn pulled at a thread on a hoodie so bleach spattered and ragged Andrew couldn't believe Mallory hadn't already consigned it to the trash.

He considered Katelyn's words. Mallory boring? Hardly. "She works awfully hard for you." He tried to frame the words as neutrally as possible, with no guilt stirred in.

To his surprise, Katelyn nodded. "She does. She worries about me, I know. And she just wants the best for me. She's worked like a dog ever since…" Here she trailed off, unable to force the words that didn't have to be said. The thread on the cuff of the hoodie grew longer, and Andrew realized that it was actually the fabric unraveling. "She's got this idea that she can't have any fun until I'm this big success. It's like, I dunno, she thinks they're gonna hand *her* the stupid diploma when I graduate from college. I can't— I love her, but I can't… I feel so *suffocated*." Again, she yanked at the thread. "Sometimes anyway."

Andrew could understand where she was coming from. "I've felt that way. When I was a kid. For all the rest of the Monroe kids, book learning came easy. Maybe Daniel and Rob would have rather been outdoors, but they aced their schoolwork. And Dad—when he wasn't working on some project, he had his nose in a book."

"But not you?"

"Not me. I couldn't sit still. And stuff like history and grammar drove me up the wall."

"I know, right? That's what I tell Mal."

Andrew continued, "Whenever I got my report card, Dad never yelled at me. He'd just look that report card up and down so hard I'd think he was going to read the print off it. And then, when I thought I might pass out, thinking for sure I was in up to my chin this time, he'd ask, 'Is this your best?'" Andrew shook his head at the memory. "Honestly, I'd have rather been grounded for a month than have to answer that question. I always wondered if, had I made straight As like Daniel and Rob, would Dad ask me that anyway?"

"Well, did he? Ask them that, I mean?"

"I don't know. That was another rule for

report card day. You didn't talk about what
marks you got or what he said."

"You've just proved my point," Katelyn
said. "You didn't make all As and you turned
out okay. You didn't go to college."

"No, I didn't, not then. But I actually have
taken some college-level courses for the department. They're more hands-on, which is
what I like. Anyway, long story short, I get
why you might want to do something with
your hands. And I don't think there's anything wrong with it. But…"

Katelyn grimaced. She spun the chair
around. "I knew it. You're going to take her
side."

"No. I'm not taking her side. You said it
yourself. She wants the best for you. My
dad was tough, and Ma, in her own way, is
equally tough on us. I never doubted for a
minute, though, that they were doing it because they loved me."

"Will you…" Katelyn trailed off, then gave
a firm shake of her head. She folded her arms
across her chest. "No, never mind. This is my
fight. I've got you in enough trouble. Sorry
for the hot water."

Andrew gave her a mock tap on the shoulder with his fist. "What's that saying about

what tea bags and people have in common? You never know how strong you are until you're in hot water?"

Katelyn's face fell. Again she unraveled a good length of thread from the cuff. "I can tell you, I don't make the cut."

"You've had some hard knocks, kiddo. Cut yourself some slack for the past, and then get right back up on that horse and ride it tomorrow."

He left her there, uncertain if he'd made her feel better or worse. One thing was for sure. He'd probably be in duck soup with Mallory for handing out more advice to Katelyn.

Resolutely he crossed the kitchen and made the turn into Ma's sewing room. It was time for him and Mallory to finish that conversation.

Only, Mallory was slumped over a sea of white fabric, her face in her hands, her shoulders shaking.

She was weeping.

LeeAnn and his other girlfriends had cried—at the drop of a hat, it seemed to him. Theirs had always been full waterworks at hurricane force.

Not this quiet defeat that was so uncharacteristic of Mallory. But for that single tear, she hadn't even cried the first night Katelyn had been in ICU. Sure, he'd seen traces of tears, and he'd heard them, raw and unshed, in her voice, then and in the time since.

But this complete unleashing of silent tears? And the way she seemed almost crushed beneath the weight of them?

Had he done this?

He stepped up behind her, touched her on her shoulder. "Hey, Mallory—"

She jumped. Scrubbing at her face as though she were a snaggletoothed four-year-old, Mallory drew in a shuddering breath and smothered the tears. "I thought I was alone."

"And crying like this is okay when you're alone?" He pulled up a spare ladder-back chair that Ma kept for the extra guests that invariably showed up at mealtimes.

"No, of course not. Crying doesn't help anything." She picked up the white silk and peered at it. "I'm tired, that's all, and I messed up this seam. I've got to rip it out."

"Here, let me help. I can hold the fabric while you pull out the seam. Ma used to press me into service whenever she needed a hand."

Mallory's chin wobbled, and her fingers clenched, swallowed up by the yards of white silk. "You don't have to."

"No." He held out his hand, waiting to see if she'd relent. After a beat or two, she lifted the puddle of silk with a sigh.

"It would make it faster," Mallory conceded. "Only, don't pull tight, or the fabric will rip. I don't want to lose this piece."

"Not too tight," he agreed.

Andrew held the silk fabric and watched as the point of her seam ripper flicked in between the impossibly tiny stitches she'd made. The going was tedious, with him putting enough tension on the seam to help her see where the next stitch was.

The pieces of fabric began to separate. Andrew thought about how strong those tiny, near invisible stitches were. That was how family was—held together by a thousand different unseen bonds.

Except when you lost someone. The stitches came out in a hurry, then. He stared over at Mallory, her nose all shiny and red, her eyes still watery, her mouth pressed together as though she might bawl any moment.

She wouldn't, though. He knew that about her now. She'd rather die inside than cry and admit weakness.

When had she started equating tears with weakness? The Monroes weren't like that at all—they roared when they were hurt, laughed when something tickled them.

Well, maybe he didn't. He was the quietest one. Still, he was a guy, and guys weren't like girls. It nagged at him, the way she thought she couldn't cry, not even in front of him.

"It's okay, you know. A good cry can help."

The tip of the seam ripper froze, poised halfway to the next stitch. With a tremble, Mallory started to work again. She didn't answer him, but he could see she was struggling not to give into those tears.

"I'm sorry, okay?" he blurted out. "I didn't mean to mess things up with Katelyn."

Mallory dropped her seam ripper and clasped her palm to her mouth. Tears spilled out of those clear green eyes and down her cheeks. She tried to fight it—but not even she could hold that much sadness back.

He pulled her into his arms, mindless of Kimberly's half-made wedding dress piled up between them. "You'll get the seam fixed, the dress made and Katelyn back in school. You're tough, Mal. You're the toughest fighter I know. You never let anything whip you."

She buried her face into the crook of his neck and muttered something. He let her stay there for a moment, then set her back, wiped away those tears.

"You can tell me. Don't keep all this bottled up."

Mallory sucked in a ragged breath, hiccupped and had to draw in another breath before she could even attempt to speak. She grabbed hold of the slippery silk before the dress could crash onto the floor, and then with her free hand scrubbed at her face.

"I'm scared," she admitted. "I don't want to let Mom and Dad down. I've screwed up so much with Katelyn—I shouldn't have let her talk me into going off to college early, but her friends at school were nothing to write home about and—who am I kidding? I can't sew a seam straight, much less get her safe and sound through high school."

Her guilt bled through her words. He knew the weight of that. He'd felt it after his dad had died, the agony of knowing that, no matter if he did live up to his father's expectations, Dad would never see it. Too late. Too little, and way too late.

"Shh. Shh." He fumbled for the box of tissue stashed on the shelf above the sewing machine.

Mallory accepted one and blew her nose.

The sound was loud and unladylike and he couldn't help but laugh at the way she turned crimson with embarrassment.

"Hey, that's the sound of a normal nose, Mal. I won't tell anybody you're mortal after all." He touched her on the chin, let his thumb stroke her cheek. "And…about the other… Ma has this rule, and it's a good one. Never try to fix things when you're upset."

"Ha. I can't fix things at all, not anymore. She's all I have, Andrew. I nearly lost her, and you'd think that would teach me to be more careful, to take better care of her, and I'm trying… But she makes it so *hard*. If I could give up, I would, but I can't. I don't know what to do anymore."

Now Mallory was crying again, guilt and pain in equal measures. He'd wanted her to feel as though it was okay to show emotion, but this scared him, the indomitable Mallory Blair at a loss. No plan A or B or C.

Later, he'd tell himself that was why he'd kissed her. Because he was scared. Because he didn't know what else to do.

Maybe. In the moment, it certainly did the trick. The second his lips touched hers, her tears stopped, with only a soft "Oh!" escaping her.

Mallory leaned in, kissing him back, gripping his arms as if she were hurtling over a waterfall. He could totally get that sensation, because as his mouth tasted hers all salty from her tears, he wanted to throw caution to the wind.

Forget his previous vows to keep his distance from beautiful women.

Forget his assurances to Daniel and Dutch that he would keep this particular beautiful woman at arm's length.

Forget that she was weeping, in part, because he had left her sister too long.

The way she felt, the way she clung to him, he could forget it all.

Mallory pulled back. Stared down at the wedding dress in her lap. "I need—"

She didn't have to say another word. He picked up the fabric and waited for her to begin ripping out the seam again.

The kiss must have loosened her tongue, because she began, in stops and starts, to talk. "I have to take care of her, Andrew. I have to make sure she's okay."

"I know that. I get it. These stitches are in the wrong place, right?"

Mallory frowned. "Yeah. That's why I'm pulling them out."

"What would happen if you yanked hard and forced them to give way?"

He heard her chuckle and the rhythmic plunk-plunk-plunk of the seam ripper started up again. "I thought you said you'd helped Ma do this before," she commented.

"I have. What I mean is… Katelyn doesn't have to do it all on some elaborate timetable. Maybe college is what she needs, but not right now. Pushing her to do something she's not ready to do—wouldn't it be like yanking out this seam?"

The last of the stitches gave way. Mallory laid aside the seam ripper and smoothed over the pin-size holes left by the threads. "Probably—no, you're right. I know you're right." She held up a hand to forestall his protest. "I don't have that luxury, Andrew. I can't let her take all the time in the world to pick herself up. She has to finish these courses or start all over again with her senior year. It's something she wouldn't have to do if…" Mallory trailed off. "We were fine. Before the accident, we were *fine*."

She didn't have to connect the dots for him. If he hadn't left Katelyn on that upstairs landing, Mallory wouldn't be faced with such an impossible choice.

CHAPTER TWENTY-SIX

A WEEK LATER, Mallory parked her car in a visitor's slot at the college. Consulting a campus map she'd printed at the library, she set off in the direction of the quad.

Today she hoped to conquer two missions—the first to run one of Katelyn's old roommates to ground, and the other to talk to her advisor in person.

The roommate, who was more than a little vague on where she'd been during the fire, could still, hopefully, solve the mystery of when the power actually got cut off. The utility company had been as creative in saying no to Mallory as the insurance company had.

Katelyn was no help, either. Even this morning, she'd refused to talk about the fire at all, despite Mallory's pleas that if they didn't get something concrete to help bolster the lawsuit, it was probably dead in the water.

"Maybe I don't want to sue. We shouldn't sue anybody, Mal," she'd told her at breakfast. "Don't you keep calling it an accident? Well, you can't blame anybody for an accident. It happened, okay? It's over. Can't we forget about it?"

After that, she'd barricaded herself in her room. Mallory had despaired of getting any current contact information out of Katelyn. If she hadn't remembered the scrap of paper with the phone number in hot pink, she would have never gotten this far.

That phone call had led to another, and that one had led her to Destiny, one of Katelyn's roommates. The girl had grudgingly agreed to meet her "at the quad" between classes. Mallory was determined to be there early, so as not to give Destiny any excuse to ditch her.

While she waited, she gazed out at the campus, its columned brick buildings situated around a rectangle of green grass. Her college experience—the single, glorious semester she'd had—had been at Savannah College of Art and Design. The buildings had tended toward the modern style, spread all over the city of Savannah.

Still, some things seemed universal. Her residence hall had featured a courtyard much like this one, with palm trees instead of the giant live oaks here. The images came flooding back to her… Girls wearing shorts and skimpy tops lay stretched out on blankets, soaking up the springtime sun, books opened but abandoned nearby. Guys, some shirtless, some in rumpled T-shirts, sent Frisbees skimming perilously close to the girls, obviously in hopes that it would attract their attention. Fast-food wrappers and pizza boxes fluttered in the breeze like corporate flags.

No one hurried. They slouched along the curving concrete pathways, lounged on benches, strolled across the grass. None of them seemed in the least concerned about anything beyond this moment.

They have no idea what the real world is like, Mallory thought. The raw bitterness that sprang up within her shocked her. She didn't regret the choice she'd made to drop out of college and raise Katelyn, of course not.

If she could have had the chance to soak up this life for a little longer…

"Hey, you Mallory what's-her-name?"

The voice beside her startled her. She turned to find that it was indeed a college student. Dressed in black-and-white chevron printed shorts and a lace crop top that came just south of her rib cage—the better to show off a belly-button ring—the girl puffed on a cigarette as she teetered on canvas wedges.

"Yes, I'm Mallory Blair." She extended her hand. "You must be Destiny."

Destiny took her hand in one of the limpest handshakes she'd ever received, along with a look up and down of intense scrutiny. "Figured it was you. You dress cute, but all businesswomanish."

Mallory couldn't help glancing down at the yard-sale blazer and the flowered skirt she'd fashioned out of thrift-store curtains. "Thanks. I think."

Destiny plopped down on the rough concrete retaining wall. She sighed with pleasure and took another drag off her cigarette. "These shoes are killer cute, but they're a pain to wear." She squinted through the smoke ring she'd blown. "You don't mind, do you? Me smoking? The buildings are smoke-free, so I gotta take advantage of the break."

Faced with the choice of possibly running Destiny off or enduring smoke, Mallory shook her head. "I just had a couple of questions. About the fire."

"I lost everything—like sixty pairs of shoes! Bum firemen couldn't be bothered to even pick up a single piece of my clothes,"

Destiny whined. "And Daddy said he wasn't going to let me have another credit card, even though I had like this much—" she held up a thumb and forefinger in a tight pincer "—left before I'd maxed it out."

Mallory swallowed hard to hold back another wave of resentment. She had to put herself in this girl's place. She had *been* in this girl's place a few short years ago, until that life-changing phone call had come. Back then, could she have said anything remotely empathetic in response to a devastating fire?

She cleared her throat. "About the fire. Katelyn is—"

"How's she doing? I guess I should have gone by and seen her, but I've been so busy." Destiny shook her head, which only resulted in one of her long, dangly earrings getting caught in her hair.

"Katelyn's doing well." Her words sounded about a hundred years old even to her ears. This girl made her feel so ancient. "She's still in therapy, but she's walking some, and she's been taking classes online."

"Cool beans," Destiny said. She flicked a trail of ash onto the walkway. "Tell her I said hi. She's a cute kid. When I moved in, I figured she was gonna be kind of a drag, since she was still in high school and all, but she was pretty okay."

"You moved in after the semester got started?" Mallory asked.

"I had a place, you know, with some friends, but this one girl, she was making moves on my boyfriend. I couldn't stay there, could I?" Destiny finished off the cigarette and sighed. "You don't happen to have a smoke, do you?"

"No, I don't. Sorry." She wasn't sorry. She was grateful to her stiletto heels. "I'm trying to make sense of something in the fire department's report about the fire. Did they ever figure out what caused it?"

"Not hardly, but it wasn't my cigarettes." She rolled her eyes, spotted someone she knew and waved them over. "You gotta have a smoke on you, please, please, please—"

The girl liberated a long slender cigarette and a lighter from her tiny purse. With another sigh of relief, Destiny lit up and drew in a calming breath. "Oh, my God, thank you! I'll do you a solid, just wait!"

The girl strolled on, her own cigarette dangling from her fingertips.

Mallory had marshaled her thoughts to ask the next question. "Anyway, what has me puzzled is that the report says that the power was off when the fire department arrived. Was it? And if it was, how could the fire be electrical?"

Instantly a cagey wariness came over Destiny's face. "I don't... What do you mean?"

"The power. When did they cut the power off?"

"Uh... Well." Inexplicably Destiny's hand shook so hard that her borrowed cigarette dropped to the ground. She swore. "Now I'll have to find another one. And I've only— What time is it?"

When Mallory consulted her wristwatch and told her the time, Destiny groaned. "I've only got ten minutes to get to my next class, and it's all the way across campus. I can't cut, either, because I've cut too many times. Are we done?"

"No. You didn't answer my question. When did the power get cut off?"

"How should I know? The place was on fire. I didn't stop to check. Listen, I gotta go—"

"Would anybody else know?"

Destiny squirmed impatiently. "If I don't find someone to bum a smoke, I'm gonna be late for class—"

To short-circuit the whine and gain cooperation, Mallory dug out her wallet and pulled a much-treasured five-dollar bill from it. "Will that buy a pack?"

Destiny snatched at the five. "It will with the two bucks in quarters I've already got. Thanks awfully!"

Exactly as she had when Katelyn was ten, Mallory held the five out of reach. "Not so fast. Was anybody else there that could tell me when the power was cut off?"

Any vestige of cheerfulness left Destiny. "That's a craptastic way of doing things. What am I, twelve?"

"Either you want this or not. A name—and a number that actually works."

"Oh, all right. My ex-boyfriend was there. He crashed on the couch for a few days. His name is Gabe Terrell." She rattled off the number.

Mallory made Destiny wait while she keyed the number into her phone, then handed her the money.

Destiny was already picking her way backward down the walkway as fast as her wedges would take her. "I don't guarantee that he'll actually answer."

Mallory shook her head to clear the foul

smell of cigarette smoke. She hoped it would be off her clothes before she met with Katelyn's academic advisor.

The advisor, a harried-looking woman with piles of paper on her desk, smiled when Mallory introduced herself.

"I'm glad to meet you. I wish it were under happier circumstances," the woman said.

Mallory frowned. "Katelyn's doing much better now—"

"No, about Katelyn's withdrawal from school. Maybe it's for the best."

A loud buzzing filled Mallory's ears. She leaned against the back of the chair for support. "Did Katelyn miss the deadline for signing up for summer classes?"

The advisor gave her a sharp look over her half-rimmed glasses. "Dear, why don't you sit down?"

Safely on the chair, Mallory asked again for the woman to explain what she meant.

The advisor folded her glasses and set them aside. She clasped her hands on the desk. "Katelyn told me that she wouldn't be able to finish her coursework—and her professors concurred. She said she planned to drop out, get her GED and go to cosmetology school instead."

The buzzing increased. "When—"

"Oh, gracious, midterms, I guess. She hasn't done any work at all since then. Maybe we were a bit too ambitious?"

"But she was working—"

The woman reached over and patted Mallory's hand. "It's probably for the best. After all, she struggled that first semester. Give her a year off, maybe repeat her senior year of high school. She would benefit from the maturation."

"She struggled? This is the first I've heard—"

"Didn't you get the progress reports from her high school? I'm sure I have signed copies." She clacked a few keys on her computer and nodded. "Yes, here they are." A printer whirred. "Reach behind you, dear, so you'll have a copy to refresh your memory. Now, you see? She barely squeaked by with a C for her first two classes, and that's with us not counting the final because of her…well, the accident. And her current grades this semester are abysmal. The poor child had too much going on."

All Mallory could do was stare at the signature. Her name—but not her handwriting. Katelyn's. Katelyn had forged her name.

"—and she told me she'd discussed this

with you, and with—oh, what was the name? Andrew? Yes, Andrew. He's… What? A cousin? An uncle? This Andrew had pointed out that maybe college wasn't for her, and that was a tremendous relief. Many adults won't be honest with kids—"

Honest? Mallory was going to be that from now on, without a doubt.

CHAPTER TWENTY-SEVEN

MALLORY PULLED UP to the farm and stopped so abruptly that a cloud of dust billowed around her car. Slamming the door, she stood, hand shielding her eyes. Yes, there was Katelyn—on a horse, with Andrew beside her.

Mindless of anything but her towering rage, Mallory crossed to the paddock. Katelyn's smile and wave faltered. Her hand dropped to her side.

"Off," Mallory ordered. "Get off that horse."

"Mal—"

Andrew interjected, "We're almost done, if you'll give me a few minutes—"

She cut him off. "You," she said, pointing a finger at him, "have done quite enough, thank you." Mallory whirled back around to face Katelyn. "And you—I am so disappointed in you. You lied, Katelyn. You lied."

Katelyn went two shades grayer. She made no move to get off the horse, but instead gripped the reins tighter. "About what?"

"You withdrew. From your classes. Without telling me. And you forged my signature on your progress reports from the school— progress reports *I* asked about and *you* told me they didn't send."

Katelyn gulped. "Because I knew you'd go all ballistic on me. You don't make it easy to tell you stuff." She turned to Andrew, the horse becoming restless under her. "You said you talked to her!"

Andrew held up his hand. "Whoa— this is not the best place to be having this conversation—"

It was the wrong thing for him to have said. "When *is* the best time?" Mallory demanded. "You're either at the station or on a horse, so when would it suit you to pencil me in?"

The horse pulled back, high-stepping away from Andrew and Mallory. "Katelyn, do you have him?" Andrew asked.

"Yeah. I'll walk him over to the other end of the pasture—away from some high-strung people!" Katelyn jerked on the reins and quickly put distance between her and Mallory.

"How dare you!" Mallory tightened her grip on the fence that separated her and Andrew. "I needed to talk to her—"

"No. You didn't. Not while she was on a horse. She's come a long way in the time she's been here, but she doesn't have the strength to control a riled-up horse." He said it firmly. Then he clambered over the fence and dropped down beside her. "And I think you'll appreciate me giving you a chance to cool off—"

"I'd appreciate it if you hadn't encouraged her to quit!" she snapped. "She quit, Andrew. She withdrew two weeks ago. And she's failing."

"Hey. Remember what I said the other day. There is no timetable. She'll get her act together—"

"There *is* a timetable! I had a plan, Andrew. She graduates high school, she gets her degree—a real degree—she gets a good, dependable job that she can do— She has so many opportunities that I never had—"

He laid a hand on her arm, looked deeply into her eyes. "Mallory, one thing my dad never did was confuse his dreams for mine."

Mallory shook his fingers off. "What do you mean?"

"Maybe…" Now Andrew stared down at the grass under their feet, kicked a loose pebble with the toe of his boot. When he lifted his head, he didn't meet Mallory's eyes. He fixed his gaze on Katelyn, who was walking the horse in a slow trot at the far end of the paddock. "Maybe you should be the one to go to college. Maybe that's your dream, not Katelyn's."

If she'd thought she was angry before, it didn't hold a candle to the fury that rose up from her core. "Andrew Monroe! Do you hear yourself? I. Can't. Go. To. College. Not until I get Katelyn settled. I can't. Because I have to work, I have to get groceries on the table and pay for health insurance and utilities and clothes—"

Her anger turned to despair. She'd thought he'd understand. A sob tore loose from her, and she pressed her hand to her mouth. She would fly apart before she cried in front of him again.

In a quieter, more controlled voice, she told him, "I can't go to college until I make sure that Katelyn has a secure future…and because of you, she's further than ever from that."

It was funny how, when she said that, it crystalized everything. There it was, the nut of the problem. She had to get Katelyn a secure future. Before Andrew had come into the picture, she'd had that goal in the fore-front of her mind, but he had distracted her.

She'd allowed herself to be distracted by him.

No more. She would do whatever it took.

She turned and started walking for the car.

"Hey, wait, where are you going?" he called after her.

"To do what I should have done a long time ago."

"What do I tell Katelyn?"

"That I'll be back tonight to pick her up, and that I'll deal with her and her forgery then."

She kept walking. Didn't turn. Didn't dare look at him because she might cry, and she didn't ever want him to see her cry again.

In the car, she backed out, pointed it toward Macon and picked up her phone.

The person picked up on the first ring.

"Chad?" she asked. "If you'll stay late, I'll come and sign those papers."

ANDREW STARED AT the ceiling of the bunk room in the firehouse. He couldn't sleep. It had been two days since the big blowup at the farm, and still Mallory wouldn't return his calls.

He suspected that she wouldn't come when she knew he was off duty, either, because he'd seen neither hide nor hair of her during the rest of his forty-eight off.

Oh, he'd reamed out Katelyn but good for her part in the whole fiasco. She'd cried and moaned and groaned, but even Ma had taken Mallory's part about withdrawing without telling Mallory and forging her signature.

"Honey," Ma had told her, "you face your problems, you don't run from them. If you turn your back on them or shove 'em under a rug, why, they'll grow twice the size they were, and then leap out at you when you least expect it."

Still, Andrew had to take responsibility for his part. While he hadn't told Katelyn to quit, and he certainly hadn't told her to forge her sister's name to her progress reports, he'd encouraged her to buck Mallory's plans.

And, boy, were those plans rigid. If he could just talk some sense into her, maybe she could see that there could be a different way. Sure, it wouldn't be as quick as her original plan, but there was no one right way of doing things. There had to be a way to get that college education she craved and still take care of Katelyn.

The alert of a call-out buzzed through the building. He rolled out of his bunk in pure reflex. Pile-up on the interstate, from the sound of the radio, with possible entrapment and a fuel leak.

"Let's go, boys!" Captain said, motioning them onto the rig. "Seconds count! What are we, nailed to the ground tonight?"

The doors slammed, seat belts clicked, and they peeled out into the dark night. The few cars dotting the streets pulled off to the side as they made their way through the main intersections of town.

"Might as well get up and answer a call," Eric grouched beside him. "The way you toss and turn on that top bunk makes the whole frame rock."

"It's because you and Jackson had the brainy idea to put those cans under it—ever since then, it's felt loose," Andrew grouched back as he watched their approach to another intersection. "I'm still cleaning up flour and Kool-Aid."

"Boys, get your mind off your high jinks and on the job," Captain ordered them. "We've got a possible entrapment, so, Eric, I want you on the—"

Whatever Captain intended to say, Andrew

never knew. He heard a shout from the fire-fighter behind the wheel, felt the whole rig yank hard, then the right side lift and they were turning and sliding, metal screeching and tools flying, until, mercifully, blackness closed in on him.

MALLORY PICKED UP the seam ripper and palmed it, a twist of pain zapping through her heart. She couldn't see this thing without thinking of Andrew and his kiss.

What did it matter about all that if *he* couldn't see what she needed? What Katelyn needed?

Nothing. She'd finished Kimberly's dress earlier in the week, and worked like a crazy woman to turn out the bridesmaids' dresses. She wanted them done so she didn't have to chance seeing him again.

And maybe soon she wouldn't ever have to see him. She'd signed the papers for Chad, explaining that Katelyn's failure had set her back and made her understand what she had to do.

"If we can get the power company to pay for Katelyn's medical bills," she'd said, "then I can start with a clean slate, and maybe, just maybe I can go back to school myself. I owe that to me and to Katelyn."

He'd grinned. "Leave it to me. You're going to have plenty of money to go back to school on…and Katelyn? She'll be set. When I get done, you won't have to worry about providing for her."

Now she set aside the seam ripper and surveyed the white dress waiting for Kimberly. This was the final fitting, the verdict as to whether Kimberly would like what Mallory had done.

The Monroe girls had made a big ceremony out of it. Mallory had gone into the sewing room and given the gown a final once-over.

It was ready.

Kimberly came in and gasped in pleasure. "Ooh, Mallory! It's gorgeous! My daughter will be over the moon…and I can't wait for Daniel to see it."

The tension in Mallory's stomach uncoiled as she helped Kimberly step into the dress. Daniel's fiancée preened in front of the full-length mirror.

"Do you like it?" Mallory asked.

"Oh, yes." Kimberly's eyes sparkled. From the other side of the closed door, the other women had started chanting, "Dress! Dress! Dress!"

"I think that's your cue," Mallory said.

Kimberly picked up the voluminous cloud of tulle and waited for Mallory to open the door. She swept in ahead of Mallory.

Oohs and aahs rewarded Mallory the moment the women and Andrew's nieces spotted Kimberly. This was Mallory's true calling. Maybe, with the money Chad had promised her, she could get a degree in fashion design.

"And…that's not all, folks!" She twirled her hands à la a game-show hostess. "I have the bridesmaids' dresses done!"

The room erupted in applause. "Mom! You look so pretty!" Marissa hollered. "Daniel's gonna swoon!"

Ma beamed. "To think you did it all in my sewing room—"

A ringing telephone cut through the festivities. Ma rose from her seat to answer it. Mallory realized something was wrong from the way Ma gripped the counter. An uneasy quiet washed over the crowd of women as they, too, felt the tension.

Ma hung up. Her head was bent, her hands shaking. "Oh, my word. Not again. Not…"

Instantly her daughters and her future daughters-in-law surrounded her. Mallory hung back, not wanting to interfere in whatever family crisis had arisen.

"That was Daniel." Ma's hand trembled. "There's been a wreck. One of the fire trucks… It's bad. Daniel said Andrew was on it when it happened—but he's okay, just a little banged up, got knocked on the head," she rushed to add. "Daniel needs me to go, though. Because…"

Mallory's breath went out of her at the mention of Andrew hurt. She was glad Ma was taking the time to search for words because she couldn't have focused anyway.

"What does Daniel need, Ma?" Kimberly pressed. Her hands were balled up in the white tulle, and her face as white as the dress she was wearing.

"Eric's hurt bad. And…that nice captain of Andrew's…" Ma closed her eyes, and her body swayed. "He's had a heart attack. Oh, his poor wife…and Eric's mama… They're at the hospital… Oh, dear, when will all this trouble be over?"

THEY'D COME THROUGH TOWN, Mallory falling in with them, though she'd insisted that she and Katelyn should stay behind. Maegan had pulled her aside and took her by the hands.

"Please," she begged. "Go in my place. Let me stay here with Katelyn. I can't see another woman lose her husband. I know I should be tougher. But all I can think about is the night we lost Dad, and…I just can't do it."

Mallory had understood. Hadn't she been that way about hospitals?

Now she stood uncertainly by Ma in the doorway of the brightly lit waiting room of the ER. She spied two women sitting between Daniel and a bandaged Andrew, bruises already sprouting across his face.

Ma took a deep breath, grabbed Kimberly's hand, then reached down and grabbed Mallory's. "Girls. This is gonna be a hard thing. Help me all you can."

Me? I'm not a firefighter's wife. I can't tell that poor woman her life is going to be okay if her husband dies, or that other woman—to bury a child, that has to be worse than losing both parents.

She didn't have a chance to hang back. She was moving in lockstep with Ma and Kimberly. Their approach attracted the attention of the younger woman, who blanched.

"No! No, please! Not my Eric, oh, please, not my husband—" she shrieked.

Ma was down on her knees in front of her, assuring her that Eric was still alive.

Kimberly exchanged glances with Ma, and then, as if there had been some elaborately choreographed plan, she drew Eric's mother to her feet. "Let's get some air. Do you need some help making any phone calls?"

Mallory stood by and watched Ma slide into the empty seat beside the captain's wife. The woman turned to face Ma, her eyes dead. She took Ma's hands in hers and said, "It's bad, isn't it? You wouldn't be here if it wasn't bad."

Ma nodded. "We've got to hope for the best, Allison. That Will, he's a fighter."

A tiny sob escaped Allison's trembling lips. How Mallory knew that sick fear the woman was experiencing now. "Ma," Allison husked. "You always said to never let 'em leave with words between you. All these years, I tried, and sometimes I'd mess up, but yesterday, I didn't. I was mad as all get-outs with him because... Oh, something so stupid. But I didn't let him see it. And I'm so glad. I'm so glad the last thing he heard was...that I loved him."

Mallory locked eyes with Andrew, realized that she had sent him off with her horrible words ringing in his ears. The room felt too close, too hot, and she had to get out of there.

Outside in the cool night air, she dragged in a calming breath. She pushed past the knot of firefighters hanging around the entrance, waiting for word on their captain. When she made it to a swing under a gazebo, she realized too late that it had been set aside as a smoking area.

The smell of stale tobacco permeated the place, and ash cans ran over with butts. But it was better than seeing that quiet resignation in Allison's face.

The swing creaked. She looked up to see Andrew beside her. Without thinking, she wrapped her arms around him. "You could have been killed!"

He shrugged. "I wasn't. A scratch. A bump on the head. Not anything at all like Eric or Cap."

Mallory sat back. "How bad is it? What happened?"

Andrew's jaw worked. "Bad as it can get. A drunk driver plowed into us. We tried to miss him and the rig flipped, slid into a utility pole." His fist tightened on the wooden slats between them. "Eric's in a coma. Doctors say...the other concussion set this one up to be a bad one. And Cap…Cap was trying to get to Eric and me…and all of a sudden, he grabs his left arm and keels over. I'm six inches away, Mallory. Six inches. And I'm jammed up in the wreckage and can't get to him."

"Oh, Andrew…" All Mallory could think about was how the awful fire that had caused such tragedy for Katelyn was still paying nasty dividends. If Eric hadn't been injured in that fire, he might not have been so badly hurt now. The captain might have not been so desperate to get to him.

"The other guy?" Andrew snorted in derision. "The driver? High as a kite. Not so much as a scratch on him."

"How could anybody be so selfish and thoughtless—you were just doing your job."

Again, resignation seemed to roll off Andrew as he shrugged once more. "That *is* the job, Mallory. Don't you get it? It could happen when we get called out for a simple kitchen fire."

A flurry of movement drew Mallory's attention to the door. The knot of firefighters parted. There under the flickering vapor lights came a sobbing Allison, supported almost wholly by Ma on one side and Daniel on the other.

As she passed, the firefighters stood straight and tall, formed two lines, executed a crisp salute.

Mallory felt rather than saw Andrew stand, as well. She couldn't tear her eyes off the crumpled figure of Allison, but she knew, from the telltale sound, that Andrew was crying softly as he saluted his captain's widow.

CHAPTER TWENTY-EIGHT

ANDREW THOUGHT HE'D come unglued as he heard the strains of the bagpipes fade to nothingness. The lone piper walked up the long dusty entrance path of the cemetery, away from the tent, the people and the grave.

Instinct made him want to break formation and check on Ma. But not even Daniel had let that salute drop, and Daniel of all people would know how hard this day would be for Ma. The death of a firefighter brought back all those memories of Dad's funeral in full force.

Finally, the flag was folded. Presented to the widow. The handshakes and grave "thank you for your sacrifice" given.

As the crowd milled around, and he saw that Ma was okay, he spied Mallory. She stood off in the distance, by herself, dressed as always in clothes perfect for the occasion.

He knew she had finally understood about Katelyn when she'd said, "You were just doing your job." She'd been sick with worry over Eric, helping Ma pack up food for the family, going with them to assist Allison.

She lifted her hand in a restrained wave. Someone jostled him, spoke, and he had to turn away to speak to them. Then there was someone else, and another, and another. When he looked back, she was gone.

Now the crowd was thinning out, and maybe this part of the day, as hard as it had been, was finally over. He joined the line to give his condolences to Allison.

Dutch tapped him on the arm. "Hey, got a minute?" He pulled him aside.

"Yeah, what is it? And don't start your usual crap about legal. That can all wait until—"

"I saw that nice little moment you had with Mallory."

"Dutch!" Andrew protested. "She's not gonna sue. Not after this. She totally gets it."

Dutch lifted his brows and rocked back on his heels. "Oh, does she?"

"Yeah." The scent of funeral flowers overwhelmed him to the point of near gagging. It put him straight back to the day of his dad's funeral.

"Well, she's got you fooled, then," Dutch

said. "Because I received notice right before I drove over here that she was suing us. Suing the county, the department, Daniel, the power company and… Hmm, who am I leaving out? Oh, yeah. You."

"What?" Andrew thought he'd pass out at Dutch's words.

"To the tune of five million dollars. That ambulance chaser of hers has already left me a message wanting to know if we're open to settling."

"No—there's got to be a mistake."

"You betcha. The mistake was you ever getting involved in Mallory Blair's business at all."

"WHAT ARE YOU doing here?" Andrew hissed as Mallory filled red plastic cups with ice. "Is this some kind of game?"

She stared at him. He'd known she was helping out with the luncheon after the funeral. Why was he suddenly white hot with barely controlled anger at her presence? "I— Ma told me— What on earth has gotten into you?"

"A little truth, that's what. Five million dollars? That's what you think this county's worth? That'll buy you a lot of shoes, won't it? You won't have to slum it in thrift stores anymore, will you? Not after you pick our bones clean."

"Andrew Monroe!" she hissed back. She slipped out of Allison's back door and beckoned for him to follow. Outside in the quiet leafy green seclusion, she asked, "What are you talking about?"

"That lawyer of yours, that's what. He's notified the county's legal counsel that you're suing us for five million dollars. Oh, and me, personally, I get listed as a separate defendant. Nice touch, Mallory. It was especially thoughtful that you'd have it served the day of Cap's funeral."

She jerked back from his anger as if she'd been stung. "I—I didn't—" The terms of the contract she'd signed came floating back to her. She'd agreed to let Chad decide the legal strategy.

"It's not what I wanted— I never meant for him to sue you—"

"Oh, yeah? Well, he did. What, you only wanted to sue people who had actual money?"

"Chad said the county's insurance would pay. Anyway, I didn't mean for him to sue the county, either. I wanted him to sue the power company."

Andrew pressed his lips together in a tight line. It took him a moment to respond. "And that makes it all right? To sue a county or a big corporation? Because they have insurance? Who pays for that insurance? What happens when the rates go up, huh? This is not a victimless suit, Mal. When you sue the county, the firefighters end up paying for it."

His words were like a stick in a hornet's nest. She couldn't control her anger. "And Katelyn should simply suck it up? She's hurt— She's lost months, Andrew—months! She may never be right again. I'm buried in medical bills. It's not her fault! Somebody should pay!"

The back door opened again, and this time Maegan slipped out. "What's going on? This is not the time or place for a lover's spat."

"Oh, you'd have to feel some love to have a lover's spat, Maegan," Andrew snapped. "Mallory only loves money." He pushed past her and headed back into the house.

"What—" Maegan frowned.

Her temper subsiding, and a wave of nausea pooling in her gut, Mallory struggled for the words to explain what had happened.

Maegan listened. "Oh, no. Tell me you

didn't do this to get money for Katelyn's therapy."

"Yes, but I never meant for the department to—"

Maegan sagged against the porch rail. "You signed a strategy waiver, didn't you?"

"What?"

"The lawyer. He told you that you had to sign a waiver allowing him to decide legal strategy. I call them strategy waivers, but they've probably got a proper legal name."

"He said that it would allow him to—"

"Negotiate a settlement?" Maegan gave her a sick, knowing look. "I've seen patients' families get roped into those. Once they do... they have no control over who that lawyer decides to sue. He's going to keep after anybody who has the potential to shell out any kind of settlement."

"Maegan—I tried to get the insurance to pay. I tried. You said it yourself, Katelyn needs the therapy."

"Oh, honey." Maegan patted her on the arm and treated her to another of those world-weary smiles. "Don't you see? It's a conflict of interest for me to continue to treat Katelyn. I'll have to discharge her. I am so sorry, but as long as my brothers are being sued, I can't risk it. You're going to have to find Katelyn another therapist."

CHAPTER TWENTY-NINE

"I TOLD YOU *not* to sue," Katelyn wailed. "I told you I didn't want to sue anybody! If you had listened, we wouldn't have to leave!"

Mallory straightened up from dropping books into a cardboard box. She put her fingers to her temples to ward off the headache that had already latched its claws into her. "Katelyn, it's a done deal. I've quit my job and I've given notice on this apartment. As for the lawsuit, I may have made mistakes, but I didn't have much choice, not after you—"

"But you can't sue! You can't! It's my fault— the fire is my fault."

Katelyn's words came out as a broken whimper. Mallory knelt down beside her. "Honey, you can't blame yourself. This was Andrew's fault. He left you on that landing instead of—"

"I deserved it, Mallory. Don't you see?" Katelyn balled up her fists. Tears streamed down her face, but she didn't bother to wipe them away. "There wouldn't have been a fire—not if it weren't for me."

"What? Katelyn, don't be silly—"

"I spent the money." The words came out in a rush. Katelyn's face went from horrified to slack with relief. "There. I said it. I spent the money."

"What do you mean? What money?"

"The money you sent for the power bill. My share. I blew it. We didn't have it. And we were, like, two months behind. And they cut the power off."

"But—" Mallory couldn't process what she was hearing.

"I was afraid you'd yell at me, or make me come home. I mean, I'd barely been able to pull passing grades, because, like, well, I was partying too much. So then Destiny's loser boyfriend, Gabe, crashed at the house. He used to work for the power company. His dad is some bigwig. He said he'd take care of it, that he knew what to do. He got some tools from his dad's truck or shop or something, and he rigged it up, and we had power. I knew it was wrong. But I couldn't— I didn't want to admit I blew the money you'd sent me."

Katelyn stared at the starburst scar on her

hand. "I'm nothing but a thief. You can't sue anybody, because it would be like a thief suing somebody for getting hurt when he robbed a house. I'm so sorry. I know I let you down. That's the worst of it—that and knowing somebody else could have gotten badly hurt. I mean, Eric—Eric wouldn't be in a coma now if it hadn't been for me."

Mallory collapsed on the floor and sagged against a cardboard box. Nausea pooled in her gut. She stared at Katelyn, who seemed at once bent over with misery and somehow older and more mature.

"Oh, Katelyn. What do we do now?"

"I know you're worried, Mal, about money and everything. But we can't sue. And—and I want to talk to the power company. Tell them what happened. Maybe if I don't, Gabe will do it again sometime and somebody might actually die."

Mallory drew in a breath. It was the right thing to do, but...

"You'll need a lawyer. I think—yeah. I should call Chad. He should go with us."

Palpable relief flooded through Katelyn. "I've been thinking about this ever since the wreck. I keep thinking about Eric, and how he wouldn't be hurt so badly. But I'd sure be glad to have Chad along."

CHAD DID COME ALONG. Though he strongly advised the two of them to say nothing, he agreed to accompany them and try to convince the power company's officials not to prosecute Katelyn as an accessory.

After Katelyn's tearful tale, the suits around the long conference table looked at each other in a guarded way. Mallory's stomach twisted in fear. Would Katelyn face jail time?

Then the silver-haired man beside Katelyn cleared his throat. "Katelyn—honey—my name is Peter Terrell, and I'm the manager here. I am so sorry. Gabe…Gabe is my son. I cannot believe— No, that's not true. He's been going down the wrong path for a while now. I knew he was capable of it, I just hoped he wouldn't ever do something like this." He put his hands to his face. "To think that all you've gone through—"

"Sir." Katelyn touched his arm. "It wasn't just Gabe. It was all our fault."

He looked up at her bleakly. "It took a great deal of courage for you to come forward. I'm going to have to pass this on to my supervisor, the district manager, and recuse myself." Mr. Terrell swallowed. "I can't promise you won't be called to testify, as it is our policy that we do prosecute…power thefts…regardless of whether it is my son. But since you came forward of your own accord, it certainly helps your case. And you've clearly paid more than enough for any crime you've committed."

Chad spoke up. "Yes, she has. As you can see, she's still in a wheelchair. Her insurance has ended her therapy, so this may be as good as it gets for her."

"No," Mr. Terrell said firmly. He looked at Mallory. "My son did this. Yes, she was culpable, but she's a teenager. My son is twenty-four years old. He should have known better. How much is the therapy she needs? I have some savings put aside. It's not much—I've already spent quite a lot of it trying to bail him out of previous scrapes, but no more. He has to face up to the consequences. It seems only fair that I cover the cost of some of those medical bills. That is…" He looked at Chad. "The suit is going away? Against the power company?"

"Oh, yes, sir. The power company has no

liability in this situation, and neither does the county or fire department."

"Then, I leave it to you to work out the details for Katelyn to get the care she needs. And I'll handle the rest."

Mallory sagged with relief. This was a miracle. Katelyn could get her therapy…but then Mallory realized that it wouldn't matter. The Monroes would never want to treat someone who had sued them. Andrew would never forgive her for blaming him when it had all been Katelyn's fault.

Katelyn lifted her chin, her resolve clear. "I swear, Mr. Terrell. I won't let you down. No more shortcuts for me." She turned to Mallory, gripped her hands in hers. There was a serious earnestness that Mallory had never seen in her eyes before. "I promise, Mallory. I'll earn your trust back, if it takes me the rest of my life."

Mallory couldn't say anything, because she had a similar speech to make to someone else.

Andrew.

CHAPTER THIRTY

ANDREW POKED AT his piece of the extravagantly frosted cake Kari had made. Usually he loved Rob's fiancée's cakes. He'd gotten the *W* of the "Way to Go, Eric" celebratory dessert that Eric's mom had dropped off at the station.

He was definitely glad that Eric was finally back in the land of the living and had shaken off the coma.

But not even Kari's confection could lift his mood. How had he misjudged Mallory so badly? Forget LeeAnn. This was truly the mother of all diva disasters.

Jackson's familiar step approached Andrew's hiding place in the bowels of the stationhouse. "Hey, buddy. You got a visitor. I think you'll want to see who it is."

Tossing the uneaten cake in a trash bin, Andrew squinted against the sunlight to see who had dropped by. He stopped in his tracks when he recognized the familiar silhouette of long legs, a flowy little skirt and impossibly high heels.

"Heck, no," he said and pivoted around. "I don't want to see her."

Jackson planted a meaty hand in the middle of his chest, blocking his escape. "I think you do."

"Is this more of your practical jokes? It's not funny, Jackson. This time, I thought she might be—"

"If you did, then you owe it to yourself and to her to see it through. You think I'd come get you for her, of all people, if I hadn't heard a preview of what she had to say? I may prank you with the best of them, but you're my friend, Monroe."

The uncharacteristic serious note in Jackson's voice turned him around. "I can't think of a thing she'd have to say to change my mind about her."

"That, boy, is an example of your complete failure of imagination." He gave Andrew a not-so-gentle shove in Mallory's direction. "Now git."

Andrew approached the bright sunlight and Mallory slowly. He could tell that she'd been crying—she hadn't even fixed her makeup.

Her skirt was rumpled, and her blouse was, too. Her hair was frizzy as all get-out.

He'd never seen her look more beautiful.

"What?" he snapped.

"I guess I've interrupted a party," she began slowly. "I saw the cake."

"Eric's mom brought it by. He's out of the coma."

"Oh, that's good!" Mallory's face brightened.

"He still has a lot of rehab to go through. They say he may never be able to return to active duty—but we'll see."

The hopeful light in her eyes faded, and she said in a diffident voice, "I'm glad." Her hands folded and unfolded a sheaf of papers. She lacked her usual spit and polish, and that kept Andrew off balance.

"You wanted to tell me something?" *That, Monroe, was cold as ice in December.*

Mallory shoved a heavily creased sheaf of papers toward him. "This—this is for you. It's the lawsuit. I got Chad to pull it."

"What?" A flicker of hope pulsed through him. He tried manfully to douse it.

She looked as though she wanted to turn and run. Still, even with no makeup and frizzy hair, she was the Mallory he'd come to know. She stuck it out, her heels planted firmly on the concrete. Mallory rubbed at her eyes. Was she crying? No, not quite, but almost.

"I'm really—really sorry. I swear, I didn't know. I should not have been looking for someone to bail me out. I should have listened to you. To everybody," she went on. "The bills were so big, and I was so tired, but that—that's no excuse."

A long beat of silence stretched out between them. He didn't dare open his mouth to ask what had happened to change her mind because he was afraid he'd say something stupid that would scare her off.

She half-turned, then turned back. "I'm sorry, Andrew. Please tell your family how sorry I am to have repaid all their kindness with…such a betrayal."

With that, she pivoted on one slender heel and trudged toward her cute little convertible. For the first time, he saw that it was packed to the gills with boxes and clothes.

"Hey," he called after her. "You should tell them yourself."

She stopped.

"What?"

"I said you should tell Ma and everybody yourself." He finally managed to un-nail his boots from the ground so that he could walk to her.

"But I—" She waved a hand to the car. "I'm leaving."

"Why would you do that?"

"Because I screwed up."

He reached over and slid a thumb along the oh-so-familiar curve of her face. "You think I haven't ever done that? If I had gone against Dutch's advice and just talked you through things, maybe we could have figured out a way to solve some of your problems. I didn't. Instead, I made 'em worse."

She caught up his hand in hers, leaned into his touch. Tears threatened to spill out onto her cheeks, but she was his Mallory. She never let them loose.

"Are you asking me to stay?"

"I guess I am," he replied. "Because I'd like to earn your forgiveness. I left somebody you cared about behind—yeah, it was my job, yeah, it was technically the right decision. But it hurt you. I want to prove to you that I will never, ever leave you, or anybody else you love, behind."

She breathed in. "I didn't figure that Maegan would want... That you would want... And even though Katelyn won't be facing criminal charges, she's got to start her senior year again, and I quit my job and gave up our apartment—"

Now he caught her other hand in his. "Wait. Criminal charges? Breathe in again. Slow down. I think I'm missing some things."

"I found out what caused the fire. Katelyn's fire." She started talking, and he heard about Gabe reconnecting the power and the offer from Terrell to pay for therapy that had come too late, after she'd quit her job and given up the apartment.

Finally her words dwindled to silence. She cleared her throat. "I can't ask you to forgive me."

"Why not?"

"Because...what I did was unforgivable."

"No. What you did was bad. Horrible. But totally understandable. You didn't have all the facts, Mallory. If you had, would you have sued?"

"No!" she cried.

"And when you knew…" He paused. "You made it right. That's the girl I love."

"You love me?" Her voice shook.

Andrew felt as vulnerable as if he were standing with one foot off a cliff. His mouth dry, he got out, "Yeah. I do. What's not to love about you? I mean, any girl who's got ingenuity and a whole lot of compassion, not to mention can keep me on my toes and looks as pretty as you do, well, she sounds like the right kind of girl for me."

Mallory brought his knuckles to her lips. "That's good," she whispered.

"That's good…why?" His heart beat even faster as he waited.

"Because I love you, too. And it was killing me to leave you behind. I just couldn't figure out how to fix everything."

"Hey, how about you let me help you figure it out? How about for, say, forever, I get an equal share in this figuring-out business?"

She leaned into him and whispered, "Forever sounds like just long enough. I'd like that a whole bunch."

He bent to kiss her—but stopped short. Out of the corner of his eye, he saw a long blue line of firefighters stretched out in front of the open bay, some of them splitting their attention between the free show and the cake they were devouring. Now Mallory saw them, too. She turned beet red.

"I think we've got an audience," she said.

"That's the understatement of the century. Guess this will have to wait, then," Andrew said regretfully.

Jackson blurted out, "Monroe, if you don't kiss that girl, I'll short-sheet your bunk for a month!"

"Would he?" Mallory asked, her eyes wide with amazement.

"You don't know a whole lot about firefighters, do you?" Andrew said by way of an answer.

"No…but I'm willing to learn."

"Fine, the first thing you need to learn is Jackson is apt to keep his word, so…" He tipped her back and gave her a kiss that drew a round of enthusiastic applause. "That's for them."

She came up for air, cheeks flushed. Before she could say anything, Andrew let his mouth slant down to hers and kissed her again, softer this time, with less flash but a whole lot more tenderness.

"This one?" he murmured as he held her close. "This one is for you…because you? You're the one for me."

* * * * *

THE GEORGIA MONROES
will be back with a final story—this time it's Maegan's turn—in Harlequin Heartwarming, coming this fall!

LARGER-PRINT BOOKS!

**GET 2 FREE
LARGER-PRINT NOVELS
PLUS 2 FREE
MYSTERY GIFTS**

Love Inspired®

Larger-print novels are now available...

LILP15

LARGER-PRINT BOOKS!

GET 2 FREE
LARGER-PRINT NOVELS
PLUS 2 FREE
MYSTERY GIFTS

Love Inspired®

SUSPENSE
RIVETING INSPIRATIONAL ROMANCE

Larger-print novels are now available...

LISLP15

REQUEST YOUR FREE BOOKS!

2 FREE INSPIRATIONAL NOVELS
PLUS 2 FREE MYSTERY GIFTS

Love Inspired® HISTORICAL

YES! Please send me 2 FREE Love Inspired® Historical novels and my 2 FREE mystery gifts (gifts are worth about $10). After receiving them, if I don't wish to receive any more books, I can return the shipping statement marked "cancel." If I don't cancel, I will receive 4 brand-new novels every month and be billed just $4.99 per book in the U.S. or $5.49 per book in Canada. That's a saving of at least 17% off the cover price. It's quite a bargain! Shipping and handling is just 50¢ per book in the U.S. and 75¢ per book in Canada.* I understand that accepting the 2 free books and gifts places me under no obligation to buy anything. I can always return a shipment and cancel at any time. Even if I never buy another book, the two free books and gifts are mine to keep forever.

102/302 IDN GH6Z

Name	(PLEASE PRINT)	
Address		Apt. #
City	State/Prov.	Zip/Postal Code

Signature (if under 18, a parent or guardian must sign)

Mail to the **Reader Service**:
IN U.S.A.: P.O. Box 1867, Buffalo, NY 14240-1867
IN CANADA: P.O. Box 609, Fort Erie, Ontario L2A 5X3

Want to try two free books from another series?
Call 1-800-873-8635 or visit www.ReaderService.com.

* Terms and prices subject to change without notice. Prices do not include applicable taxes. Sales tax applicable in N.Y. Canadian residents will be charged applicable taxes. Offer not valid in Quebec. This offer is limited to one order per household. Not valid for current subscribers to Love Inspired Historical books. All orders subject to credit approval. Credit or debit balances in a customer's account(s) may be offset by any other outstanding balance owed by or to the customer. Please allow 4 to 6 weeks for delivery. Offer available while quantities last.

Your Privacy—The Reader Service is committed to protecting your privacy. Our Privacy Policy is available online at www.ReaderService.com or upon request from the Reader Service.

We make a portion of our mailing list available to reputable third parties that offer products we believe may interest you. If you prefer that we not exchange your name with third parties, or if you wish to clarify or modify your communication preferences, please visit us at www.ReaderService.com/consumerschoice or write to us at Reader Service Preference Service, P.O. Box 9062, Buffalo, NY 14240-9062. Include your complete name and address.

LIH15

REQUEST YOUR FREE BOOKS!
2 FREE WHOLESOME ROMANCE NOVELS IN LARGER PRINT
PLUS 2
FREE
MYSTERY GIFTS

✿✿✿✿✿✿✿✿✿✿✿✿✿✿✿✿✿✿✿✿✿✿✿✿✿✿

HEARTWARMING™

✿✿✿✿✿✿✿✿✿✿✿✿✿✿✿✿✿✿✿✿✿✿✿✿✿✿

Wholesome, tender romances